A FAMILY AFFAIR

They'd been trying to avoid it all day, the same as they wanted to avoid touching. But it was too late. They both came to the realization in the same moment. Brenda flew into his arms, knowing she couldn't live one more moment without his touch, without his mouth on hers. She turned her head seeking his kiss with the same fierceness as she felt in him.

Frantically they sought and found each other. With a force more powerful than the two of them, their mouths melded. Brenda felt as if her soul had fused with Wes's, as if she had been seeking him her entire life and not known it. Finally she'd found him and knew that life would not be the same without him.

She didn't know how long the kiss went on, how long Wes's hand massaged her back, how long her hands raked over every part of him. Everything within her had liquefied until she was a writhing, formless mass of feelings.

Other Books by Shirley Hailstock

WHISPERS OF LOVE
WHITE DIAMONDS
LEGACY
MIRROR IMAGE
OPPOSITES ATTRACT
HIS 1-800 WIFE

Published by BET/Arabesque Books

A FAMILY AFFAIR

SHIRLEY HAILSTOCK

BET Publications, LLC
http://www.bet.com
http://www.arabesquebooks.com

ARABESQUE BOOKS are published by

BET Publications, LLC
c/o BET BOOKS
One BET Plaza
1900 W Place NE
Washington, D.C. 20018-1211

Copyright © 2002 by Shirley Hailstock

All rights reserved. No part of this book may be reproduced, stored in a retrieval system, or transmitted in any form or by any means without the prior written consent of the Publisher.

If you purchased this book without a cover, you should be aware that this book is stolen property. It was reported as "unsold and destroyed" to the Publisher and neither the Author nor the Publisher has received any payment for this "stripped book."

All Kensington Titles, Imprints, and Distributed Lines are available at special quantity discounts for bulk purchases for sales promotions, premiums, fund-raising, and educational or institutional use. Special book excerpts or customized printings can also be created to fit specific needs. For details, write or phone the office of the Kensington special sales manager: Kensington Publishing Corp., 850 Third Avenue, New York, NY 10022, attn: Special Sales Department, Phone: 1-800-221-2647.

BET Books is a trademark of Black Entertainment Television, Inc. ARABESQUE, the ARABESQUE logo and the BET BOOKS logo are trademarks and registered trademarks.

First Printing: August 2002
10 9 8 7 6 5 4 3 2

Printed in the United States of America

To my sister, Marilyn Hailstock, for being my sister, and because I finished this book on her birthday.

Descendants of George Johnson

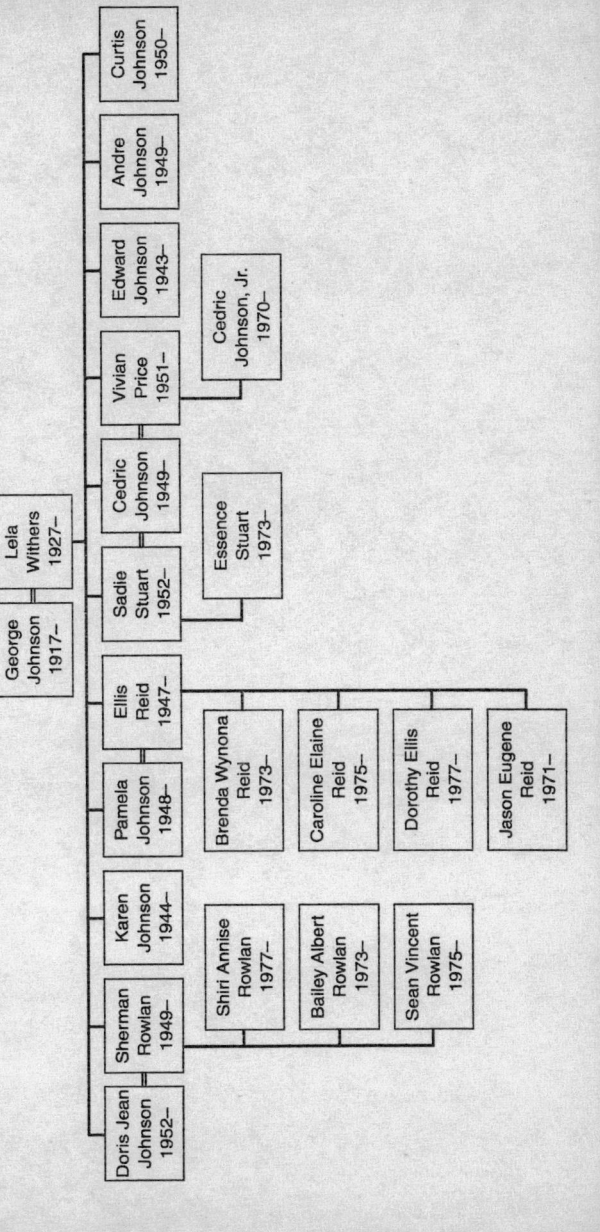

- George Johnson 1917– — Lela Withers 1927–
  - Doris Jean Johnson 1952–
  - Sherman Rowlan 1949–
    - Shiri Annise Rowlan 1977–
    - Bailey Albert Rowlan 1973–
    - Sean Vincent Rowlan 1975–
  - Karen Johnson 1944–
  - Pamela Johnson 1948–
  - Ellis Reid 1947–
    - Brenda Wynona Reid 1973–
    - Caroline Elaine Reid 1975–
    - Dorothy Ellis Reid 1977–
    - Jason Eugene Reid 1971–
  - Sadie Stuart 1952–
    - Essence Stuart 1973–
  - Cedric Johnson 1949–
  - Vivian Price 1951–
    - Cedric Johnson, Jr. 1970–
  - Edward Johnson 1943–
  - Andre Johnson 1949–
  - Curtis Johnson 1950–

PROLOGUE

He absolutely hated it when she was right. And she'd been right all his life. His older sister. She'd told him to find a wife while he was in college, but what healthy nineteen-year-old male had marriage on his mind while he was in college? Sex, yes. For sure. But marriage? There was plenty of time for marriage when he was an old man.

When he was nineteen he thought thirty-two was old. By the time he got that old he'd be married with children, a mortgage, a minivan and a dog. Well, he had a mortgage, but no children, no minivan, no dog, and no wife.

Wesley Cooper enjoyed learning. He'd spent his college years closeted in a lab most of the time. Oh, he'd made time for dating, Saturday night movies, dances, fraternity parties. He'd had plenty of women, but he'd never really been serious about anyone. Now he wanted a wife and he couldn't find one. He hated it when his sister was right. He *should* have found a wife when he was in college. But what did his sister know anyway? At thirty-six she had yet to do the white-dress-and-rice thing. Well, she *was* engaged, but that didn't mean marriage was a certainty.

At his age dating should have been a thing of the past. And blind dating should be outlawed regardless of age.

But he'd done his share, computer dates, chat rooms, singles bars, *and* blind dates. His brother had proved smarter than both him and his sister. He'd met his wife during his first week at Stanford. Six weeks after graduation they were married. But Wes had had his head in too many books, spent too many Saturday nights in the lab instead of finding the right woman, and now he was paying for it with blind dates. Well, no more. Tonight's was the end, the last. He was out of the business.

One more time, he'd told himself earlier this evening. One more blind date. After all, this one could be the one. But she wasn't. Wes climbed the four steps to Isaiah Lambert's front door. He'd agreed to meet Ms. Monica Banks. *Damn*, if he knew then what he knew now, he wouldn't have wasted his time. And now he had to face the guys. He'd come to Isaiah's straight from dropping Ms. Banks at her front door. He knew they'd start in on him the moment he walked in. It was a guy thing. Wes had to take his medicine. There was no way of getting around it.

The guys were playing poker. He would have been here with them except for his date. He'd opted to come here instead of going home, to take the ribbing now and not wait for some moment that would come at the most inopportune time. Here he had some form of control. Not much, but at least there was no female audience the way there had been the last time they decided to get on him about his quest.

Wes didn't remember dating being this hard when he was a teenager. He'd had zits then and if someone turned him down, his confidence was shaken. He was no longer a teenager. At thirty-two he discovered dating hadn't changed much and although he could handle rejection, tonight had been the worst date he'd had in sixteen years. Monica Banks talked incessantly about her last boyfriend, someone with whom she had unresolved issues. She told Wes how much he reminded her of her father, ate loudly, stepped on his feet when they danced, and sang off-key in his ear.

If he hadn't been thinking of quitting this type of socialization, Monica would have pushed him to it. He was done with dating. There had to be an easier way to find a wife, but he would invest no more time in pursuit of the perfect woman. Somewhere tonight he'd decided he didn't really need a wife. He was a geneticist. He could have a family even if he didn't have a wife. He'd talked to JoAnne weeks ago about helping him. All he had to do was call her again and set another plan in motion. A wife would make his parents happy. His sister and brother were bound to lecture him on his decision, but he could handle them and he didn't need a wife for his purposes. He could do just as well, probably better, without one.

Wes knocked once and opened the door. A sudden burst of laughter rose as he stepped across the threshold. He could hear the noise all the way to his car. Laughter and friendly cajoling greeted his entrance. It was too loud for anyone to hear him. The noise came from the back. Wes knew they were in the kitchen. It was customary to stay near the beer. Isaiah's kitchen was huge, with a circular table they could all fit around. Wes was already smiling. Playing a couple of hands would help raise his spirits.

He stopped at the kitchen door. Smoke hung in the air like an opaque horizon. Five men sat around the table playing cards. These were the science guys: biology, physics, biochemistry, genetics, and math. Math was allowed in only because of its connection to physics. Intelligence levels or number of degrees didn't matter. They could be adjunct professors, heads of departments, or the guy washing petri dishes and test tubes. The only requirement was that they were associated with the sciences and male. Like women, men needed time to themselves. This weekly game was their ritual. Since Wes had come to Meyers University they had gotten together every week for a friendly game of poker. The group had few rules. No women and no talk about work. Consequently, the talk centered on work and women.

While the temperature outside was in the thirties, these guys had discarded sweaters for shirtsleeves. Wes pulled his tie to the side and loosened it.

"Fold." Chase Morris, math professor, closed the fan of cards in his hand and threw them facedown on the table in front of him.

"Me, too." Tate Levy from biochemistry did the same.

Cards slapped on the table as one by one the players folded.

"Call," Isaiah from physics said with a straight face. Isaiah had uncanny luck. He often won. His face was so straight they kidded him that he could bluff his way out of a fire with a lighted match.

Rupert Cross from biology spread his five cards faceside up over the Formica surface, smacking them down one by one to reveal a royal flush. A roar went up, laughter and groans mixing with the smoky air. Rupert raked in the pot of cash from the middle of the table.

"Hey, Wes." Rupert noticed him. "What are you doing here?"

"Yeah, man, I thought you had a *date*," Tate Levy added.

Wes advanced into the room, hearing the snicker that followed the comment. They all knew he was looking for a wife. They'd been privy to his methods for some time. While they teased him here about looking for a wife they only talked about the dates in public. Most of the faculty thought he was playing the field, dating a lot and taking no serious interest in anyone. He wondered what they would think if they knew the truth.

He took a chair, spun it around, and straddled it. "That's the last one," he said. "I'm done with dating."

"Didn't go well, I gather?"

"In a word, the pits," he told Rupert.

Isaiah put a long-neck beer bottle in his hand. "You'll feel differently in the morning."

"No," Wes said, taking a long swallow. "I've done blind dates, computer dates, chat rooms, and singles clubs. I'm convinced there's no compatible woman out there."

"There's always Olivia," Tate Levy said with a laugh. The entire congregation joined him. Wes was the only one who didn't laugh. Olivia Harris worked in biochemistry with Tate. Everyone knew she had a crush on him. At their ages he wondered if it was still called a crush. He knew she wanted him. She made no secret of her feelings. Unfortunately he had none of those feelings for her.

"This is unlike you, Wes. Giving up. I never thought I'd see it."

"Oh, I'm not giving up, Jerry. I'm just changing focus."

Gerald Cusack, whom everyone called Jerry, worked in the genetics lab next to Wes's. The two had never really hit it off. They were colleagues, but not friends. Wes wasn't really sure why. They didn't work on the same projects. He knew Jerry hated him although he had no idea why. Personality differences were all he could think of. Wes understood that there was something inside people that brought them together or kept them apart. Male bonding, that's what his sister would call it. He couldn't argue with her. He and his assistant Glenn had become fast friends. They thought alike, worked well together despite Glenn's ribbing him about his dates, while he and Jerry Cusack meshed about as well as a fly on flypaper, stuck together and struggling to get free.

"Changing to what?"

"Instead of looking for a wife, I'm putting my efforts into finding the perfect mother candidate."

For a second there wasn't a sound. They all looked at him as if he'd just announced he was pregnant. Then the roar of laughter spontaneously seized the group and the sound bounced off the walls in thunderous bedlam.

"Doesn't one of those involve the other?" Rupert asked when the hilarity died down.

"Only if you're talking biology." Wes smiled. He took another swig of his beer feeling uncomfortable under group scrutiny. "I'm thinking genetics."

"Genetics?" Jerry said.

"I'm going to find the perfect subject."

Tate shuffled the cards. "A surrogate?" He stopped and lifted an eyebrow as he looked at Wes.

Jerry threw his head back and laughed. "I'll bet you," he began. "I'll bet in the next year you can't find a woman to have a baby for you."

"I already have a surrogate."

Jerry was baiting him. The smile froze on his face, however. Wes enjoyed seeing that. Jerry loved having the upper hand. He was good at throwing out insults, but when someone came back at him, he was often at a loss for words.

"Then what's your problem?" Isaiah asked.

"The perfect subject," Wes said.

From a moment they all waited for him to continue.

"All right, I'll bite," Chase said. He leaned forward,

his arms on the table. "I know I'm only in the math department and totally illogical at this state of inebriation, but what is the perfect subject?"

"Beautiful woman, highly intelligent, logical thinking, yet with a fiery passion, accomplished in more than her own field of expertise."

"Wow," Isaiah said, lifting his hands as if from a hot plate. "Bite me."

"You believe such a creature exists?" Jerry asked, his face set in seriousness.

Wes nodded.

"How drunk are you?" Tate asked.

"I'm serious about this."

"She must have been a dog of a date," Rupert said.

"She was very good to look at." Wes felt the need to defend his taste in women, even if she was a blind date. He had nothing else good to say about Monica Banks. He wished her well and hoped she could resolve the issues with her former boyfriend.

"First you have to find such a prodigy," Jerry began. "Then you have to convince her to have a baby with you without the ceremony of falling in love. Man, I'd lay odds you can't do it."

"You're on," Wes said quietly. "I'll bet you that twelve months from today I will have found the perfect subject to produce a highly intelligent child and the terms will be agreed to by both parties."

The room seemed dreadfully quiet after he made his declaration. Only the smoke hung in the air like an ominous cloak banding them together in some unholy alliance.

"So what are the stakes?" Chase asked.

"Make it easy on yourself, Wes," Jerry said, sounding every bit like he meant the opposite of what he said.

"You're expecting to win?" Wes asked.

"I'm expecting you to lose," he said with a grunt that had always irritated Wes.

"My research grant," Wes offered.

"No." Tate Levy stood up. "This is a friendly game and a friendly wager. Let's not take things too seriously."

Wes ignored him and so did Jerry. The two men stared at each other as if they were the only ones in the room. "You've always wanted it," he told Jerry. "If I can't pull this off in a year, it's yours."

"No, Wes. That's too much to think about in our state. If you want to do this let's sleep on it and talk about it in the morning." Tate spoke to him, but Wes's attention was on Jerry. He knew his friend was trying to keep him from making a mistake.

"I'm not drunk."

"You're also not thinking clearly," Tate pointed out.

"Yes, I am."

"You all heard him," Jerry said, taking up the gauntlet.

"There's one more thing," Wes said.

"What?" Jerry's eyebrows went up as if this were the trump card Wes had been holding.

"Suppose I win?"

"What do you want?"

"I want your promise that you'll treat everyone, from the secretaries to the head of the department, with the respect they deserve as members of the scientific community."

Jerry smiled as if he'd already won. "Is that all?"

"That's a lot, Jerry," Wes said. "You act like people don't exists. You treat the staff as if they were your personal servants. It stops if I win."

Jerry stared at him. He looked from one face to another. Wes knew he wanted to say something, contradict him in some way, but he must have thought better of it.

"Deal," he said.

The room was silent. Every pair of eyes looked at the two men. Jerry smiled as if he held all the cards.

"One year from today, you'll either have a baby on the way . . ." Jerry paused for effect. Wes knew his tactics, knew how he liked to gain attention with his carefully timed pauses. "Or you'll be knocking on foundation doors."

ONE

Three months later

"You haven't seen her yet?"

Wesley Cooper shrugged out of his lab coat and hung it on the hook behind the door of his office. He didn't have to ask Glenn Steuben, his assistant, who "she" was. The male campus population had buzzed with Brenda Reid's attributes since she first set foot on campus almost a month ago. Wes had yet to run into the siren queen.

He would later tonight. There was a party in her honor at the president's house. She'd managed to elude him for a month, but her time was limited.

"She's exactly what you're looking for," Glenn continued as Wes straightened his tie. There wasn't time to return home and change. He'd go from here. "It's been three months and you haven't come up with any prospects."

Wes laughed. "You sound like a nervous bridegroom."

"More like the mother of the groom. I'm the one who's worried that you won't fulfill your promises."

"Don't worry, *Mom*." Wes slapped his assistant's shoulder.

"I got a look at her file," Glenn said. Janelle over in

personnel had it on her computer screen when I went to see her one day."

Wes turned to Glenn. "Janelle let you look at it?" Wes doubted that. Janelle Jones could keep a secret and she never gave out unauthorized information.

"She was out of the office, getting coffee," Glenn confessed.

"And you just read the file?"

"Curious minds want to know." As Wes looked at him he raised his eyebrows several times, then seeing the expression on Wes's face looked a little nervous. "I didn't read anything confidential. Only personal stuff," he rushed to explain. "All right, it was wrong, but everyone is talking about her and here was information just sitting there. It was like finding money."

Glenn had been his assistant for five years. He trusted him with everything in the lab. They worked on projects that weren't top secret but groundbreaking, and he wouldn't want them revealed to anyone. He knew Glenn was trustworthy. In the case of Brenda Reid he was just curious. And scared.

"I understand you wouldn't breach a confidence here, Glenn."

"I never would. I wanted to know about her. She's got an IQ of 212, genius range. Graduated from MIT, third in her class. Got her PhD at age twenty. Taught at MIT for four years, then went to work for Cleage Observatory at Connelley University. She remained there for five years before coming here to Meyers. She's twenty-nine, long dark red hair that's often pulled back into a ponytail, but boy it has possibilities. She's thin—"

"I'm sure good teeth is next on the list," Wes said, interrupting. He had to stop his assistant. He was interested in what Glenn was saying and felt he shouldn't be. It was like eavesdropping on a stranger.

Glenn ignored his sarcasm and went on. "She's got a spitfire personality, looks great in a pair of jeans, and doesn't wear an engagement ring or a wedding band."

"I'm sure that wasn't in her file."

Glenn shook his head, his mouth smiling.

"And last time I looked you *were* wearing a wedding ring." Wes pointed at Glenn's left hand and he glanced at the gleaming gold ring resting there.

"I was just looking, my friend. There's no law against it. Wait until you see her."

"It won't make a difference. She already sounds too good to be true. But it doesn't matter. She could be the most beautiful woman in the world and she'd still be out of bounds. She works here and by default she's immediately off the list."

"You haven't got much time. You've done nothing in the past three months. There are only nine left."

"Enough time," Wes said, consoling him.

"I thought you were serious about this."

"Not as serious as you, apparently." Wes slipped his arms into his suit jacket. Since he'd made the bet with Jerry, Glenn had been nervous. He'd tried to find him women, looked on the Internet for possibilities, even had his wife scouring the area for any woman who would fit his requirements. "Don't worry about it, Glenn. I haven't exactly done nothing."

"What have you done? You haven't been on any dates." Glenn stared at him. "Have you?"

"Not in a while."

"Then what have you done? I don't want to work for Gerald Cusack."

"You won't. You'll have your own research going in a couple of months."

"What?"

Wes smiled. "It came in today." Glenn had been waiting for this. His research grant had come through. Wes had seen it when he was in the director's office. The money wouldn't actually arrive until the fall semester began in two months, but Glenn could count on it. And Wes would need another assistant.

Glenn's smile widened. "Now you really need to see her."

Wes thought the news of his grant would force all other problems out of his head, but apparently it didn't. Wes had been doing things, but most of what people expected wasn't the method he'd chosen or even the one he'd considered. He'd always known what he planned to do. He just let Glenn and the guys believe he was on a mother safari.

"I will see her. The party, remember." He paused. "Beautiful, long hair, looks great in jeans . . ."

Glenn smiled. "Wait until you see her."

Brenda Reid never knew what to wear to these shindigs. She couldn't remember what was appropriate when. Did she wear white before or after Labor Day? When were patent leather shoes acceptable? She much preferred her jeans and a T-shirt to this piece of air that was as light as a cloud. And it was red. Was it all right to wear this color now? But if her cousin Shiri hadn't sent it to her she'd have nothing to wear. Everything she owned was too old, too tight, too short, too high-necked, too revealing, or just too something. She'd finally decided on this twenty minutes ago. Would it be acceptable?

She was often underdressed or overdressed, never quite managing to find that middle ground where everything jelled.

She looked at herself in the mirror, holding the dress in front of her. It felt good against her bare legs. What would she look like in it? Oh, why did they feel they needed to have these affairs anyway? She'd just as well start her job without the fanfare. But this was a university. And universities were known for parties, not the beer busts and bootie calls of the students, but the faculty needed little or no excuse to get together. Tonight it was her turn to stand front and center. It was her formal introduction to the staff. She'd just as soon skip it, but she couldn't.

Brenda checked her watch. She didn't have much time. Slipping the dress over her head, she zipped it up while trying to push her feet into sandals. She decided against nylons. It was too hot. The dress swished about her legs. She smiled as she turned and looked at her reflection in the mirror. It didn't look like her. Her hair hung about her shoulders and neck and her eyes looked larger with the makeup she had on. Ever since Essence had come to Connelley and taken her for a makeover, she was surprised at the woman in the mirror when she got dressed to go somewhere other than the observatory. She wasn't as much of a stranger now as she had been, but she still looked like someone Brenda might be related to, and not herself. She'd seen photos of her mother when she was younger. The face in the mirror looked a lot like her.

Minutes after leaving the house, where she was still walking around unpacked boxes, she found a parking space outside the university president's house. There were cars up and down the tree-lined block. She cursed under her breath. Rushing down the street, she checked her watch. Late, she thought. She was the guest of honor and she couldn't get to a party on time. Now her appearance would be doubly noted and in this outfit. If it didn't fit in, her first impression on her new colleagues was bound to be a disaster.

At the door Brenda took a deep breath and smoothed her hair down. She'd had little time to do anything to it. She hadn't found a beauty salon yet and she was hopeless at styling it herself. It fell straight down her back with only the smallest curl on the ends. She usually pulled it back into a long ponytail that kept it off her face while she worked. She rang the doorbell and the door was immediately opened as if the person on the other side had been waiting for her to ring.

Brenda looked up, then farther up. There was a man smiling at her. He was tall and *gorgeous*. She opened her mouth to say something, but not a single thought formed in her head. Where was her brain? She hadn't been attracted to a man since her fiasco with Reuben Sherwood ended so badly. She gaped at him. Bright, white teeth in a face that was as dark as rich chocolate. Dark chocolate. Godiva chocolate. Her breath caught. And for some reason she was hungry.

"Hello, we've been waiting for you." He leaned lazily in the doorway, one shoulder against the jamb, a wineglass balanced in his hand. Brenda couldn't get past him without brushing against him and the thought sent delicious shivers through her system. He was wearing a suit that looked great on him. Maybe her dress would be all right after all. It was July in northern California and unusually hot. The red confection had spaghetti straps that connected to a scalloped bodice. It was fitted to her waist, then billowed out in layers of chiffon as it fell to her knees. She liked the rustling sound it made as she walked. Shiri said it was elegant and fitting for any after-five occasion.

"Sorry, I'm late," she said, finding her voice a little high.

"I'm Doctor Wesley Cooper, genetics." He shifted the wineglass to his left hand and extended his right to her. "Wes to my friends."

Wes Cooper, she thought. Brenda let his hand hang in the air for a moment before she took it. So this was Wes Cooper. She hadn't been on campus twenty minutes before his name had come up. She could see why. The man was open-your-eyes-wide-and-take-him-in gorgeous. And he was the one who wanted to date her. According to campus scuttlebutt Wes Cooper was a ladies' man, dating constantly and never more than once. For some reason he wanted to date her, sight unseen. She wondered what he thought of her now. So far she hadn't given her name, but she was probably the only new face in the crowd.

"So, Wes-to-my-friends," she repeated. "I'm Doctor Brenda Reid, astronomy, cold fish. I'm an I-don't-date-my-coworkers kind of woman." She gave him a dazzling smile. "And I especially don't date those who think they can use me as the subject of a bet."

She dropped his hand and brushed past him into the room. Brenda didn't breathe until she was well out of Wes's sight.

"Doctor Reid," Phillip Langley took her hands in both of his and welcomed her. The Meyers University president was a distinguished-looking man with white hair and dancing blue eyes. He was short by her standards, but he had a presence that made people notice him, listen to him when he spoke, and take heed of his words. His wife, Amanda, also smiled and shook her hand. Together they looked like brother and sister. "Let me introduce you to some of the staff," he said.

Several colleagues she'd already met during her first two weeks at the university, and she was introduced to everyone else. There was no way she could remember all of them. Names blurred like an out-of-focus movie screen and she'd never been able to remember people's names. Give her a constellation or a portion of the sky and she could name all the stars in it, but someone she met five minutes ago she couldn't recall the name for more than a second.

Everyone was friendly, making small talk with her, asking if she was settled into her new surroundings and if there was anything she needed at the school. A couple of people asked about her previous job and one woman wanted to know if they had shared any of the same professors at MIT. Brenda didn't know any of the names she mentioned and eventually they each moved on to other groups.

Brenda longed to be gone, away from this crowd that pressed in on her, turning the cavernous room into a claustrophobic closet. Everywhere she looked there was Mr. Gorgeous smiling at her, looking every bit as if he had a secret. Her secret.

"So you know about the bet," he said from behind her as she found herself momentarily alone. Brenda was forced to turn around.

"It's been mentioned." More than once, she thought. In fact she hadn't been able to go anywhere without hearing about Wes Cooper and his bet to date her. Now that she'd seen him she wondered why he even needed a bet to get a date. He was obviously good looking enough to get dates on his own. But not with her. She had sworn off dating men she worked with.

She'd sworn off men in general, but Essence convinced her that Reuben Sherwood was not worthy of her quitting the entire sex. Yet since her breakup with him she hadn't entered another relationship. It had been harmful and she knew she didn't want to put her heart in that kind a risk again.

"It's a harmless procedure," he said.

"Especially when none of you will win." She didn't know how many others were involved, but campus gossip told her there was a group of guys who devised this game.

"I could take that as a challenge." He sipped from his wineglass, yet his eyes never left her face.

"Don't," she warned. "It's not meant to be."

Wes shrugged his shoulders. "Well, it only proves we're still red-blooded human beings."

She didn't doubt that for a instant. Not the way her blood pressure was reacting to him. It made her nervous. She wanted more than ever to get away, mostly from him. The other members of the faculty didn't have nearly the effect on her that he had, and she didn't like it.

Brenda arrived on campus two weeks before the summer session started. It would be good to start in the summer, she'd told herself. She'd teach one class and have plenty of time to work in the observatory. There wouldn't be many people on campus and she could ease into the job. If she could get through this party she wouldn't have to see most of these people again until the fall semester started or the next party she couldn't get out of attending. She was leaving in a month anyway for a two-week vacation and a week of family reunion. She'd return in September and that feeling of newness would be gone. Life would settle into routine and everyone would be too busy with a full load of classes and personal research to worry about whether she attended faculty parties or social functions.

"Dance with me?"

Brenda had been lost in thought. She hadn't noticed Wes Cooper was still standing in front of her. In a flash she heard the music, a soft slow song. She didn't have time to refuse. He took her hand. Instinctively she resisted. His touch was dangerous. He pulled harder and unless she created a scene she had to dance with him. Brenda followed him to the floor. She turned into his arms, feeling as if he swallowed her completely. His size was massive compared to hers. His body heat seeped into her and she could smell his cologne, warm and tantalizing. The room seemed to recede. The danger she felt was lost in the heated air around them. Voices muffled to a white noise and then to silence. All she could hear was the music. She moved with Wes. Swaying back and forth, being carried away by the feel of his arms holding her securely against him and the smooth voice of Luther Vandross singing in her ears, spinning his tale of love directly to her.

There's something about the feel of a man, the smell of maleness, something rough and tender, protective and explosive. Something dangerous. And exciting. She couldn't define it, distill it into words that made sense. She could feel it in the way he held her, in the strength of arms that could crush her, yet safeguarded her in their embrace.

Brenda wanted to run her hands over his arms, feel the tight cords of power that ran the length of him, and know that he held a greater strength, a control that could harness all that strength. This was insane, she told herself suddenly, stopping the train of thought that had no terminal in the present or the future. It had been years since anyone had made her feel like this. She wasn't sure she'd ever felt like this. She couldn't let it happen. Not again.

She felt welcome here. She liked Meyers University, had liked it the moment it had come into view as she drove over the mountain for her interview. She didn't want anything to get in the way of that, and the man holding her in his arms, making her want to dissolve into him, was one way to lose her future here. She'd been down this road before. Following the same path twice in a lifetime was foolish.

She wasn't foolish. She could almost hear her cousin, Essence Stuart, saying it. "You'll never let anything as common as a man turn your head." It was also Essence who'd told her she only saw the stars in the sky. Never those in a man's eyes.

Reuben Sherwood was a tenured professor in the psychology department at Connelley University. She'd had an affair with him. When it ended, life at Connelley was terrible for both of them. The number of functions where they were together was too much. Their colleagues tiptoed around them. The situation was uncomfortable for all. One of them had to leave. Since he was tenured and she was looking for more than the university could offer her, she began making applications. Meyers was her first choice.

Wes's arms tightened around her. Brenda felt the comfort of them. She wanted to thaw the ice she had around her heart and continue to let it melt, but thoughts of Reuben and the pressure of Wes's arms brought her back to her senses. She pushed back, giving herself breathing room and looking about to see if anyone was taking notice of how intimately he'd held her. And how much she'd enjoyed it. While there were other couples dancing she felt as if every eye was focused on the two of them; certainly the male eyes were on them. She wondered how many of them were in on the bet. If Wes did manage to get a date with her, who would the winner be?

"Anything wrong?" he asked.

She looked up. She could think of nothing to say. Then the final notes of the song came to her aid. "The music stopped." She moved out of his embrace completely. "Thank you, Doctor Cooper."

"Wes to my friends," he said.

"Wes," she said and backed away. She needed something to drink—*and a cold shower.* Brenda headed for the bar. She ordered a tonic water with a twist of lemon. She wanted to chug it the way she did when she worked out, but this room was full of polite company so she sipped it through the small straw the bartender had put in the glass.

"I see you and Wes are getting along."

Brenda turned around to a too-thin blonde with a beak nose and limp hair. Her only saving grace was her smile, which showed even white teeth and a dimple in her left cheek. She had come to stand next to Brenda, who couldn't remember her name or in which department she worked.

"We danced." She moved away from the bar. The blonde fell into step with her.

"I noticed."

Brenda stopped and turned to look at her. "Are you two . . ." She raised her eyebrows and pointed her finger at the blonde and then the man on the other side of the room. "Are you two an item?" She noticed the woman wore no rings. She'd also noticed the same thing about Wesley Cooper. Naturally she assumed he wasn't married and from his reputation she was sure of it. She also thought that he didn't see anyone on a steady basis, but the beak-nose woman in front of her acted as if there were things she didn't know about.

"Oh no," she said, her eyes squinting and her head shaking. "He's a friend. That's all."

Something in the way she said it made Brenda think of regret. It was there underlying her words as if she wanted it to be something more. Brenda glanced at Wes. At that moment he looked her way and flashed those even white teeth. Brenda returned the gesture before she thought of doing anything else. Wesley Cooper was a man who commanded attention. It was impossible to be in the same room with him and not feel his presence. When she turned back to the blonde the expression on her face was pure anger. It disappeared in a moment and the smile was in place. The change was so rapid Brenda felt it was a practiced action.

She'd said there was nothing between them. That didn't mean she didn't *want* something to be between them. Brenda was sure she did. She understood jealousy when she saw it. It wasn't often an emotion that was directed at her, but when it was it was fully recognizable.

"I'm sorry," Brenda confessed, "but I don't remember your name."

"Olivia Harris."

Biochemist. She suddenly remembered. Olivia worked in the biochemistry department. "Well, Olivia, biochemistry and genetics aren't that far apart. Just keep your eyes open." She glanced at Wes and smiled at the woman. The blonde smiled shyly back as if an understanding had been reached between them.

Brenda was captured for a dance by another doctor in genetics. Then she danced with the university president. She saw Olivia dancing with Wes. The woman looked as if she were in heaven. Brenda understood. No one she had danced with tonight had even remotely evoked the feelings in her that Wes had.

She put that on hold and continued to talk to the other faculty members. Amanda Langley checked to see that she was having a good time. Brenda smiled brightly and nodded. Around eleven the party broke up. She was relieved. She would have skipped this function or left as soon as it was correct to do so, but as the honored guest she was required to stay until the end.

"Let me walk you to your car, Brenda." She recognized Wes's voice. Unable to stop herself she stiffened.

"That won't be necessary," she told him. She grabbed Olivia as she started to pass them. "Walk Olivia to her car. She was telling me earlier she had a hard time getting her car started tonight. I wouldn't want her to be stranded." Brenda was sure the woman wouldn't mind the small lie.

Wes acquiesced with the chivalry of a southern gentleman. The two of them left and Brenda smiled to herself. The expression on Wes-to-my-friends' face was priceless. Turning to Doctor Langley and his wife she said good night. "Good night, Doctor Reid," Mrs. Langley said. "I'm sure you made the right choice coming to Meyers."

"Thank you. I'm sure I did too."

Brenda started to leave, but Mrs. Langley stopped her. She left her husband and walked out on the porch with Brenda. "By the way, Doctor Reid." The silver-haired woman glanced down the street. Brenda could see Wes and Olivia Harris walking away from the house. "In addition to biochemistry, Doctor Harris loves speed. She drives a vintage Corvette, red and white convertible, 1966, with a silver grill. It's got a big engine. I can't tell you the particulars, but Doctor Harris knows everything about it, right down to the number on the engine. She does all the maintenance herself." The older woman smiled at her. "And Doctor Cooper, along with everyone else on the faculty, knows that."

Wes pulled his tie off as he closed the door of his house. It had been an interesting evening. More interesting than he anticipated. He hadn't expected it, but he felt as if he were walking on air. He'd only allow this feeling to overtake him tonight. Brenda Reid was beautiful and he was nearly tempted to try the dating scene again. She satisfied all his requirements, except one. He already knew she was intelligent. She had a lively wit. She was beautiful. He liked her laugh, the soft drawl of an accent that she'd probably tried to lose. She danced well and was light in his arms. But they both worked at Meyers. She had a rule against dating colleagues and so did he. He knew it wasn't a good idea.

But she sure did get his juices flowing!

He hadn't known she was at the door when the bell rang. He'd been passing it and opened it because no one else was around. Despite his cool, he'd been bowled over by her striking appearance. Glenn Steuben's comments in the lab before the party had been right on the money. Her hair was pulled straight back and off her face leaving it open to inspection. Her eyes were an affecting shade of brown, like transparent amber, deep and openly mysterious with depths that reached back eons.

He'd wanted to dive into them and find the source of their wisdom. She stood a step down from where Wes stood, but with her head near his chin she was tall for a woman. He discovered how leggy she was when she walked away from him giving him a mouth watering view of her long legs and the promise of curvy hips under the hissing red chiffon. The color sizzled on her and Wes could almost imagine a fire in her soul. He could certainly feel it in his own.

The sprinkling of freckles over her nose had him wanting to kiss each of them individually. Their color dotted her very light brown skin, which had a ruddy redness underlying it. But it was her hair that completed the package. Auburn in color, and the sunlight behind her added to the fiery redness and made it look as if it were burning. Wes felt as if she could blister him if he got too close, yet he had an almost uncontrollable urge to run his hands thought it.

Vulnerability, however, showed in the small scar bisecting her right eyebrow. She covered it with makeup but he'd been close enough to see it and see that there was pain in her life.

She'd issued the challenge, verbally and with everything her body said. Dancing was only one indicator. She fit in his arms. He liked the way she smelled, the way she felt as he held her. He couldn't keep his mind from following his thoughts to places neither of them would go. Brenda Reid would be a challenge. One he had to disregard.

Now he understood everything Glenn had said about her since she arrived. She was perfect for his needs even if he didn't develop any emotional ties. She had the looks and the IQ. She was in good health. And she knew about the bet. She thought it had to do with a date.

Boy, was she wrong!

TWO

Brenda was used to being up all night. The light show hidden during daylight hours was there for the taking while most of the world slept. The party last night had disturbed her balance with the division of day and night.

She'd found it hard to sleep after she got home from the party. Her backfired white lie made her feel foolish. More so when she realized the smile on Wes Cooper's face was probably a smirk. But on him it looked good. And that was a problem too.

Everything on him looked good—so far as she could tell.

By the time sleep took her the tinge of red was washing up the mountains in the distance. When she woke it was time for her class. She'd rushed to it expecting at every step to see Wes Cooper striding toward her. He hadn't made an appearance. Brenda didn't know if she was glad or disappointed. Her eyes constantly darted to the door as if she expected him to come looking for her. Although why she should feel like this she didn't know. They'd only met last night. She'd danced with him once. The experience had been frightening. She could hardly breathe in his arms. There was something about him holding her close, his breath on her cheek and his body against hers, that she hadn't known could happen. Especially to her.

She was the bookworm. She didn't have emotions for anything except the coldness of space. She wasn't moved by men. Even as a teenager she hadn't been the hormonally controlled adolescent. Once she'd thought she had a crush on Alex Carter, another gifted and talented student who appeared to share her interest in astronomy. He'd touched her hair one night as they stared at the open sky. She'd nearly fainted from the feelings that tore through her like a train jumping the tracks. But Alex was only flicking away a firefly. He wasn't interested in her at all. He was interested in Gloria Fledstone, the head cheerleader. The fact that Gloria was dating the captain of the football team and so far out of Alex's league he might as well have been on Pluto did nothing to assuage his desire.

Was that what she felt for Wesley Cooper? Desire? Did it happen this fast? With a first look?

With Reuben it was nothing like last night. It had been gradual. And he'd pursued her more than she thought of him. Yet she had been enamored by him. She thought she loved him, but she wasn't sure any longer. One night, a couple of hours, and a smile had changed her entire thoughts on the male species.

And on one man in particular.

But Wesley Cooper was the forbidden fruit of her Eden.

The day passed without incident. Brenda went about her class, teaching, advising students, greeting and talking to colleagues, having lunch with Professor Diggins, another astronomer in her department. In the entire day she saw nothing of Wes Cooper. She should feel relieved, yet somehow inside her there was an unsettling, a nervousness she couldn't explain or even name. And now she found herself here. In her sanctuary.

Dowers Observatory sat at the highest point of the university. Up a steeply winding road to the top of the mountain peak that shared its name with the observatory and the family who founded the school in 1893. The observatory hadn't been built until 1910, but it was a cornerstone of the university. It could be seen from almost every point on campus.

Brenda entered the vacuous rotunda. The building housed a 200-inch telescope. Tonight the dome, rising to 135 feet, was open. She could see a rectangular patch of sky through the opening.

Brenda walked across the floor. Her crepe-sole shoes making no noise as she moved. Getting into the giant chair, she worked the automatic controls that lifted her off the ground and raised her to the telescope's eyepiece. The highly oiled mechanism made a quiet whirring noise. In the 137-foot-diameter dome only she could hear the sound.

Stepping onto the platform she peered through the lens. The heavens came into view. Brenda marveled at the vastness of the sea above her. She stood five feet ten inches in her stocking feet. She had no measurement of the sky, no way to tell how far it extended, and if there was an end what came after that? She felt no insignificance in this setting.

Brenda stared at the sky. The points of light never failed to amaze her. She knew they were burning gases, that they would eventually cave into themselves and create a black hole, but tonight she didn't care for the scientific explanation. Tonight they were just beautiful. Despite her cousin Essence's assessment of her, that she saw more in the sky than in a man's eyes, tonight there was a man. And he *did* have beautiful eyes.

When Wes Cooper opened that door last night she all but gasped at the sight of him. People had mentioned his classic good looks, but she hadn't been prepared for the reality of him. Of course it was her own fault. She hadn't really been involved with anyone. Her head was in the stars. Even her affair with Reuben had been an attempt to prove Essence wrong. It hadn't worked and she was worse for the experience, but she was here now, at a new job, starting over.

And not about to make the same mistake twice.

She stared at the constellations. Usually she only looked at them as starting points, a sort of direction finder for her to locate other things in the sky. She'd mapped areas of the heavens at Connelley, looking deeper into the spaces that only appeared as darkness to the naked eye.

Ships used to sail by the stars—men went around the world using star charts and the rising and setting of the sun. Brenda saw them as galaxies. One huge system existing in the cosmos for some purpose unknown to her, but it had an order, a regularity of events, and it had exceptions. Like most things in life, rules could be applied ninety percent of the time. But it was the ten percent that was interesting.

It was like love. She stopped. Cocked her head. She hadn't thought of that before. She loved the stars. They were hers. They defined her. She traveled with them, watched them move across the heavens as if they were expressions moving across a face. Often their beauty took her breath away. She was blessed to be able to indulge her heart in something she loved. But tonight there was another galaxy occupying her thoughts. Wes Cooper was his own universe. He was the unknown, the galactic mystery that could either have her soaring through the heavens or reduce her to cosmic dust. He was an enigma, but not as much as her reaction to him. She looked back at the sky. He scared her a little and she didn't know why.

Brenda got lost looking at the sky. The world on earth receded and she was part of the sky, part of the heavens. There was something that happened to her up here in this vast room close to the sky. She became part of it. She felt as if her feet left the platform and she floated off, suspended in the stars.

Time had no meaning when Brenda was lost in the stars. She didn't know how much had passed while she stood there. She wasn't researching, looking for new galaxies, or checking for changes in those she knew. Black holes, sunspots, nuclear explosions on distant stars had no measure in her mind. She was stargazing. Something every child had done once or twice in a lifetime. She could have been lying back in her bed in Birmingham, Alabama, staring at the sky. It was only slightly different here. For most people the stars looked the same no matter where they were. Only she and those in her profession knew the differences. Like sunrise and sunset. They were vastly different, yet most people equated them as one and the same.

Finally Brenda stepped back from the telescope, back onto earth, her head returning from the spatial void to the firmness of the ground. She locked herself in the chair and started her descent. She needed her feet on the floor, her mind returned to logic, her thought processes devoid of illusions.

As the chair reached the floor, Wes Cooper stepped away from the shadowed wall and started toward her.

Brenda blinked to make sure he was real. Her heart accelerated. She'd been thinking of him and not sure if she'd conjured him up in her mind, but he kept coming after she opened her eyes, his shoes making the same quiet sound hers had.

"What are you doing here?" she asked as he came to a stop in front of her. Brenda remained in the chair, for a moment forgetting to unhook the basket and stand. He looked every bit as good in the shadows of the dome as he had in the doorway of President Langley's house.

"Just being friendly."

She looked at him with skepticism.

"I can see you don't believe me." He reached down and released the lock on the chair.

She stood. "Why should I? I already know you have an ulterior motive."

"This has nothing to do with the bet."

"Come on, Doctor. I'm smarter than that." She was standing in front of him now. She usually stood tall enough to intimidate most men, but with Wes she had to look up. "Tell me, have you ever been here before?"

"Here? In this dome?" He looked around, up at the huge telescope.

She nodded. He didn't look the least bit out of place. She couldn't tell from the way he carried that straight body of his if his answer would be yes or no.

"Never."

"And you're here now because . . ." She purposely left the sentence hanging, raising a single questioning eyebrow.

"Friendship."

Brenda crossed her arms and looked at Wes. She immediately regretted the action as she noticed his eyes going to the tightness of her T-shirt. She dropped her arms.

"I thought I'd already met the welcoming committee."

"I thought we could go for a cup of coffee, get to know each other, and . . ." He smiled. "I could listen to that wonderful voice of yours."

Brenda lowered her chin and opened her eyes fully. She'd seen Essence look at men this way and was surprised at how naturally the gesture had come to her.

"Would that be a date, Doctor?"

"No."

"It sounds like a date. I've been asked out before, even on an impromptu basis. And this has that date kind of familiarity." Brenda turned and walked away. Her blood pressure was vaulting as high as the domed ceiling. Wes Cooper fell into step beside her as she headed for the door.

"It's only a cup of coffee, not a marriage proposal."

Brenda stopped at the door and faced him. She liked hearing him talk too. She had practiced her words after she left for college. So many people had mentioned her accent that it began to bother her. She made a point of thinking before she spoke so she could be sure of the pronunciation. She still had an accent. She knew that. But it wasn't as pronounced as it had once been.

Wes, on the other hand, was probably never teased about his speech patterns. It took a moment to get used to the cadence of his speech and translate it into words instead of being mesmerized by the sound.

"I'm busy. I have a class to prepare for and many things to get done before the summer ends."

Again she turned and went into the night. The stars felt closer outside. There was no structure to slice them into manageable chunks of sky. Out here they were a vast network of diamonds spangling the skies above her, yet feeling close enough to touch. Brenda pulled her car keys from her pocket and pressed the button that popped the door locks and turned on the interior lights. Wes was right behind her. She turned as she reached her Jeep. "Good night, Wes. Thanks for the invitation."

"You could still reconsider. It's only a cup of coffee."

"Doctor. Cooper." She raised her hand, stopping him from repeating the Wes-to-my-friends litany. "Let's get this straight. You have an ulterior motive for following me around. We both know it. I'm not interested in your bet with the guys. We both work here. So let's not start something neither of us can finish."

"What does that mean?"

"It means I'm not interested."

"Two days, two challenges," he said, grinning.

"This is no challenge. I've been down this road before. I won't go down it again."

She slid into the driver's seat, started the engine, and drove away.

She cursed to herself as she turned out of the parking lot. Why had she said that? She didn't want anyone to know about her affair with Reuben Sherwood. The experience had been humiliating enough in private. She wanted it behind her, never to be thought of again. She did not want to share it with anyone, especially a man who had eyes as insightful as Wes-to-my-friends.

Running into Wes on campus as Brenda went back and forth to classes proved steady and often. The man was persistent. He was like a chameleon. No matter where she went he was there. He'd shown up twice at the observatory, with one offer for a cup of coffee and another to accompany her to a faculty party. It was summer, but the skeletal faculty in residence seemed to find a reason to get together at every turn. She'd managed to hedge off both of them because of her work schedule in the observatory. When she was alone and being truthful with herself, she wondered about her decisions. She thought about Wes a lot, more than she cared to admit.

Brenda checked her watch. She had half an hour before her class. She'd gotten to campus early, hoping to enjoy a silent cup of coffee before working with students who weren't really interested in the subject of astronomy. They were only here to pass the course and get in a few weeks of summer vacation before the fall semester began. Brenda sat in the student lounge. She sipped her coffee and thought about her own plans. She'd be leaving as soon as the summer semester ended too. She was going to her family reunion, looking forward to seeing her cousins again. She, Shiri, and Essence were close, but now that they no longer lived in Birmingham she didn't get to see them often enough. Essence was a massage therapist and Shiri on the fast track as a petrochemical engineer. And she had yet to meet Shiri's new love, J.D.

It looked like there was going to be a wedding in the family. Brenda suddenly frowned. This meant gowns and fittings and looking like a peacock. She was glad Shiri had found someone to love. She deserved it and she was sure Shiri would be devastated if Brenda and Essence weren't part of the wedding. So she'd grit her teeth and not show up wearing her jeans. She'd even have her hair done.

"Hair!" she said out loud, clutching the straight strands that fell down her back. She got up quickly, checking her watch as she gathered her belongings. Her cell phone was in the Jeep. She'd left it on the car's charger since she forgot to charge it the day before. She needed to call and make an appointment.

"Where are you going in such a rush?"

"Wes." She sighed, forgetting that she rarely turned around without finding him on her heels. "Don't you ever work? You seem to be underfoot at all hours." And he was always disconcerting. Her stomach should have become used to his presence by now, but each time she saw him, it went into a kind of acrobatic plunge. She wasn't sure why, but she knew that no medical doctor could treat her for the symptoms. And how would she describe the affliction?

"My research is there when I need it. Like yours, there is a timetable it works with and I have some assistants."

"I'd love to stand here and compare timetables and assistants with you, but I have an appointment to make and a class to get to."

She moved to pass him. His hands came out and closed around her upper arms. She was essentially trapped in front of his massive frame. Her breath caught in her throat and she held it. He wasn't holding her tightly. His hands weren't imprisoning her, yet she couldn't move. She could feel a weakness growing down her body, taking the strength from her legs. What was it? She hadn't ever reacted to a man this way before. She'd never wanted to run her hands up a man's arms and find out what it felt like to have his mouth on hers. She felt inadequate. If she had it to do over she'd pay more attention to the boys who made passes at her when she was a teenager. At twenty-nine she should have had more control over her emotions.

Wes dropped his hands and Brenda let out a breath. "I just wanted to remind you of the end-of-term party next week."

A FAMILY AFFAIR

"I can't make that. I—"

"You can't have anything pressing to do. The term will be over. It's traditional for the summer staff to attend the final closing."

"I was going to say I'd be leaving campus right after the term ends and I have too much to do to get ready to go to another party. So forgive me." She looked at her watch again. "I have to go now or I'll be late." She didn't actually leave for two weeks after the last class, but she did have a lot to get done. She was still getting settled in her house, unpacking and hanging pictures, buying curtains and finding the right spot for everything. She had work in the observatory. She needed to prepare for the fall semester all within the two weeks before she left on her cross-country train ride.

Brenda rushed away. She felt as if she couldn't stand in Wes's presence any longer. Whenever they were together he took up all the air. The family reunion would be good. First she'd have a two-week vacation to spend just lying about doing anything she wanted or doing nothing at all. Then her entire family would show up. Shiri would come and Essence, too, if they could convince her to join them. Essence wasn't really a cousin, but the three of them had grown up together and Essence practically lived at her house when they were children. She was as much a part of the Johnson clan as any of her aunts and uncles.

"Brenda."

She heard her name called. She knew it was Wes's voice, but she kept walking. She'd ignore him. She didn't want to admit how much she wanted to talk to him, to be in his company, to go to that party where she could see him, possibly dance with him one more time.

"Brenda."

The voice was closer. She turned abruptly so he wouldn't touch her, wouldn't slip his hand under her arm and swing her around. But she was too late. He was too close. When she turned he walked into her. His arms enclosed her, and Brenda found her body up against his. She smelled his cologne mixed with bath soap and the fragrance of male. She swallowed hard, recognizing the weakness that would have her lying against his shoulder if she didn't move.

"Wes, I'm already late." Her voice shook and her body was extremely hot. The heat had come instantly. The moment his arms closed around her, she felt as if the two of them could fuse together. She hadn't known it was possible to be this hot without melting or bursting into flame. She had to get out of his arms. Pushing away she took several steps backward. "I have a class," she finished weakly.

"Think about it. You wouldn't want to tempt tradition. There's a curse that will unleash itself on any faculty member who doesn't attend."

She laughed at the playfulness of his words. "I assume illness and legitimate excuses are excluded from this powerful curse."

"Of course, it's a benevolent curse, at least to the sick and shut-ins," he said, smiling. "You only need to stay a few minutes. Everyone will excuse you if you have to leave."

"I'll think about it," she said. At this moment she was willing to agree to almost anything to get away from him.

"Shall I pick you up?"

"Don't you ever give up?"

"Occasionally," he said. "I know when to throw in the towel."

Obviously, this was not the time, Brenda thought, but

didn't want to make the comment. He'd led her to this place. He wanted her to say it, issue yet another challenge so he'd have an excuse to continue the pursuit of his bet, but she wouldn't. And she wouldn't go to that party either. She'd start a new tradition.

Steering clear of Wesley Cooper.

THREE

The night was soft and clear. Stars winked in the heavens. Wes stood in his den, his shoulder leaning against the jamb of the French doors that led into the backyard, looking up at the stars. He couldn't help facing the part of the sky where the observatory's telescope searched the galaxy. He could see it from his doorway, and he wondered if Brenda was there.

She'd occupied his mind a lot lately, ever since her reception. Since he'd opened that door and found her standing there. Since she'd knocked the socks off him.

Wes went back to his desk. The laptop was open. He put his hands on the keys and read the part of the letter he was composing, a message to his sister and brother. While his sister was in college and he was still in high school he used to write her letters. He looked forward to her replies. The electronic age changed that and now they communicated instantaneously over electrical pulses. She lived in Portland, Maine, while his brother had settled in Nashville, Tennessee. He'd told them both about the bet and instead of his finding an answer through his computer the phone had rung. As soon as he answered and heard his sister's voice shouting in his ear, his call waiting beeped and he knew it was his brother. His sister could read faster and dial faster. Hers was the first call.

Both of them berated him for his foolhardy impulse. He'd listened to their assault by conference call.

He'd explained his method of completing and winning the bet. Now he could tell them he'd found the perfect subject. He hadn't had to travel all over the United States or the world as his brother had said. She'd arrived on campus as if he'd ordered her thorough a catalog and the UPS guy had brought her directly to his lab. If she wanted to volunteer, Wes would refuse her.

He pictured Brenda Reid in his mind, heard her soft drawl as she said his name. He also remembered the details of Glenn's unsolicited e-mail that had come weeks ago, but that Wes had committed to memory. The woman had a genius IQ, yet she didn't act or *look* like a nerd. She was five feet ten inches tall, and combined with his height the two could practically guarantee tall sons. Beautiful, with a quick wit, a smile to die for, hair that begged his hands to plow through it, and a mouth that should be governed by a city ordinance.

He liked everything he could see, the way she walked, moved, smiled. That lazy way she had of saying his name. The way her hands floated through the air as if they were about to conduct an orchestra. Her hobbies were music and swimming. Wes also liked to swim. Immediately his mind saw her body clad only in the skimpiest of swimsuits.

He adjusted his position in the chair and drew his concentration back to the letter he was writing. Brenda Reid was too distracting. What a distraction though. He would have to get a handle on his thoughts soon and his reactions. Right now these were running in the direction that in only nine months the two of them could make the perfect baby.

* * *

A FAMILY AFFAIR 51

There were distinct disadvantages to living in small, secluded towns, Brenda thought—when those towns were like Lake Vista, high in the Sierras and populated by 12,000 people, 10,000 of whom were college students and faculty members. The local services available were designed for their comfort and their parents' ability to pay.

Lake Vista, California, was no different from any other college town. It had a video store, a twenty-four-hour all-around office supply and copy shop, every fast-food chain known to man, and more pizza parlors than Brenda could count. What it lacked was a single hair salon for African-Americans. Since Brenda had always lived in places where having her hair done was open to choice, she found it necessary to travel down the mountain and into the town of Klamuth Falls, Oregon, for her bimonthly touch-ups.

The family reunion was barely a month away and she didn't want her hair freshly relaxed. She needed a few weeks for it to fall, redevelop its body, and be manageable. As manageable as she could fanthom with her lack of skills.

Brenda had changed her appearance after her breakup with Reuben. She needed a change, needed to feel good about herself. Essence had come to visit her and had convinced her to submit to a makeover. Essence said she would enjoy the revenge when she saw the look on Reuben's face when he saw her. And she was right. Brenda got a perverse satisfaction at seeing him staring at her, longing for what he'd missed. He'd even tried to renew their association, but it was too late.

She began to take care of her hair and makeup after that. She was adequate at makeup, but her hair needed constant care. Only a remedial course could help her there.

She felt powerful with her new looks. She came to Meyers a different person from the one who'd left Connelley. She wasn't as glamorous as Essence and didn't have the natural confidence of carriage that Shiri possessed. She didn't expect to find a man in a month, someone she could talk about when her unrestrained cousins asked about her love life. At least if her face and hair met with their approval they wouldn't accuse her of spending all her time with men like Orion the Hunter.

Wes Cooper's face suddenly jumped into her mind. He was no Orion, but there was definitely a hunter in him. Brenda stepped on the brake as the road ahead dipped downward. She clenched her teeth and not necessarily at the turn in the road. For a moment she wondered what Shiri and Essence would say if she showed up with someone who looked like Wes. Not only would he have their tongues hanging out like panting puppies, he could stand up under any intelligence tests her two cousins might unconsciously—or consciously—devise.

Brenda smiled to herself as she negotiated a sharp curve. As she came out of it she wondered what Wes would say if she invited him. The thought had her laughing out loud. He'd been trying to date her all summer and she'd refused. Asking him out was ironic. Of course, she wouldn't do it, but it would be almost worth it to see the look on his face. And there *was* the bet to consider. She wouldn't date him, but she could have her fantasies. There was no harm in that.

Brenda went down another hairpin turn. Two more came up in rapid succession and then she pulled her Jeep onto straight and flat ground. Twenty minutes later she crossed into Oregon and headed for Klamuth Falls. She angle-parked in front of Elzeta's Hair and Nails. The building was a free-standing shop several blocks off the

A FAMILY AFFAIR 53

main street. Elzeta Washington couldn't have weighed more than 103 pounds soaking wet. Her skin was like polished walnut, both in color and tightness. She had to be fifty years old, yet her skin had a firmness to it that only came from a hearty and enviable gene pool.

"Doctor Reid?" she asked.

Brenda nodded, returning the older woman's smile that showed an overlapping front tooth. Brenda instantly liked her.

Three hours later Brenda came out of the shop knowing the intimate details of people she had yet to meet. Elzeta's was the hub of African-American female activity for the town. There was a bid-whist game going on for the entire time she remained in the shop. People came and went, but the game never ended. Brenda was sure it went on from opening to closing. They'd asked her to join in while she waited for her turn, but she refused, having gotten all the way through college, grad school, and postgraduate studies without learning to play a single card game. She felt inadequate for the first time in a long while and made a mental note to learn to play.

Elzeta Washington knew everything about everybody, and while Brenda tried to remain quiet Elzeta was obvious more adept at getting information than Brenda was at concealing it.

Brenda had to admit, the woman had magic hands. Her hair looked better than it ever had. It looked fantastic. She moved her head from side to side, loving the feel of the bouncing curls. Her hair framed her face and fell in neat curves over her shoulders. While she often draped it down her back, Elzeta brought it around the front and let it come together just above her breasts. Brenda liked the look of it and it made her feel sexy.

A few doors from the salon was a dress shop. Brenda

stopped at the window and looked at the display manikin. She also saw the reflection of herself. The dress wasn't her. She thought of herself as the jeans and T-shirt kind, but she did have a reunion coming up and she needed something to wear that didn't come from one of her cousins. She hated it when they criticized her clothes. They never did it with words, but with presents. Instead of getting earrings or a nightgown for Christmas or her birthday, she got a ball gown or a business suit as if she had no fashion sense at all.

The bell rang as she opened the door. The shop was empty except for a woman behind the counter. She looked up and smiled. Brenda nodded.

"Can I help you with anything?" the woman asked.

"Do you mind if I just browse?"

She shook her head. "I'm Lorris. If you need help, just call me."

Brenda hoisted her purse on her shoulder and headed toward the back of the shop. If it had any evening dresses they would be there. She passed skirts, jeans, and suits. It was hard not to stop and look through them, but she wasn't here for that. A sale rack set in one corner displayed summer wear. It was August in the mountains. The chill of winter was already testing the evening air, although the days remained warm and comfortable.

At the back of the store Brenda was surprised to find an L-shaped enclave that led her into another room. This one was full of evening wear, tuxedo pants sets with satin or chiffon sleeves, sequined gowns, and even a section of beaded wedding gowns and a full rack of mother-of-the-bride dresses.

Brenda turned away from them. She went toward the chiffons. The dress Essence had sent her was chiffon and she liked the feel of it. She pulled out a dark blue one

A FAMILY AFFAIR

and held it up to herself. She frowned in the mirror when she saw it against her skin color. Blue was not her color, unless it came on jeans. She put it back.

How many changes of clothes would she need? Immediately she began calculating the number of outfits she would need for her Florida vacation and the reunion. She would be there for three weeks. Two of them on her own so she could wear shorts and shirts every day. When her family arrived, there would be activities, dinners she had to attend, family outings, and unexpected exhibitions. The actual reunion called for at least one fancy dress. Brenda thought she'd better plan on two, three to be safe.

"Cruise or wedding?" The clerk from the front of the store stood in the archway.

Brenda turned to face her. "Family reunion."

She smiled. "Let me help you."

The woman proved a godsend. Her name was Lorris and she found things that Brenda liked on sight and loved when she saw herself in the mirror. Once she got started Brenda realized she needed everything from the skin out. For the first time in her life she bought Victoria's Secret underwear. She supposed she could call it more Lorris's Secret, but it was skimpy, sexy, and she felt like she was hiding a secret while she wore it.

Leaving the shop, the bell tinkled as she angled three large boxes and several shopping bags out into the afternoon light.

"Thanks for coming in," Lorris called.

"Bye, and thanks for all your help," Brenda said. Lorris closed the door and Brenda turned toward her Jeep. She could barely see for all the things she carried, but the Jeep was only a few steps away. She headed for it trying to get into her purse and find her keys to unlock to doors. She heard another bell tinkle and thought Lorris was coming after her. Had she forgotten something? She tried to look back. Then she hit something. A wall. She bounced off of it and stumbled backward. She was going to fall. She knew it in the second she had to save herself. She let go of the boxes and packages and pushed her hands behind her trying to break her fall. She twisted, but the ground came up faster than she could adjust. Her hands made contact and she sat down hard, hurting her tailbone and scraping her hands as she slid across the rough cement.

"I'm sorry," someone said from above her. "Are you all right?"

Brenda hadn't looked up. She'd closed her eyes over the pain in her rear, yet that voice had her snapping her eyelids wide open.

"Wes!"

"Brenda!"

They both spoke at the same time. He bent down next to her, his face level with hers.

"What are you doing here?" she asked, wanting to rub her backside, but generations of manners prevented her from doing it. A crowd gathered. Men poured out of a shop and surrounded them.

"Is she all right?" someone asked.

"What happened?" someone else wanted to know.

"Doctor Reid?" She recognized Lorris's voice. "What happened?" She could see the concerned frown in Lorris's face. "Are you hurt?"

"I'm all right," Brenda said, nervous at the attention she was causing.

"Why don't you come back inside?" Lorris asked.

"Can you stand?" Wes asked in a low voice.

Of all the voices around her, Brenda heard Wes's the

most. He spoke softly as if a harsh sound would disturb her.

"Yes," she said strongly. She knew standing would hurt, but she'd do it. She didn't like the crowd, the stares.

He didn't ask to help her. He put his hands under her arms and lifted her up. Brenda lay against him, biting her lower lip to keep the pain inside. "Pick up her packages," he told someone. Brenda could feel his voice as it reverberated from his body and into hers. She tried to turn away, but Wes kept her against him. "Just be still for a moment," he whispered as if he understood her need for comfort and the subsidence of pain.

"She was in my shop," Lorris explained to Wes as if he were the one in authority. "You can bring her back. I'll take care of her until she can drive."

"It's all right," Wes explained. "We work together. I'll get her home."

"You're sure she doesn't need a doctor?" one of the men asked.

"No," Brenda said. "I'm fine. I was just winded." She turned her head and looked at the man who spoke. He was wearing a white uniform shirt with *Bob's Barber Shop* stitched on the breast pocket. "I'll be fine."

Pushing off Wes's chest, Brenda stood alone. "Thank you," she said, looking up at him. He looked concerned. His face was stern and solid, almost frozen in place. She looked back at the group. "I'll take the packages," she said. "My Jeep is just over there." She was thankful all the boxes and bags were intact. She didn't want Wes seeing her lacy underwear spread over the ground.

She looked about for her purse. Lorris handed it to her. Quickly she found her keys and pressed the button that unlocked the doors. Wes moved to the Jeep and supervised the boxes and packages as they were placed inside. Brenda didn't want him to see her when she moved. While his back was turned she walked gingerly toward the driver's door.

The crowd, realizing the drama was over, returned to the shops. Brenda assured Lorris she was all right and the boutique owner made her way back inside her door. The sound of tinkling bells died in the afternoon air.

"What are you doing here?" Wes asked when they were alone. He came around to the driver's door. Brenda had been unable to get inside. Jeeps were made like trucks with a step up in order to get inside. Raising her leg hurt.

"I had an appointment for my hair." She ran her hand over the length of it wondering what it looked like now. Her scraped hand picked up single strands and hurt. She winched and pulled it away. Wes grabbed first one of her hands, then the other, turning them over to view the cut and reddened skin.

"You need something on these."

When she looked up at him she noticed that his hair was also different. He must have been at the barber's while she was in the salon or the dress shop. He still held her hands. She looked down at them. "They're all right." She tried to pull away.

"Do you have a first-aid kit?"

"Of course I do." She spoke a little sharper than she meant. Brenda wanted him to let her go. Her hands did hurt, but the fire that went through them burned even deeper while he held her.

He yanked the back door open, found the white box with the red cross on its center, and opened it. With the precision and speed of an emergency room doctor he removed something to clean her wounds and a salve to prevent infection. Without asking he took charge and administered aid to her hands.

"You've done this before." She watched him work. He was efficient, holding her hand firmly yet being careful not to inflict any further pain. As he bent over her hands she noticed a few shaved hairs on his shoulder. His hair had been recently clipped. Black barbers must be just as hard to find at the university as salons.

"A few times," he said without commitment.

"Where? To whom?"

"I have a sister and a brother. We like camping."

"Well, with all these mountains and trees around you're in your element."

He finished her hand and looked her in the eyes. Brenda almost gasped at the smoldering fire she saw there. She pulled her hand free and stared at it to give herself something to do. She thought he was detached, ministering to her the way an intern she'd meet for the first time in the emergency room of a hospital would. But he hadn't. There was a fire between them and they both knew it.

"Can you sit?" he asked.

"Let's just say I won't be riding any horses for a couple of weeks." She tried to joke. After the look in his eyes she needed something to lighten the mood.

"What about this horse?" He indicated the Jeep. "It's a hard ride back up the mountain. You got a cushion back there?"

Brenda shook her head. "Do you have one?"

Wes shook his head. "Why don't we go somewhere and rest until you feel better?"

Brenda rolled her eyes and turned toward the open car door, away from Wes. As she climbed into the seat a pain shot up her back. She clenched her teeth and avoided looking at Wes until she could relax.

He was leaning into her window. "Are you always this stubborn?"

"Persistent, Doctor Cooper. Not stubborn."

"Don't forget your final projects are due next Friday." Brenda spoke amid the slap of closing books, the click of laptops shutting, and the general noise of students gathering backpacks and purses and moving toward the exits of her classroom. Several students always hung around with questions. More of them seemed to need attention since she'd had her hair done. She noticed the outright appraisals from several of her male students. It was hard not to think of Wes and whether he thought she looked better after she'd been to Elzeta's. He hadn't mentioned her hair when they were in Klamuth. And she hadn't seen him since her return.

Brenda answered each of the students patiently and as if their questions were the most important ones of their young lives. Finally, the last one left and she was alone. She sighed, thinking it had been a long day. Or a long week.

She hadn't seen Wes the entire time. The drive up the mountain had taken longer than it did to go down it. She became familiar with every bump in the gouged pavement. Brenda was glad to get home, to a place where she could sit on something soft. She'd treated herself to a bubble bath and by morning she could walk normally— slowly but without the pain each step had taken as she got out of the Jeep when she'd pulled into her driveway.

Somehow she expected Wes to remain persistent. She was almost sure he would call her, follow her up the mountain, or show up at one of her classes or the observatory. She didn't want to admit that she expected him to do the expected, follow the plan of action he'd established. He did none of those things. She'd become used to seeing him on campus, finding him staring at her from a distance, or discovering he was right behind her in the cafeteria line.

His total change unnerved her. She thought of calling him, casually stopping by his lab. He'd come to hers. He'd arrived unannounced. She could do the same. She hadn't. She wanted to. Once she'd even gotten up and headed toward the door. She'd stopped herself each time. Brenda wouldn't allow herself to think that she missed him. It felt good to have a man interested in her, especially a man who pursued her as openly as Wes Cooper did. And he was gorgeous. She really had no reason not to go out with him. None except the bet and her policy of steering clear of men she worked with. She felt that decision crumbling. Several professors at the university were married to each other and others were actively and openly dating.

As small and isolated as Meyers was from a large city, did it really make sense to voluntarily exclude herself from male companionship because she worked on the same campus as a man she was attracted to? Brenda picked up her notebook. She remembered Reuben and the pain and humiliation she'd been left with when her affair with him ended.

Their friends didn't know how to talk to them. They were awkward and uncomfortable when the two of them were in the same room. Invitations must have been easier since Reuben always accepted and she always declined. Yet she felt left out, abandoned by people she included as friends.

Shaking herself out of the past, she tidied up her papers and left. It was Friday and she had two days before she needed to worry about seeing Wes Cooper again.

Wes slumped back in the chair, his head against the chair rest, his eyes closed. He'd run the numbers on the computer eighteen times and eighteen times the returned results never wavered. The cells were dying.

Things weren't going well in the lab. He had lost a third of his experiment and the rest of it was in jeopardy. A whole year's work was about to go down the drain and there was nothing he could do about it. He hadn't left the place for a full week, nursing petri dishes, warm-water baths, keeping the temperature at a controlled level, willing his cells to live by sweat and determination. Yet he was losing. He knew he was losing, but he refused to give up. There had to be something else he could do.

Glenn had spent nearly every minute with him. The two of them had tried everything known to their collective sciences and none of it worked. More cells died or mutated than could be saved. Those that didn't die were badly deformed.

Wes threw the pencil in his hand on the desk. There was nothing humanly possible that hadn't been done. He'd worked day and night nursing those cells. He thought he'd had it. He thought he'd found a way to regenerate them. But they were dying. For no reason. At least none he could come up with. What had happened? He checked the incubator temperatures. The gauges were set at 98.6. The room temperature was within the normal range. Everything looked clean and in working order. There was nothing to account for the falling activity level. The cells were dying and he didn't know why.

it was possible that at this stage of the development this happened and the reasons for it could be beyond him. But he didn't feel this was true. He knew when to throw in the towel. This didn't feel like that either. He and Glenn had carefully checked those cells every day for nearly a year. Until a week ago they were progressing as expected. The two of them had begun outlining their joint paper. They had research, results, and every reason to believe their hypothesis would become fact. But it wasn't to be.

Wes looked at the computer screen again as if the results would change. He stared into the lab through the glass walls that separated his office from the laboratory. Sighing he knew there was nowhere else to go. All experimentation was a gamble. There was the risk that things wouldn't work out, that there was some flaw in the theory. That what they discovered might not be what they wanted to find. This had to be the case. Wes reached the end of the road. It was time to cut his losses.

He'd sent Glenn home at midnight. The results had been run six times by then. He'd run them twelve additional times. He'd put the cells under a microscope and hoped for activity. Sample after sample either were dead or seriously deformed. Even the deformed ones were weak and unviable.

Wes pushed himself back from the desk and stood up with a sigh. He went into the lab and stared at the score of dishes. These had been his children, his hopes, and his dream to stamp out birth defects. It wouldn't stamp out all defects. He could only work on one at a time, but the cell generation could be instrumental in preventing defects in the fetuses of pregnant women.

It wasn't to be. Not in this go-round. If he was lucky,

maybe there would be another chance, but he knew better than to think so. At least not for him.

Wes reached for the controls. He held the master switch in his hand, staring into the room, looking at all the lives that could be affected by what he was doing, thinking of the millions of parents and children who could have a better life if this project had worked. Sorrow engulfed him.

He switched the control off.

This was a mistake. Brenda knew it the moment she saw Wes walking toward her. Everything about his body, the slump of his shoulders, the way his head was bowed, the slow way he moved toward her, told her his week had been hell. She had no real reason for being here. She'd been in the sky, up in the stars, her own playground, but her week of looking for Wes at every turn had him on her mind.

She'd seen his car, a lonely sentinel in the parking lot. Brenda felt good at seeing it. She smiled and pulled in next to it. It was late on Friday night. Wes couldn't be in there much longer. It was almost two o'clock in the morning. She'd come straight from the observatory. She'd only waited ten minutes when she saw him. She would have left, if she could have gotten away before he saw her, but with their two vehicles the only ones in the lot, escaping was out of the question.

"Bad week?" she asked when he stopped in front of her.

He stuffed his hands in his pockets and leaned back on his heels. "I lost a year's worth of work tonight."

Brenda, who'd been leaning against the hood and bumper of her Jeep, stood up straight.

A FAMILY AFFAIR

"I'm sorry." It sounded weak. She didn't mean it that way. She truly felt bad for whatever he'd lost. She never asked about his work, knew nothing of the specifics of what he did. She wanted to hug him, take him in her arms, and put the mischievous smile back in his eyes. She didn't, didn't even move. "Would you like to talk about it?"

For a long moment he looked at her, searching her features. Brenda knew they hadn't been the best of friends. Mostly they'd been adversaries, but if anyone needed a friend tonight it was Wesley Cooper.

"Get in," she ordered.

He looked at her, still saying nothing.

"Get in," she repeated. Although her voice was stronger, the hand that touched his sleeve communicated the tenderness she felt. He moved toward the passenger seat. Brenda got inside and drove to her house.

Wes was silent during the drive. He'd remained that way while she made coffee. He broke the silence when she set a tray on the coffee table in front of him.

"If I drink that I'll be up all night."

She handed him a cup. "The night is nearly over anyway." Brenda sipped from her own cup. She leaned back, curled her feet under her, and waited.

Wes picked up a cup and drank from it. He didn't speak for a while. Brenda could be patient. Her job had taught her patience, so she knew not to rush him now. Then he started.

Brenda listened quietly. Wes's voice didn't have the strength it usually did, nor did she hear that happy lift that often teased her. He told her about the birth-defects research, about his dreams for the outcome, about the mutated cells, and his and Glenn's work trying to save the research. But it was all useless.

Brenda wanted to go to him, put her arms around him, and hold him close. But she knew that wouldn't change things, so she remained sitting where she was.

"Is there nothing that can be done?"

"I've run the computations every way possible. I've looked at the cells through an electron microscope. There is no mistake. Somewhere too far back to repair, some kind of rip or breakdown occurred in one or more cells." He sighed, resolutely. "When they divided they also mutated and according to U.S. Law number 89576-907-58 covering gene splicing and resultant mutations, the cells must be destroyed."

"Did you destroy them?"

He leaned his head back against the sofa and closed his eyes. "I turned off the incubators as I left the lab. Without the proper heat and light, they'll die before morning."

Brenda glanced at the windows. Light leaked in around the sides of the shades. It was already morning, but Brenda saw no need in pointing that out.

"What will you do now?" she whispered.

He opened his eyes and rolled his head sideways to look at her. A little of the old Wes stared at her from the depths of his dark eyes.

"I'll have to make a report to the university and the foundation"

"Foundation?" she said, interrupting.

"Reeves Foundation for Scientific Research. They contributed the three million dollars that's freezing in my lab as we speak."

"They aren't going to look kindly on tonight's events, I take it."

"You bet they aren't."

Brenda slipped her feet to the floor and leaned her

arms on her thighs. "What will happen to your research?"

He sat up and faced her. "It'll be set back, but I'll survive it."

"How?"

"I don't know right now. I'll have to apply to other foundations, hope the university will still contribute their share."

"What about the teaching?"

"I'll still teach. In fact, I'll have more classes this fall than I'd expected to have." He gave her a quick smile that said he'd rather spend that extra time at the experiment that was no longer viable.

Brenda moved a seat closer to him. Her knees nearly touched his. "Wes, I'm really sorry." She took his hand unconsciously, yet once she was holding it she felt the strength of his hand clasp hers.

"It'll work out," he said. Then he stood up, keeping her hand and walking toward the door. "It's time I go. I'll have plenty to do tomorrow."

"Tomorrow's Saturday."

"Those cells in the lab don't know that," he whispered conspiratorially. "Cleanup can't wait."

"Want some help?"

He stopped, turned to face her, stared. He was still holding her hand. They were very close, closer than Brenda thought. She could feel his body heat, feel her own temperature rising.

"You're too much of a distraction." His voice broke the trance she was in. "If you come I'm not sure I wouldn't want to experiment on your cells."

Brenda's throat dried up like a drop of water sinking into the massive sands of the Sahara Desert.

"You should see your face," Wes said. "It looks like I scared you to death."

He did scare her. He scared her more than any man ever had. She missed him when she didn't see him. Her heartbeat accelerated when she did. A week ago he'd held her in his arms and tonight she wanted to repeat the situation.

"Don't worry, Brenda." He stepped closer to her and pulled her into his arms. His hands wove through her hair. "The last thing I want to do is scare you."

Brenda felt him take a breath and expel it. She closed her eyes and let her body go slack. Her arms went around Wes's waist. She held her breath not wishing to let him know how comfortable she felt, how good it was to feel his arms, lay her head on his chest, take in the tantalizing male smell of him.

He was the one who needed comforting. He'd lost everything tonight. She should be holding him instead of the other way around.

Brenda didn't know how long they stood like that holding each other, yet saying nothing, communicating the way lovers did, with silent hearts, not spoken words.

Suddenly Wes laughed. Brenda felt the rumble of his voice in his belly, which pressed against hers.

"What's so funny?" she asked.

He pushed back and looked at her. This was not the face of a man who'd lost his hope tonight.

"The bet," he said, continuing to laugh. "Now it doesn't matter if I lose."

The receiver rocked back and forth as Wes replaced it. He sat on the side of his desk back in the lab. He'd talked to Glenn. It wasn't necessary for him to come in.

There was nothing left of the experiment. It needed to be disposed of and he would do that alone.

He'd walked home from Brenda's. The sun was already up when he left. A new day had begun and Wes had to face it. He hadn't gone to bed. He'd sat on the sofa and thought sleep would come. His body was tired, his mind was exhausted from trying to come up with a logical reason for what happened, but it hadn't. And he hadn't slept.

He turned on the television only to find nothing that interested him. He thought of calling his sister. Camille would understand. She always did, but it was too early to call her and she might not be alone. She was engaged. So he got up and walked to the lab.

His truck sat silent and alone in the lot. The building loomed above him like a sterile monster. Wes entered the glass doors as he had done for the past several years. Today he dreaded even the look of the place. Unlocking his lab he went inside. He'd oversee the cleanup. He didn't want anyone with him.

Turning around he looked across the dark room. The lights had been burning in those rooms for the last three hundred days. Now they were dark. He had to go in there, turn on the lights, and clear away everything. Wash, sterilize, burn if necessary any residue that might survive. He left the desk where he sat on the corner and headed toward his task. As he came out of his office he saw her.

Brenda stood at the door. She wore jeans and a T-shirt. A jacket was slung over her arm. Her hair hung around her shoulders the way it had when he discovered her in Klamuth. The same way it had last night when she leaned against her Jeep.

He opened the door.

"I thought a distraction might be in order," she said.

He smiled at her audacity. It felt good to let his body relax enough to smile. Wes realized how uptight he was about the task at hand. Maybe she was right and he did need something to keep his mind off what he was about to do.

Brenda walked to the windows that looked into the labs. Row upon row of petri dishes sat in straight lines on long tables. Others were inside small see-through cases.

"It's like looking at a nursery," Brenda said.

Wes's head snapped around to look at her. He knew she was very perceptive.

"Does each of the sections represent a different disease?"

Wes turned the lights on. "We can't control more than one at a time in the same space. This area is only dealing with one disease."

"Which one?"

"Spina bifida." He rested his hand against the glass wall separating them from the lab. "One out of every thousand children born in the United States has this disease. Yet it is determinable prior to birth and could be reduced in about seventy-five percent of the cases with a simple vitamin."

"Why isn't it?" Brenda asked.

"Most people don't know when they get pregnant. Some, such as teenage, are unplanned. Even adults planning a family don't consult their doctors until they're already pregnant and have had it confirmed with over-the-counter pregnancy tests. Folic acid and vitamin B6 taken during the period before and during pregnancy has shown remarkable results. My experiment was to generate the cells to prevent or replace the defective ones."

"This would save a lifetime of health care for the children, save the parents of special-needs children the financial hardship of caring for their needs when society forces both parents to work, and reduce the amount of health-care insurance that would be spread to many more participants of a plan. It would also give these children normal, healthy lives."

"Exactly." Wes knew she'd understand. She'd grasped the central point of his research as quickly as she would have stepped over a puddle in the rain. He'd spent days writing his proposals to gain research money, preparing statistics, and drawing charts to show the effect a successful research program would have on the lives of families and the reduction in health-care costs. Brenda had reduced it to two concise and easily understandable sentences.

For a moment she stared through the window, looking into the lab. Neither of them spoke. Wes wondered if she could see what he saw. If she understood the enormity of his loss. He thought she did. In the lab the world at large had no faces. He didn't have to look into the large eyes of a child who didn't recognize him, who couldn't hold its head up. He didn't have to stare at the rounded shoulders of a mother and father who fashioned their lives around the care of a child who needed constant care. He'd seen it more than once and it was enough to put him on this course of study.

It was his own mother. For three years she'd taken care of his youngest sister, born with spina bifida. Her shoulders were perpetually slumped and tears wet her eyes making her look old and tired. The baby died three years and five months after she was born. To look at his mother today no one would know that she'd given her life to a child. Wes remembered her sacrifice and he didn't want another family to go through the hardship they had endured.

His education and interests led him to study genetic frailties. Unfortunately, it wasn't paying off today.

Wes moved. His throat was clogged and he turned away to compose himself. He went into his office and came back a moment later with rubber gloves and carefully stored emotions.

"You'll need to put these on."

"Is anything in here toxic?"

"No." He didn't joke with her. It was a question that should be asked by every scientist. "We are going to have to burn some of the residue. There's a closed area for that."

Brenda put the black gloves over her hands. She held them up. "Ready," she said. "Just tell me what you want me to do."

He really wanted to answer that question. He wanted to tell her that he'd like her to stand there with her eyes closed and let him kiss that section of her neck framed by her hair. He wanted to put his hands in the deep red of her hair, and start by kissing each of the freckles on her nose. From there he'd progress to other parts of her face until he reached that mouth that drawled words that made his blood skitter through his system. He wanted to say a lot of things, but he didn't. He opened the door and went into the room.

Surveying the dishes and incubators as he'd done for the past year, he checked to see if there was activity in any of them. Then he began the sort. He moved the ones that needed incineration to one side. He'd handle those. The others could be washed and sterilized.

"This section can go into that first machine." He took her over to the dishwasher and showed her how to load it. "After they come out of here, they automatically go into this unit." On the side was written the name of the manufacturer. Wes hardly noticed it. To him it was the sterilizer. "When this light goes out, the process is complete. The dishes will be hot. Don't burn your hands."

"I think I can probably handle this."

Wes left her and went to the other end of the lab. Brenda turned to her task. He looked at her. She did look good in a pair of jeans.

It took three hours to clean everything up and put it away. The tables were washed and sterilized. The equipment was cleaned and ready for the next user. Wes wondered who that would be. He had a stack of forms to fill out for the foundation and the international scientific community, not to mention the government. Then he would need to begin filling out grant and foundation forms to try and get money to begin again.

"What's next?" Brenda asked.

"I was thinking of all the paperwork that needs to be completed now."

"That I do know about. I'd help you with it, but I really think you should get some sleep. You look exhausted."

He felt it too. His mind had been pretty clear while he worked, but looking over the clean room only made him think of what he'd just done and why he needed to do it.

"Why don't you go home and get some rest?"

"I think I will." He'd been up all night and so had she. She'd been up with him. He hadn't asked her why she'd been there last night, or rather, early this morning, when he'd come out of the lab. He was so glad to see her, and later as he told her all about the experiment he was glad to have someone to talk to.

They left the lab together, walking silently to their two vehicles waiting like obedient siblings. Wes went to Brenda's Jeep with her. She turned at the door.

"Promise me you'll get some sleep?"

He raised his right hand. "Scout's honor."

"Were you ever a Boy Scout?"

He shook his head. "I did get plenty of training though. Remember the woods, camping, my brother and sister?"

She nodded.

"Thank you," he said.

"You're welcome."

"I don't mean for helping me clean. I mean for helping me."

Brenda stared at him then. She reached up and put her hand on his cheek. Then she kissed a spot on his cheek close to his mouth. Wes shivered in the sun's warmth.

"Any time you need a distraction, just call me."

FOUR

Wes had enough time if he hurried. He looked at the clock in the corner of the computer screen. Time rushed forward. He had only a couple of hours to get off this mountain and make his train. He was going to Florida, Orlando specifically, a child's playground and the exact place Brenda Reid was heading. He supposed it was ironic that he had to meet his sponsors in the land of Mickey Mouse and make-believe. He'd stuffed boxer shorts and socks, a couple of shirts and pairs of slacks into a bag. He'd rejected a suit, then thought better of it and added it to the swim trunks and shorts in his suitcase.

The Reeves Foundation was located in Orlando and they wanted to see Wes. He assumed the written report hadn't been enough. For their three million dollars they wanted him in person. He knew they wanted a full accounting of the events that led to the loss of their investment. If he were in their shoes he'd want one. Wes wasn't looking forward to the meeting, yet he'd quickly packed and was now throwing every research file he had on the project into his briefcase, making sure his laptop was fully connected to the network and all pertinent files had been downloaded to the laptop's hard drive.

"Got everything?" Glenn asked, coming into Wes's office.

"The file's just finished." Wes shut down the laptop and disconnected the electrical cords.

"What do you think they'll do?" Wes noticed the nervous tremor that underlay the question. Glenn's new research project was along the same lines as Wes's. He was interested in recombinant DNA studies too, with an emphasis in diseases that attack unborn children. If the Reeves Foundation looked unfavorably on Wes, they were unlikely to advance more money.

Other foundations would likely look at requests for grants with more scrutiny. The effect would mean the coffers dried up. Money would be hard to find. Research would suffer and ultimately children and families would pay the greater price.

"I don't know. I've told you everything they said on the phone. I'm to see a three-man committee. My report arrived and they want to see me in person."

"More likely they want to castrate you."

"Hopefully it won't come to that," Wes said dryly. "They probably want to discuss the details that weren't in the report."

"We put everything we knew in it."

"Three million dollars is a lot of money. They're bound to have questions we haven't thought about." Wes hoped he had the answers. His explanation was incomplete. He had no reason to give for what had happened. He could only give the progress up to a point; then everything had suddenly, without forewarning, turned to disaster.

"You sure you don't want me to go with you?" Glenn asked.

"I was responsible for the money. I was responsible for the research. It was my project. I'll take the responsibility for its failure."

Glenn looked as if he wanted to say something more,

A FAMILY AFFAIR

but didn't know quite what it was. Wes understood. The two of them had the same temperament. He wanted to reassure his friend that things would work out, but Wes wasn't an illusionist. He knew how bad things looked and how bad he expected them to get when he arrived for his reprimand in Florida.

Wes looked around. He zipped the laptop case and hoisted the shoulder strap on his arm. Then he reached for his suitcase.

"Oh," Glenn said, searching through his pockets for something. "I picked up your tickets from administration." He handed Wes a red, white, and blue envelope. "And I checked on her train."

"Whose train?" Wes felt heat on the back of his neck. He knew Glenn had been acting like a matchmaker. He thought after Glenn received his own funding he wouldn't try to keep Wes's job for him, but he apparently was still at it, even in the face of imminent loss.

"Don't tell me you don't know she's leaving for Orlando today, *by train?*" Glenn gave him an incredible look. Wes covered himself by slipping the tickets in his breast pocket. "I thought that was why you decided to travel by train," Glenn added.

"I need time to think, go over this research, and see if I can find out when and where it went wrong."

"I believe that." Glenn spoke in a voice that said the exact opposite.

"All right, I'm following her. Is that what you want to hear?"

Glenn's smile was as wide as train rails.

Brenda's compartment on the Silver Limited was small. Sunlight shone through the huge picture window in an attempt to create the illusion of spaciousness. It would be fine for the trip to St. Louis where she'd pick up another train to Chicago, then on to Washington and a final train for the last leg of her cross-country trek to Orlando. She hated flying, a fear she shared with Shiri. She also loved old trains. The romantic nature of traveling in compartments, meeting people, and watching the scenery go by fascinated her. It was one of the few times she looked at the mountains, trees, and plains instead of turning her head skyward. The trains she'd be traveling on were new and modern, with showers, televisions, and private video movies. Yet she imagined they were the old ones, with gas lights and smoky chandeliers in the dining car.

She felt young and happy and excited. She was on her way home, back to the South. She loved California, loved the lush green trees that crept up the mountains, loved the clean smell of the air blowing in from the distant ocean, but it wasn't home. She couldn't wait to see the rolling hills, smell the sweet grass, and hear the night music of the cicadas singing in the shadow of the pecan trees.

The peaches would be ripe, their fragrance perfuming the air. Brenda giggled to herself. She sat cross-legged on the compartment seat and stared at the platform. Soon the train would pull out of the station and she'd be on her way. She felt like a small child taking her first train ride. This wasn't her first trip, but she was going to see her cousins, her parents, grands, greats, the firsts, and seconds, and the twice removed. All of them would be there. The oldest, the newest, the sweetest. And Shiri and Essence would be there. She hoped Essence would come. She needed a good dose of family and there was an addition. She couldn't wait to meet the man who'd turned Shiri's head.

Immediately, she thought of Wes. Had he turned her head? Is that what this feeling was? She would miss him. She already missed him. Their friendly banter had become enjoyable and since the morning they'd cleaned his experiment she smiled more often when she saw him. She'd looked forward to finding him on campus.

She noticed there was a slight difference in him, however. He looked a little tired, and his teasing wasn't as playful as it had been. She expected it was due to the experiment and his investors. He'd only mentioned them once when she'd run into him in the campus post office. He told her he'd just mailed his final report. He hadn't asked her to have a cup of coffee with him or tried to get a date. He'd smiled quickly and left her.

Since then she hadn't seen much of him and when she did, it was at a distance. Brenda looked forward to leaving, leaving Wes behind, both in thoughts and in person. She hadn't been the same since she'd set eyes on him, and a little distance, like the length of the country, should be enough to put her back on course with the even-tempered, logical, intelligent woman she knew herself to be. She wouldn't have these mood swings or the need to try and understand what was going on in his mind. And she would need to fight her own feelings each time their paths crossed.

Brenda watched as the platform slowly moved outside the window. She was on her way. In minutes there were only trees outside the windows. The train picked up speed, although the modern engine and quiet ride didn't make her dizzy as she looked at the scenery moving sideways. Five days from now she would be in sunny Florida. Meyers University and Wes Cooper would be behind her.

She'd have time to clear her head. She could talk to Shiri and Essence, although both of them would tell her to forget her rules and date Wes.

Brenda pulled her suitcase down. She might as well unpack and not think about the man she was leaving behind. She'd packed one suitcase for the train, putting everything she would need for the five-day trip together, and everything she'd need in Florida in another one. The room was engineered tightly and it took almost no time to get everything put away. She had magazines, books, her computer, and quilt scraps if she wanted to spend her time sewing them together. She didn't find any of the options appealing.

She sat and watched the trees go by, looked at the mountains as she moved farther and farther away from them, and refused to let her mind return to the campus. Twenty minutes later there was a knock on the compartment door. Grabbing her ticket she was ready to prove her right to space on this train. She pulled the door open.

And got the surprise of her life.

Wes Cooper stood there looking every bit as good as he did the night he'd opened the door to President Langley's house. Brenda was shocked. She'd been thinking about him, but he was in the past. He wasn't here. She closed her eyes. When she opened them she knew the conductor would be there. She only imagined Wes was on the train. It was her mind, a trick of the light, her imagination conjuring up her subconscious. A second later she opened her eyes. He was still there.

"I'm real," he said.

Her throat went dry as she stared. She couldn't believe it. She also couldn't believe what was happening to her heart. It was hammering in her chest. She was glad to

A FAMILY AFFAIR

see him and angry that he was here. How could she feel both emotions at the same time?

"Does that frozen-face look mean I've so surprised you that you're speechless?"

"What are you doing here?" she whispered as if someone might hear them.

"Ah, you *can* talk." His wide smile angered her. He had no right to smile. Not after the way he'd been acting on campus. He'd scrambled her brain, and now he showed up without a word of warning and she was supposed to smile and act as if nothing had happened.

"Stop it," she shouted, her hands chopping the air. She expected peace and quiet on this trip. She expected her heartbeat to normalize, the dampness that gathered between her breasts at the sound of his voice to dry up, that rush of anticipation that followed her every time she left her house to vanish. She expected 4,000 miles to separate them and that in three weeks she could return to Meyers U. as the calm, no-nonsense person she knew herself to be. There was nothing between them and there would be nothing between them. How could there be? She hadn't known him long. They both worked for the same university and more importantly he wasn't really interested in her, just her ability to reproduce.

Brenda took a calming breath. "Why are you here?"

"I didn't want to surprise you when you found me sitting at your dinner table later tonight," he said.

Brenda wouldn't speak. Her throat closed completely. Hundreds of questions went through her mind, none of them staying long enough to form a cohesive thought. Her emotions rocked from pleasure at seeing him to the cold fear of knowing she would be spending five days in his company.

Wes glanced down the hall. "Do you think we can discuss this inside?"

"Well, I suppose you're not a serial killer," Brenda muttered to herself. She stepped back. She didn't want him in the small space. It was designed for two if they were married or lovers or wanted to be together. If they didn't want to be together it was too close a confinement. She felt awkward like she didn't know where to look or if she should sit or stand. She decided to remain standing. Wes walked to the center of the small space. She closed the door and stood with her back to it.

"At the last minute I discovered I have to go to Orlando," he began.

Brenda cocked her head and folded her arms, her stance telling him she did not believe that for a minute.

"At the last minute suddenly you have to get to Orlando and you rush off the mountain in a sure-fire hurry to get on this train? What happened, did Mickey call you personally needing an emergency clone of the Disney crowd?"

"Not exactly. The foundation that supports my research is based in Orlando." He paused with a little of the mischievousness she'd come to recognize in his eyes. "And I don't do cloning."

Brenda couldn't believe this. He was going to be with her for the next five days *and* in the close confines of a train. She couldn't stay in the compartment all the time. And he'd already told her he was assigned to her dinner table.

"If they called at the last minute, why aren't you on a plane?"

"I'm afraid to fly."

She stared at him. The smile on his face irked her.

A FAMILY AFFAIR

He was lying. She was the one with the mortal fear of airplanes.

"How did you know?" she asked.

"I'm sure you know how small our campus is."

It wasn't exactly a secret. She'd arrived at Meyers by train. And over the summer she'd had more than one conversation with people about her trip back East. Any number of people on campus could have told him of her fear of flying.

"You have no fear of airplanes."

"You're here," he finally said, the tone of his voice low and commanding. A small ache tickled the back of her throat and ran a tremor down her back.

The fight went out of her, like a kid letting stale air out of a three-day-old balloon. Brenda didn't want to fight with Wes. She didn't want to fight against her own feelings.

She remembered the night he'd told her about losing his experiment, about the investors in his research, and now he had to travel across the country to talk to them. She sat down.

"Wes, I need to make this clear. I'm not interested in an affair with you. Or anyone," she said.

Wes didn't respond with words. His eyes looked her over, up and down, slowly rolling over every inch of her until her ears were burning and she was sure the sweat collecting between her breasts would dampen her blouse.

"I'm not interested in an affair either," he whispered. He was interested in something else. Brenda refused to ask what it was. She didn't want to know, didn't want to have the words take form, especially didn't want to hear his answer.

"Then we have five days to enjoy the changing scenery.

And I suppose if you have a meeting in Orlando, you have to prepare for it during this time."

He nodded. I brought everything with me. I'll explain what I think happened and hope they will back me again."

"Is there a chance of that?" Her voice was hopeful.

"There's always a chance."

He was the most optimistic man she had ever met. She hoped when he got to Orlando the investors would be willing to continue to support him, but three million dollars with no return on investment wasn't something anyone took lightly. Most people, even the superrich, didn't look at losing that kind of money as a drop in the bucket.

"We won't worry about it now. We have five days to not have an affair."

The train rocked from side to side. Brenda loved the sway. She could feel it inside her like some beating rhythm. She'd traveled on trains since leaving Birmingham when she went to college. The dinner car was set with tables for two and four against the windows. Glass chandeliers had been anchored to the ceiling. They swaged only slightly. Not like the romantic light that played against the darkened windows of the trains from the nineteenth century. Brenda remembered the first time she had ridden on one. She was in college and on a date. A blind date that her roommate had set up. The four of them decided to ride a vintage train that was part of an exhibition. It only went five miles in one direction, but Brenda discovered she loved the sway of the cars and the relaxing nature of traveling from one place to another.

A FAMILY AFFAIR 85

She hated commuter trains where people were herded like cattle into tight spaces for their twice daily rides into and out of centers of commerce. The train she was on was a hybrid of those two. It was functionally comfortable and had a certain amount of ambience.

Brenda waited for Wes to join her. *Five days to not have an affair.* His words came back to her. She looked out the window. Only her own reflection looked back at her. For the first time in months she looked at herself. What did Wes see when he looked at her? Did he think she was beautiful? She'd always thought her neck was too short, her legs too long, and her hair unmanageable.

She was new at Meyers. Maybe that was the novelty. She frowned. She'd only been there for the summer session so far, but people talked and no one mentioned anything that would give him the reputation of campus gigolo. She grinned at that. She'd heard the stories about his dating a lot and she wondered if his bet had anything to do with that. The bet had begun before she arrived on campus, but afterward it appeared as if she was the focus of it. Maybe that was only in her mind. Although Wes loved to play off of her. He was constantly underfoot and he knew he was getting to her. The night she'd shown up at his lab was nothing if not a dead giveaway. Still, she hadn't given him that much of a chance. She wondered if she should.

He got her juices flowing. The couple of times she'd been in his arms she wanted to stay there. She wanted to spend time with him. She'd gone to his lab that night with her defenses reduced. It was his problem that saved her, kept her from telling him how she was beginning to feel. Yet was she really saved? Here she was staring into the darkness waiting for him, looking forward to talking to him. When he took her to her cabin tonight would she invite him in or were the five days to not have an affair going to be five torturously lonely days?

Brenda knew the logical answer. She didn't need to risk her heart or the possibility of remaining at Meyers. Keeping Wes Cooper at arm's length was the safe thing to do. She had only just relocated to Meyers after a relationship gone wrong. And as much as his smile turned her heart over and his arms made her knees go weak, she needed to keep her head.

It might be five days to not have an affair, but in the end it would be worth it. Her brain told her that.

The woman frowning into the night wasn't so sure.

The small mirror over the sink in Wes's compartment threw his image back at him. He'd shaved and brushed his hair and remembered the talk he'd had with Brenda. *Affair.* She'd brought it up. He had thought of having an affair with her. In fact, he couldn't get her out of his mind. That was why he was on this train. Right after he'd hung up the phone with the Reeves Foundation he'd called and secured a ticket on this particular train. This was the one she would be on. He'd checked to make sure Brenda Reid also had a reservation, that she hadn't changed her plans.

Now he was about to have dinner with her. He was looking forward to it. When he was with her she commanded his full attention. There was no room for the haunting thoughts of the past few weeks or the word that had taken root in his consciousness since he discovered his experiment was not viable. He'd searched for solutions, spent the night trying to find a reason for the large deviation from the expected results, but he could no longer hide the word from himself.

Sabotage.

He had no other explanation. He'd spent the afternoon reading through his research and calling Glenn on his cell phone to check facts. He didn't like the message, the confirmation that formed in his mind. He was on his way to meet with the foundation executives. They'd want to know the truth. He wanted to know it too. He wanted to be sure, wanted to know without a doubt that there was nothing he did that caused it, that there was no other involvement that caused the year's worth of work to go so infallibly wrong that there was no way possible to revive it.

He hadn't shared his thoughts with Glenn. Soon he would have to. Glenn asked questions. He was inquisitive and logical like any scientist worth his graduated cylinders had to be. Sooner or later he would come to the same conclusion Wes had reached. Someone had tampered with the experiment.

But who?

And why?

Wes returned the brush to his travel bag and checked his watch. It was time to go. Brenda was waiting. She was probably the only person who could get his mind off his problem. His compartment was two cars away from hers. He was closer to the dining car and she'd agreed to meet him there.

He saw her through the center window in the door. Pausing he looked at her. All thoughts of Glenn and his experiment went on hold at seeing the smile on her face. Wes hadn't felt like this before. He'd known few women and those he dated weren't nearly as memorable. The night she showed up outside his lab she'd looked like a dream. She was just what he needed. Wes wondered if he could fall in love with her. He'd never been in love before. While the guys thought he was the lucky one, he didn't agree with them. And looking at the fair-skinned woman sitting at the third table, he thought there was something that he liked seeing and wanted to see more and more of. He didn't understand it and didn't feel the need to explore or analyze the feelings. They were there and he was happy with them. She smiled at one of the waiters. An unfamiliar tightening constricted his heart. He opened the door and went through it. She looked his way. He was sure her smile widened just a bit. She was happy to see him. He'd seen her only a few hours ago and he'd missed her.

Walking toward her he realized he didn't know very much about her. The information Glenn had sent him only gave him the facts. He knew she was compassionate and that he liked the feel of her in his arms. She was soft and smooth and smelled of flowers. But of her life he knew little.

"What are you going to do on your vacation?" he asked after the waiter took their order.

"It's not totally a vacation."

Wes raised his eyebrow. "Work?"

"A little. I've been asked to consult with some NASA scientists on some star maps I made before I came to Meyers."

"Sounds impressive."

She smiled. "I'm impressed. Whoever thought a little black girl from Birmingham would be going to consult with NASA?"

He could tell she was dying to talk about it. "I guess they don't ask a lot of people to consult."

"I don't know. I know they called and asked me, told me they were interested in some of the work I had done.

In fact, a lot of the work astronomers do is used by NASA for space missions."

"Even what you're doing at Meyers?"

She nodded.

"Before coming to Meyers I worked on a portion of the sky beyond the documented star charts. I wrote a paper on it detailing my theories and my findings. It was published in a trade magazine, *Astronomy Today*. One of the astronomers at NASA read it and called me for a consultation."

"Congratulations. I'm sure good things are in store for you."

Wes understood how movement took place in the academic and corporate worlds, especially when those worlds intersected with the U.S. government. If they liked what she did, if she had knowledge they needed, they'd offer her anything to get her to come and work for them. Brenda could possibly be on her way to another job.

If his experience had gone to the result he expected, he'd be sought after by every major pharmaceutical company in the country. Wes had seen it happen to other scientists who broke through with revolutionary cures or treatments for diseases that had eluded man for decades, even centuries. He was waiting for the cure for leukemia, diabetes, or Alzheimer's Disease to be discovered. The scientist who finds any of those cures can write his own ticket.

But the lure of fame and fortune hadn't been Wes's reason for going into genetics. He was paid well at the university and when his grandfather had died and left him a third of his insurance money, Wes had invested it wisely. He had a nice income to support himself beyond Meyers University. Wes had gone into genetics because of his lost sister and a high school teacher he admired.

And as that teacher told him because of "a thirst to change things." He loved discovering the human makeup, finding out how things worked in the body and how to fix the things that nature threw out of balance.

He wasn't sure if after he had completed his research he would take any of those offers. Luckily he didn't have to wonder about that yet. Maybe never.

Brenda had only been at Meyers for a few months. She might be leaving sooner than she thought. NASA wasn't interested in many people and rarely were they called. NASA had many consultants. Usually they went there looking for work. The National Aeronautics and Space Administration had a staff of astronomers. If they wanted to consult with Brenda, she had done something truly extraordinary.

Wes's insides constricted. He didn't want her to leave. There was nothing keeping her at Meyers. She hadn't formed any relationships she was worried about leaving. Wes wanted her too. He'd tried valiantly to get her to look at him as more than another faculty member. She was friendly, but he wasn't sure where her allegiance lay. Florida was closer to her home and family than Meyers. She'd be able to visit her cousins more often. She did appear attached to them and valued their opinions. And she'd be far enough away from home to have her own life.

Wes was sure she'd take it if it was offered. "Why did you come to Meyers?" he suddenly asked.

He noticed her change. It was subtle. She was trying to hide it, but she went for her water glass. She'd been looking directly at him. Now she focused on the goblet. Something happened to make her leave her other job. He wondered what.

"It was a better position. More freedom to explore the

things I'm interested in. Meyers offered me more research time and less time in the classroom."

"From what I hear the students love you."

"I've only taught one class. How much could you hear?"

"Word gets to me."

The waiter returned then and placed drinks and salads in front of them.

"What kind of word?" she asked when he'd gone. "I imagine you have spies all over the university." She paused. "Not just in administration."

"I—"

She held up her hand to stop any denial he might have raised. "I know Glenn got the records, but he did it for you."

"He's concerned about me."

"How?"

"He thinks I should be married."

"Why should that have anything to do with me?"

"He thinks you're the perfect candidate."

"Please tell him I'm not applying for the position."

"Why not?" he baited, leaning forward in his chair and staring directly at her. "Don't you find me attractive?"

She put down her fork and smiled at him. "You are full of yourself, aren't you?"

"I don't think so. And you didn't answer my question." He'd meant to tease, but suddenly he really wanted an answer.

"Doctor Cooper, I find you devastatingly attractive."

Her head shook while she said it. Wes wasn't sure she meant it. There wasn't that usual seriousness to her demeanor that he loved throwing off balance. Her soft southern drawl could be facetious—or she could be telling the truth. He'd have to hold out on the decision until later.

"But—" he prompted.

"No but."

"Just that you're immune to devastatingly attractive men."

"Absolutely."

"Who was he?"

She went for the water glass again. "He?"

"The devastatingly attractive man who shot you, through the heart, I presume, and left you with antibodies against all future devastatingly attractive diseases."

She smiled, then picked up her fork and went back to her salad. "You know this train ride doesn't give you any rights to probe into my personal life."

"Have you ever told anyone about him?"

"I don't live in a complete vacuum, Doctor Cooper."

"Wes."

Wes let the conversation go. Brenda called him attractive, devastatingly attractive. She was indeed beautiful, yet he had the feeling she didn't know much about men. In the same way he hadn't had many relationships, he felt she matched him in her knowledge of the opposite sex.

He wondered why. He could tell she was attracted to him, yet whatever name went with "he" was part of the reason she held men at arm's length.

"What about you?" She interrupted his thoughts as the waiter removed their salad plates and replaced them with their dinners. "Tell me about your family. You said you often went on camping trips." Wes thought she was going to ask about the women in his past, but she didn't. Opening that line of questioning would mean she had to tell her story and apparently she had no intention of doing that. At least not at the moment.

"It was in the Maine woods. Have you ever been to Maine?"

She shook her head. "It's very cold there. I'm from the South where it's warm."

"You live in the mountains now. It's going to get plenty cold this winter. You might need something to warm you up during the coming months."

"I'll get an electric blanket. Go on."

"My dad took us the first time. Cammie hated it. Jule dug up worms to terrorize her."

"Cammie and Jule are your sister and brother?"

"Camilla and Julian." He nodded. "We got used to it and after a while we looked forward to going. Every year we'd go camping with my dad. Summer in the woods with the animals and time to talk. I loved it." He smiled remembering how much fun they had laughing, cooking the worst meals in the world, and eating food no human should consume. But it was a fun time.

"Tell me about your dad."

Wes's memories of his dad were wonderful. He leaned back in his chair. "He's the best dad a guy can have. Unlike most dads who are so busy working they never have time for their families, my day put us first. He always had time to talk to us. He came to all our games, even the practices. Sat on everything, the PTA, the booster club, scholarship committee."

"What does he do? For a living, I mean."

"He's a pharmacist. Runs a drugstore in a small town near Portland."

"Sounds like a happy childhood."

"It was wonderful. We did things my mother would have had a cow over if she knew."

"Ah-ha. Secrets were forged in the wild, wild woods?"

"Like you've never kept a secret from your mother."

"I swear." Brenda laughed. "I was a model child. I never did anything my mother wouldn't approve."

"And you said it with a straight face too." He knew she was lying. Even a woman with stars in her eyes had secrets. And unlike the secrets he kept from his mother, he wanted to know hers.

"Your father didn't tell your mother what you'd done?"

"Some of it he still doesn't know about. My mother either. Good thing too."

"What happened?" Brenda asked.

"What?"

"The expression on your face. Something happened?"

"Something always happened. Usually nothing catastrophic. Nothing we'd ever tell her about." Wes paused. "Except that one time."

"Don't stop there. Tell me." She was sitting on the edge of her chair, leaning forward on the table and staring at him.

"There was that time we almost killed Jule."

She laughed. He liked hearing the soft sound. "You're kidding, right?"

"Mostly. We were always getting hurt, scraped knees, cut hands, brambles across the cheeks." He reached over and smoothed her right eyebrow, the one that had a scar bisecting it. She'd never mentioned what happened to cause it. She closed her eyes when he touched her, but didn't flinch. "All of us had to learn how to take care of wounds that happened in the woods. One day we decided to prove who was the best woodsman. Dad was at the campsite and we were out gathering firewood. Along the way we started playing our own version of *Survivor*, making up the obstacles as we went along."

He stopped, remembering how badly things could have turned out that day.

"Survivor could be pretty physical?" Brenda asked.

"There are many hills and mountains in Maine. At one of them we decided to jump across a ravine."

"A ravine?" Brenda's eyebrows went up.

"It's not a ravine now. When I go back and look at it, it's only a small opening in two sections of rock, but when I was twelve the gap looked as wide as the Grand Canyon. Jule, who was small for his age and forever proving he was as tough as the rest of us, did whatever Cammie and I did."

"So when you and Cammie jumped over this ravine, your very young and very small brother Jule followed right behind you in the grand Cooper tradition."

Wes nodded. "He fell fifteen feet into a rock bed. He broke his leg and both arms. They had to rig a rescue bed to get him out and he was helicoptered to a trauma hospital that was sixty miles away from where we lived. He was critical for three days."

She reached across the table and took his hand. "You must have felt awful."

"I did. Both of us did. So much so that we spoiled him rotten."

"Where is he now?"

"He lives in Memphis. Married. Wife's pregnant."

"Is your sister married too?"

"Engaged."

"So there's to be a wedding in your family too."

"Next June. When's yours?"

"It was last July, just before I moved to California. She and her husband are spending their honeymoon at the reunion. We're all looking forward to really meeting him."

"Wow," Wes swallowed. "Taking on a whole family at one time, all generations in one place. This is brave man."

"I know what you mean. You haven't met the Johnsons. We can be a pretty diverse bunch." She smiled when she said it. Wes knew all families have their eccentrics, but he was sure in Brenda's family every personality was unique and she loved them all.

"It's a good thing Shiri already married J.D."

"Good, how?"

Brenda rolled her eyes. "My aunts and my mother. They would have just taken control. All Shiri had to do is set a date and the terrible trio would be off and running."

"I gather they are a take-charge group."

"You have no idea. They are sisters and when they get on a roll, it's like a single bulldozer. They take no prisoners. The rest of us just step aside and beware of the Johnson sisters." She paused with a smile. "What about your mother? Did she go on these camping trips too?"

Wes noticed she batted the conversation away from her own family and back at his.

"My mother never went. She's the fashion model type. Her idea of camping is checking into the Beverly Hilton when the pool is closed for cleaning."

Brenda laughed. "I think she'd be right at home with my mom."

Wes lifted his fork and continued eating. "My mother runs an art gallery. She gives gala parties and entertains visiting dignitaries and VIPs."

"What did you do with your mother, since she never went camping?"

"She took us to see ballets and operas, plays and baseball games."

A FAMILY AFFAIR

"Did you like them, the operas and ballets?"

He hesitated. Real men weren't supposed to like that stuff. "One or two," he confessed. "She likes high fashion and traveling, but she also came to everything she could get to. Despite her long fingernails and perfect makeup and hair, she'd grab a baseball bat and ball and go into the field with us."

Brenda smiled. Her teeth were even and her smile was beautiful.

"Where does the baseball come in?"

"Her father played minor league when he was young. Apparently he instilled in her a love of the game. She's got season tickets for the Boston Orioles. She and Dad go regularly."

Wes wanted to know more about Brenda's life too. He'd told her about his family. Now it was her turn.

"Tell me about your family." He expected her to go for the water glass again, but she didn't. She cut her steak and started talking.

"We're a big clan. I used to call us the Johnson tribe when I was a kid. We'd get together for everything, reunions, weddings, sometimes just Sunday dinners. There was so much flash and color with aunts and uncles and cousins, and Aunt Rosie was the gang leader. She's a character. Even now in her seventies she's as close to a free spirit as you can get. She's a retired cook, but in her day, which began after her husband died, she moved to Mississippi and taught herself to drive. After that there was no stopping her. Oh, the stories she tells. You never know how much is true or how much is pure fabrication, but I love her."

"Sounds like you had fun growing up."

"Oh, I did. Me and my partners in crime."

"You . . . crime, in the same sentence."

"Well, actually I was the law. My cousins were the criminals."

"Male or female cousins?"

"Shiri and Essence, female cousins. Shiri is the one who just got married."

"Are they meeting you in Florida?"

She nodded. "The whole tribe is coming, even Aunt Rosie. We're having a family reunion. Although I'm not sure about Essence." She frowned.

Wes wanted to smooth lines away. He could tell Essence somehow worried her. More than Shiri did. "Why isn't she coming?"

"She's not really a relative. Her family lived close to mine and she often spent hours at our house. Her mother died a while ago and I'm not sure she's over it. We all love her. She's been part of our family so long that few of us remember she isn't a Johnson by blood. No one ever points it out, no one except Essence."

"Have you talked to her?"

"Not in a while. She's been in school, getting her certification as a massage therapist."

"I could use a massage." He rolled his shoulders back. "Do you think she'll give me one?"

"You are not invited to the reunion," she told him with a smile that showed she could be playful shining in her eyes.

"Touchy about the family?"

"No, they're a great clan."

"What about your parents? You said your mother was a lot like mine."

"My mother is the city planner. She orders people around all day, keeping a hundred projects on schedule and within budget."

"Is that a quote?"

"Exactly, I've heard it a million times. She's dressed us in more party dresses and sun hats to take us to openings, groundbreaking ceremonies, dedications of parks, or ribbon-cutting ceremonies than you can imagine. It took me years to convince her I'm really a jeans kind of girl."

"But she never quite gets it."

Brenda shook her head. It appeared they had something in common. Mothers. Yet there was a deep and apparent love for her mother. She didn't have to say it. It was there in her speech.

"If you met Pamela Reid she'd immediately retie your tie and check to make sure your pants had a razor-sharp crease in them."

"Your father must love that."

"Oh, he does. He's the exact opposite of her. Yet the two of them are a perfect mix. They love each other, laugh a lot, especially when my mom forgets she's home and not in her office and my dad finds some subtle way of reminding her."

"Are you more like your mother or your father?"

"My father, hands down. We both like comfortable clothes and staying away from parties. My brother is the same way. But those two in the middle are Mommy clones."

"Brothers and sisters?"

"One brother, the youngest, spoiled rotten, and two sisters. I'm the oldest. I'm looking forward to seeing them again. When we get together it's one big party."

"So NASA wasn't your only reason for taking this trip?"

"NASA is just the icing on a very sweet cake."

To tell her she was the sweetest chocolate icing he'd ever seen was probably out of line. He held the comment, knowing he'd like nothing better than to reach over and taste her. And her family sounded eccentric. They were probably a lot like his, fun to be around, loaded with practical jokes, but fiercely loyal to each other.

He had a sudden picture of his mother pitching baseballs in a pair of red high heels and his father playing catcher while he held on to his fishing rod. He smiled at the thought.

And made a mental note to call them tonight.

FIVE

Brenda's knees hit the wall. The jarring woke her. Recoiling, she instinctively pulled her legs up. Opening her eyes, she wondered where she was now. During the night the train had lulled her to sleep in the tiny bed. She was used to her big bed in her comfortable house back in California. When she moved from Illinois she'd sold a lot of her furnishings. She wanted to begin fresh, with everything new, from the walls out. The one thing she'd kept was her bed.

She wondered how Wes was making out. Did his huge frame fit into the tiny Murphy-type contraption the porter had opened while they were at dinner? She remembered dinner and stretched with a smile, her body yawning like a waking cat until again she contacted the unforgiving wall. Wes had walked her back to her compartment after they lingered over coffee and warm snifters of brandy. At first Brenda thought he was trying to get her drunk, but after the warming liquid made her relax they talked. The dining car cleared out, leaving them the lone occupants. The waiters checked with them infrequently, but in no way hurried them along. Brenda listened to Wes tell her about his work and he seemed genuinely interested in what she did. He also appeared to understand when she explained black holes and event horizons. His immediate translation of the speed of light into space-normal speed and doubling the speed into warp one had her laughing. She liked laughing. There was a time when she didn't think she'd do much of it again, but Wes had come into her life with his optimism and his quiet approach that let her know life could be fun again.

The passageway was small leading to her cabin. They walked silently and slowly to her door. Brenda turned to say good night as the train lurched. The motion was slight. She doubted if it would wake anyone, but in their state of inebriation it was enough to throw them off balance and into each other. Brenda clung to him, immobile, taking in his scent, savoring it. Wes ran his hand up her back and into her hair. She felt all the breath in her body leave it. Brenda couldn't remember feeling like this before. Just being in his arms and she was losing all her senses. Her muscles seemed to dissolve and she wanted to go on lying against him.

Then his hand massaged her neck. Her head lolled around like a rag doll's. She felt his mouth on her forehead and again on her cheek. Brenda knew it had to stop. In a moment he'd really kiss her and she wouldn't be able to hold back what was happening to her. As his mouth turned to meet hers she turned her head and pushed away from him.

"I'm sorry, Wes. It was the train."

But it wasn't the train and they both knew it. He graciously didn't call her on it. She opened the door and slipped inside, her heart pounding and her body washed in heat.

Sitting up, Brenda threw the bedcovers back and raised the shade to find lush green hills and the constant and reminding mountains in the distance. She wondered where she was. She knew the itinerary. The train had started out in Oregon but had traveled south into California and was considerably south of Lake Vista, but still in the state. She hadn't seen much of it, one trip to Los Angeles to see the Dodgers play. On her trip West the train had gone across Wyoming and taken her down into Klamuth Falls, Oregon.

She was looking at the mountains in wonder when someone knocked on the door.

"It's me."

She recognized Wes's strong voice even muffled through the door. Brenda grabbed the robe matching her silk pajamas and threw it on. She opened the door intending only to crack it, but Wes swept right past her and closed it.

"Did you see the mountains?"

Brenda finger-combed her hair back. She hadn't expected company. "Wes, we live in the mountains."

"Did you see the snow?"

"There isn't any snow." She looked at the mountains. It wasn't late enough for snow, but in winter the scene would be something out of a Christmas card. "I've seen snow before." She started to laugh. He was teasing her. Usually she hated people making references to Birmingham being a small town in Alabama where nothing much happened or where the residents of it didn't understand cold weather and snow. With Wes it was different. He was acting young. It was charming.

"Do you know how great you look in the morning?"

"I'm a grouch in the morning," Brenda said, but it didn't stop the blush from heating her face. Even her ears warmed to the compliment. "I haven't even brushed my teeth yet," she said, her voice scratchy.

The air in the compartment changed. The happy-go-lucky energy was gone. Electricity snapped around them. Brenda didn't know what to say. She was unsure where she wanted to go from here. She'd searched her soul yesterday. She'd let her mind guide her, but her mind had no chance against the presence of the man in front of her. Tall, dark, solid, and apparently waiting for her to say something. She needed to make the next move. She needed to let him know she was willing. The same way she'd lain in his arms last night, then pulled away, he needed to know now that she wouldn't pull away.

"Wes, last night—"

He raised his hands and stopped her. "I know what you're going to say." He closed the distance between them. Brenda wanted to move back, out of the realm of magnetism that robbed her of reason and had her swaying toward him. "I won't push you. We're coming into Martinez. We have a three-hour stopover here. Want to grab something to eat and sightsee?"

Brenda nodded.

"Be ready in half an hour."

Wes didn't immediately leave. He raised his hand and ran his knuckles down her cheek.

"What are you doing?" she asked, hoping to control her breathing enough to keep from giving away the fact that his touch was sending her blood rioting through her system.

"I'm seducing you," he answered honestly.

"I thought you said you're weren't going to push me."

"This isn't a push. This is a press." Then he bent down and kissed her cheek.

"Brush your teeth," he said. "I might want to really kiss you later."

The air was pungently sweet. If Brenda had been in a building it would be overwhelming, but outside in the open air the smell of grapevines and soft earth was fragrant. Wes had hired a car, apparently before the train stopped, she found out. Quickly they were crossing the Benicia Bridge and heading up Interstate 680 toward Napa Valley.

"This is just beautiful," Brenda said. She got out of the car and surveyed the land around her. Fields and fields of grapes grew in every direction. To think the entire valley was settled by wine-producing families when she couldn't see any buildings other than the ones along the side of the parking lot. The air was comfortably warm and suitable for the grapes, nestled between high mountains, to grow and thrive.

They took the guided tour that led them through the fields and into the limestone caves where vats measured in stories of grape juice turned itself into wine. Finally they came out into the tasting room. Brenda tried several varieties. Sweet, dry, chardonnays, merlots. She liked the merlot best and decided to buy a bottle to take with her.

The tour concluded in the gift shop where presumably people would buy one of the wines they'd just tasted. Brenda walked around in a building that gave the impression of a converted Spanish mission. She checked labels and read the histories that were sometimes printed on them. Wes seemed to know exactly what he wanted.

She saw him near several counters as he pointed out wines that a clerk had to get for him.

She'd never cultivated a love of wines. Her parents loved wine. Her father even had a small cache in the cellar, but Brenda never took to it. Seeing the sign that said WE SHIP, Brenda decided to send him a few of the wines she'd tasted. She found a clerk and completed the transaction at about the same time Wes finished his.

Brenda left the building carrying a box that hung from her arm on a softly twisted fabric rope and a plastic bag with books. Wes also carried a roped box. They went back to the vines where they were permitted to explore on their own. Brenda must have looked awed, because she was. She wouldn't have thought twice about walking through a field of beans or growing cotton, but these grapes captured her attention. Their endless turning and twisting as they climbed the trellises touched something inside her. Something she wouldn't have known was there if Wes hadn't burst into her compartment this morning and told her they were taking a tour.

She looked over her shoulder at him as he bent down to avoid an overhanging branch.

"Thank you," she said.

"What are you thanking me for? I didn't make it beautiful."

"Thank you for bringing me. If I'd been on the train alone, I would never have ventured further than the station."

"Aren't you the adventurous type?"

She shook her head.

"I've noticed how orderly you are," he said. She glanced at him. "Your office," he explained. "Don't you ever want to spice things up, do the unexpected, add adventure to an ordinary day?"

"You mean like jumping over a ravine?"

Brenda wished she could have answered yes to that question, but she'd never been adventurous. She played it safe, never venturing further than necessary, often staying close to the familiar. She couldn't explain the fear that had engulfed her when she left to go to college. While most of the other students' parents' had driven them to school, Brenda had arrived by train and alone. Her mother had shipped her clothes, computer, microwave, answering machine, even a compact refrigerator. Everything she would need was delivered to her door. But she was on her own to get there without family or friend to lead the way.

Brenda understood her mother was cutting the proverbial apron strings, pushing her out into the world, forcing her offspring to take a chance on her own. She'd survived it, but it didn't make her more prone to wander the world engaging in new experiences. After college she'd taken the job at Colgate Observatory in Pennsylvania where she stayed until the appointment to Connelley in Illinois. At both places she only knew the people she worked with. Going to Meyers she made a pact to meet more people, but other than Elzeta and Lorris and the ladies of the bid-whist game she hadn't met anyone unconnected with the school. Yet with Wes . . . with Wes she wanted to go rushing into the unknown.

"Do you like wine?" She changed the subject, not the one they were discussing, but the one in her head.

"Some," he said. "I don't get down here often and they have a very good selection."

"Better than the French?"

"Did you know that French farmers traveled all the way across the Atlantic protecting the roots of grape plants, then arduously crossed the unforgiving land of the United States just to plant their precious vines right here in this soil?"

She looked down at the ground. "As a matter of fact I did know that. It was a question in Trivial Pursuit."

"Trivial Pursuit?"

"We played it in college," she told him, wondering again if he was teasing her.

"Did you also know that when there was a blight in the French wine industry the California vines were returned to the home country to save the day?"

"Do you think there's going to be another one?"

"Another what?"

"Blight. You shipped a lot of wine."

He laughed. The sound was deep in his body. Brenda had a sudden urge to put her hands on him and feel it. She could tell herself it was experimental, that she wanted to do it to test the warm sound of his voice. But she felt the heat of it pouring over her like honey.

"I sent a couple of cases to Cammie. Her fiancée loves Napa Valley wine and it'll soon be my brother's anniversary so I sent him a case."

"And how many cases did you send back to the university?"

"Man does not live by steak and eggs alone." He stood up tall to make a point of what man did live on.

She raised her hand with three fingers in the air. Wes grabbed it and held on to it. Brenda should have pulled free. She told herself she didn't want to struggle with him, but the truth was she didn't want to let go. Wes wasn't holding her that tightly. If she wanted to drop his hand she could. She liked the way his hand felt. It wasn't a hard, work-worn hand, it had the feel of a doctor's, strong and sure, and hers fit perfectly into his.

"I sent a case to the Friday night poker game."

"The place where bets are made," she reminded him.

"The other two are mine. Winter will be long and hard. I'll share one with you sometime."

She didn't say anything. The suggestion was sexual. Pure and simple. And the mark hit where it was supposed to. Right between the shoulder blades.

"You sent a healthy amount of wine too."

"My parents like wine. I sent them a case. And I sent a couple of bottles to my two aunts."

They walked through the vines, looking up as the sun darted in and out of the overhead frames and through the leafy branches. It felt good on her face and neck. Brenda didn't know when Wes dropped her hand or how his arm got around her waist, but somehow the two of them were walking hip to hip through the sandy earth, down the aisles that had a sacredness to them. They went on for miles, in straight rows, with only the sound of the breeze, the whisper of the leaves, and the soft pounding of her heart.

As they neared the end of their allotted time Brenda was sad to see it close. She and Wes had to return to the train, and while they would still be together there was something magical about the vines. She'd grown up in Birmingham where there were many farms only a short drive from downtown. Part of the Johnson clan still lived and worked farms and Brenda had been to them many times. She understood the ground, the water, the cycle of growing. Yet she'd never felt as close to the earth, as one with the bridal veil of plant life as she did under the mantle of fragrant leaves with Wes. He'd been silent as if the vines formed a cathedral and the two of them paid quiet homage to the fingers of the Divine.

With Wes's arm around her waist, they went back to the hired car. Brenda rode in silence watching the green fields turn back into highway, then into streets and finally the station.

"Jump out. I'll turn the car in and meet you on board."

Brenda gathered her things, the souvenirs she'd bought, a couple of books on wine making and the history of the Napa Valley, and took the wooden cask holding four bottles of wine that Wes had purchased.

"I'll take everything so you don't have to worry about it."

She smiled at him and closed the car door. He drove away. Brenda climbed the stairs to the station platform. The train was sitting there. The platform was virtually empty except for the porters and engineers. Everyone must be on board, she thought. Out of the corner of her eye Brenda caught a movement. It was a man running. He jumped on the train as if only arriving in the nick of time. She glanced at the clock above her head. It was an old Bulova clock that hung from the station ceiling on a tarnished golden coil that had an electrical wire running through it. Wes had only five minutes to make the train. Panic set in. How could they have cut it so close? Why didn't he tell her she needed to hurry when she was dawdling around the gift shop? Or when they were straggling in the fields.

She rushed on board and dropped everything in her cabin. Then she went back to look for Wes. She didn't see him. Checking her watch against the clock on the platform she could see the hands matched exactly. It was almost time to leave and in her experience trains usually left on time. If they were late, they would be late arriving, but would either leave right on schedule or only stop long enough to disembark and load passengers.

"Wes, where are you?" she asked under her breath.

A FAMILY AFFAIR   111

Her knees pumped unconsciously as if the gesture could make him appear. Her head swung back and forth looking for his long-legged stride to come up the same stairway she had come up. Heat intensified in her body as the minutes ticked by and Wes did not appear.

"Board." She heard the elongated word called out by a porter to signal the engine driver. For over a century that single word had been used as a warning that the train would be leaving the station. That those who should be on board should get on and all others should leave.

Brenda stood in the doorway, holding it open with her body. Where was Wes? Could the train start if the door remained open? The old trains she loved were a thing of the past, of memory and museums or rides that led to nowhere, depositing their passengers in the same place where they were picked up. This was a modern train. It had some of the old details that historic train buffs loved to point out, but the doors were electric. They opened and closed on a rush of compressed air. Wes couldn't come into the station, running to hop on board a train that had already begun to move. Those were actions for the cowboy days and most where creations of the Hollywood western. If this train moved, there would be no hopping onto a caboose or jumping onto the steps and swinging his body into the space between cars. He'd miss it altogether.

"Board." She heard it again. This time the door tried to close, but Brenda forced it open.

"Wes," she shouted. "Wes!"

The door pushed against her slight body. She strained against it as if she were trying to keep a star from going nova. The train jerked, then rocked, throwing her off guard. The door stared to close. She jumped for it, pushing it open with both her hands, her legs braced to anchor her forward strength. It went back into the recess, then immediately came forward again. She caught it, holding it like some wild animal that needed taming.

"Brenda!" She looked up.

"Wes." He was running along the platform. The door was jerking in and out of her hands. He only needed a few more seconds and he'd be here. His long legs sprinted, his feet making contact with the concrete. She strained, gritting her teeth and holding back the forces of physics and an electric closing mechanism. Wes continued to run. All the other doors were closed. This was his only way in. The train fought her. Brenda's strength was weakening. She didn't know how long she could keep it from closing. She saw the conductor looking through an open window, probably wondering why the door light on his panel was still illuminated. Why the train had not begun the steady movement it did day in and day out during his trips along this route.

She glanced back, fighting with the mechanism. Wes was closer and still running. "Come on," she said aloud, the words giving her strength to hold on another second and another.

He reached her. Jumped inside, crashing against the inside wall as his body's momentum continued its forward movement, unmindful of the fact that he'd reached his destination.

Brenda let go of the door. It jerked, then closed. She flinched, raising her hands away from the black rubber binding as if its purpose were to drag her hands through the opening and cut them off. The image scared her.

She turned toward Wes and threw herself into his arms.

* * *

A FAMILY AFFAIR

Wes closed his arms around her and breathed in. His eyes closed. He buried his face in her neck and held on and as if his life depended on it. There was a sweet scent of something she had on her hair, the damp smell of relieved fear, the faint odor of sunshine, grapes, and earth. Underlying it all was the unique scent that could only be Brenda Reid.

Wes found it intoxicating. Stronger the longer he held her. They were standing in a public vestibule. He'd been afraid of missing the train, afraid of losing Brenda. She would go on without him. Wes continued to hold her. He wanted to do more. He wanted to run his hands into her hair and turn her mouth onto his, but he knew better. She'd stopped him last night. She wasn't ready. And he couldn't start something in this public area that he couldn't finish. If he kissed her he wouldn't stop at that. There was too much adrenaline running through his system. He couldn't be accountable for his actions right now and neither could Brenda. He hoped his timing wouldn't always be off with her. This was the wrong place, but it wouldn't always be wrong. Never had he wanted anything more in his life than to kiss Brenda.

He pushed her back, congratulating himself for having more stamina than a weight lifter. She stared up at him. Her eyes were dark and confused looking. He was sure his looked the same. He was confused. He'd never met a woman he wanted to know more about or one he'd been more attracted to. In research he'd met some women. There were plenty of them in the field these days and more joining every day. None of them turned him on the way Brenda Reid did. He felt as if he'd known her for years and that there were still things he wanted to know.

"Are you all right?" he asked.

"Just a little out of breath," she responded. Wes had the feeling her breathlessness had nothing to do with holding the door. His didn't.

"Come on. I'll take you to your cabin."

"I'm all right," she protested. "I can go—alone."

She turned quickly and walked away from him. Wes let her go. Their afternoon had been wonderful. He enjoyed walking through the vineyard with her, having her leaning on him, laughing. Now she wanted to put distance between them.

She'd held the door, forced it open so the train couldn't move without him. She'd held an entire train for him. Should he read more into it? He wanted to. He wanted to think she wanted him around. That her life would be irrevocably changed if the train left the station without the two of them on it. Yet her retreat after being in his arms didn't go with the theory. Did his arms banding her to him communicate what was going on inside him to her? The rapid beating of his heart could be due to his hundred-yard dash to reach the open doorway, but he knew it had more to do with the soft, warm body in his arms. Then he thought of the bet. Was that what stood between them? Did she still think he was pursuing her because of it?

What else could she think? Wes asked himself as he went into his own compartment. His entire presence since he met her had been about the bet. His presence on this train, even today in the valley. She thought he was trying to seduce her into a date. And she had to feel what he felt when he had his arms around her. There was no denying he was attracted to her, no denying he wanted her. But the bet stood between them. He'd explain at dinner that their afternoon had nothing to do with the bet.

A FAMILY AFFAIR

* * *

Wes drummed his fingers on the white tablecloth in the dining car. He checked his watch. She was late.

"Excuse me," he said, stopping a waiter. "My dinner partner . . ."

"Ms. Reid elected to have her dinner in her compartment, sir."

"Thank you." Wes wanted to know more. He wondered why she'd chosen to eat alone. Was she ill? Had the afternoon been too much for her? She usually spent nights in the observatory. The train had left early and when they got to California he'd immediately hauled her off the train and taken her to the vineyards. Maybe the day had just been long and she was turning in early. Yet he didn't think so. He thought it had nothing to do with the day and everything to do with the hug in the train doorway.

And there was no time like the present to find out.

Wes ordered the waiter to put his dinner on a tray. He took it and knocked on Brenda's door. He waited long enough to think she wasn't inside or had chosen not to answer. He knocked again and she pulled the door inward. Sweeping by her, he went inside. Her hair was down, no longer in the ponytail she often wore. Dressed in a pink robe that fell to the floor, she looked small and vulnerable.

"I thought the day may have been tiring so I ordered dinner on a tray. Mind if I join you?" He put his tray on the small fold-down table next to hers, which was still covered with the white napkin.

She looked down at her robe. "I'll put something on." Wes let out a breath when she didn't order him out of her room. Hastily grabbing clothing from the closet she went into the tiny bathroom.

He lifted the napkins. She hadn't eaten. Her food was nearly cold. She had a deluxe compartment identical to his. During the day there was seating that converted to beds during the night. In addition to the sleeping arrangements Brenda also had a television on which she could select an array of videos to occupy her time during the trip. The machine was silent and dark.

She came out of the bathroom wearing jeans and a T-shirt. She'd wound her hair into a knot and clamped it with some type of comb. He much preferred it loose. Her face was unframed and unadorned. She had the most amazing eyes he'd ever seen, yet they were totally unreadable. She smiled, but Wes had the feeling she was uneasy.

"It's my turn to say thank you," he started, at a loss for anything else to say. He wondered why it was that each time he saw her it felt like the first time, like rushing around a corner and colliding with the unexpected.

"For what?"

"For holding an entire trainload of people with your bare hands so I wouldn't miss it."

She made a muscle and laughed. "It was the least I could do. Shall we eat?"

Wes felt as if the mood had lightened. She walked to the table and pulled the napkin aside. She made no comment on the food. They ate discussing the day, the vineyards and wine. Wes thought of them as safe subjects. Brenda appeared uneasy. She looked about the small space avoiding looking at him. He wondered if he should have come. Maybe he should have respected her privacy and gone to his own compartment. Maybe he should have let her invite him in instead of brushing past her without an invitation.

The truth was he didn't want to be refused. He wanted to spend the time they had together. He wanted her to know him and he wanted to know her. Yet she was reluctant. He could see that. Often she steered the conversation away from herself.

"Would you like to watch a movie?" she asked when they'd finished eating and the conversation seemed to fall into a dead zone. Wes was staring at her. He hadn't heard the question. He was watching the way she moved. The way her hands floated through the air as if she were conducting music.

"Do you always wear your hair like that?"

Instantly her hand went to the clamp securing it.

"Before coming to Meyers I looked totally different."

Wes raised an eyebrow for her to go on and explain. Brenda turned away, going to the window and staring at the passing scenery. It was getting dark and more of her was reflected back into the train than could be seen outside. It was also the first time she'd volunteered anything personal about herself.

"What did you look like before?" He couldn't imagine her looking any way but beautiful.

"More like the country bumpkin. Straw in my teeth and hair."

She was kidding, he was sure. "That's not possible."

She turned to face him. "Oh, I assure you it is."

"And what caused you to change?"

He saw her face cloud. It was a fleeting change, faster in time than it took the 4,500-ghp 7FDL engine to pull the train the distance from one railroad tie to the next.

"My cousin Essence came to see me. We went to one of those places that does makeovers; everything from head to foot is bathed, exfoliated, vacuumed, oiled, perfumed, combed, and redone."

"Ouch. Sounds painful."

She laughed. "It's supposed to be relaxing."

"Were you relaxed?"

She thought for a moment, then nodded. "I was amazed when I finally saw myself in a mirror." She looked at the window again. This time she surveyed her own image, not the distant trees and lack of cities.

"I can't believe that. You're beautiful. You must have been told that thousands of times."

"Sure," she agreed. "Thousands of times." The flatness of her voice assured him she spoke the truth.

"Is something wrong with the men in Birmingham? Are they blind?"

"Let's just say I bloomed late in life and leave it at that."

Wes thought she was cocooning again. She was pulling the conversation away from the personal, gathering all personal data and folding it inside herself. He didn't want to go there. He wanted to know more about her.

"Was there a man?" He knew this was the reason. She'd alluded to it before, but when he tried to get her to tell him, she turned off.

"Why would you ask that?"

"There was a man," he stated.

"There was a man," she admitted after a long pause. "His name was Reuben Sherwood. We worked together at Connelley." Her voice was soft, quiet. Wes stood behind her. He could see both their reflections in the glass. They looked like a portrait. "I'm the bookworm of the family. No one expects me to marry. I'm too into my work. I'm dedicated and conscientious and have no time for men." She paused. Wes could almost hear someone telling her that. He wondered who it could be. "Reuben was the first man to really pay attention to me," she went on. "At least what I thought was me. I found out later he really wanted to horn in on my research. He was the tenured one, but I was the one making strides. I was new and still idealistic, he told me. There had been some scientists on campus. They were from NASA and they'd expressed an interest in my research. He concealed the information from me and used me to try to get in on the deal any way he could."

Wes had a sudden urge to strangle a man he'd never met. He also had the urge to move across to Brenda and take her in his arms.

"We broke up. Essence came to see me and I told her all about it. She said the best revenge was letting him see what he'd missed out on. So she convinced me to do the makeover."

She didn't have to tell Wes her result was a success. He could see it.

"Reuben's reaction was priceless," she said, interrupting his thoughts. "He couldn't even talk when he saw me."

"Did he call you?"

She nodded.

"Did he try to seek you out on campus? Find you in the cafeteria?"

Again she nodded.

"What about the faculty parties?"

"I refused to go to any."

"You couldn't completely avoid him."

"No, we saw each other in classrooms and sometimes off campus. I avoided him every time, but he'd come over and try to talk to me."

"Then it was a success."

"I don't know." She looked at the floor, then up at him. "I don't have much experience with these kinds of things."

Wes thought that was the most telling comment she could have made.

"I don't know why I'm explaining this to you. It's not like you're a close friend."

"Maybe you're trying to tell me why you refuse to have coffee with me."

She didn't answer.

Wes took a step toward her. She looked confused. Needing. Wanting someone to comfort her, put his arms around her. He knew he shouldn't. Knew her confusion wasn't ready for a solution. Yet he found himself eliminating the space between them. Just as he reached her she turned to face the window. Wes's chin was level with the comb holding her hair. He hesitated. Her actions stopped him.

"What happened with the NASA people while you were there?"

"I don't know. Reuben wouldn't give me any information on who they were or what research they had been interested in. I had a good idea because he asked more questions about the maps than anything else. I tried to call NASA, but got nowhere. I dropped it assuming they were no longer interested in anything or they would have followed up."

Wes still wanted to touch her, to remove that clamp and let her hair fall down. She was speaking to the window, telling him not to do it. He should understand her plight. She'd lost an opportunity that could have changed her life. He'd lost an entire experiment. He should understand. Yet things were working out for her. NASA had again approached her. She was getting a second chance. Inside him was a voice telling him to leave it alone. But there was a stronger voice speaking to him. It was an unfamiliar voice. One in his own head that had him reaching for the brown plastic contraption. He squeezed it open and pulled it free.

Sweet, fragrant hair fell to her shoulders, over his hands. Wes pulled her back against him, slipping his arms around her waist. Her head fell on his shoulder. Heat washed over them like a burst of steam. She was soft and warm and she seemed to melt into him. Wes bent down and kissed the skin at the base of her neck. He felt a tremor run through her and listened to the delicious throaty sounds that issued from her unconsciously.

He wanted to taste her, assure her of her beauty and her attraction to men, turn her around, and feel the full solid length of her body against his. He wanted to undress her slowly in the boiling heat of the room, reveal each inch of her to his touch, his eyes, and his mouth. He wanted to stretch her out on the small bed and make slow, delicious love to her from sundown to sunup.

Yet when he turned her around, when his mouth moved from her neck and his hands ran over her breasts, she said the one word that stopped him as forcefully as if he'd been hit by a tidal wave.

"Don't."

SIX

Brenda had never thought of her hair as sexy. She stood looking at herself in the mirror over the bathroom sink. Wes had had his hands in it and she could still feel them threading through the curls. She'd washed it since he'd left her almost a day ago. Staying in her compartment she'd tried to work, watched videos she couldn't concentrate on, tried to read, and looked through the window at the red and gold landscape that might as well have been gray for all she could see of it.

Her mind was on Wesley Cooper and no amount of distraction could deter it. She combed her hair, tossing the curls about her face and looking at the differences she could achieve with just the use of several different makeups and framing her face with her hair. She told herself she wasn't doing this for Wes. That she had changed her appearance before she ever met him, but she knew that wasn't true. She knew she wanted him to—what? Put his hands in her hair again? She wanted to succumb to the feelings that overwhelmed her just a day ago. She wanted to raise her head and feel his mouth on hers.

Reuben Sherwood had never evoked the kind of feelings she had for Wes and she hadn't known him nearly as long. She thought she'd been in love with Reuben.

She was hurt when she discovered his betrayal. Now she knew that was only puppy love. At twenty-nine she was discovering what every high school student knew. Yet she wasn't in love with Wes. She was sure of that.

What scared her was that she could be. She didn't understand why that should bring on fear. Maybe because of Reuben. He'd wanted something from her and hid his reasons. Wes was open with his. He only wanted a date to win a bet. A date wasn't so bad. But where did it go from there? Last night if she'd let him kiss her, where would it have led?

What if she did fall in love with Wes? If what she felt for Reuben wasn't love, the feelings of shame and disappointment and hurt would be tenfold. She couldn't go through that.

She couldn't stay cooped up in this compartment for the next few days either. When they got to Chicago they would change trains, and although the setup might be slightly different she was going to be in close quarters with him until they got to Orlando.

Brenda put the comb down and added a light lipstick to her mouth. She had done everything Essence showed her how to do. She looked great, better than she ever thought she would. Her dress clung to her curves, which she would have denied having a year ago, and her heels made her legs look as long as the distance from the top of the sky to the earth. Essence said men loved women with long legs.

She was ready to go. At the door Brenda saw her full reflection in the mirror. She nearly gasped. What was she doing? She looked like she was about to seduce someone. Had that been her real reason for taking so much care with her dress? Had she unconsciously wanted to seduce Wes?

A FAMILY AFFAIR   125

Heat funneled up her body, into her ears and hairline. She knew the answer.

She did.

Brenda yanked the door open and swept through it like a Hollywood actress making an entrance. The tight hallway was deserted. She turned toward the dining car and went straight there. At the door she hesitated, taking a deep breath. Wes sat with his back to the door at the table they were both assigned.

She pushed the door in and smiled at the waiter, who looked up at her. Walking toward the table she stopped and faced Wes.

"Is this seat taken?" she asked.

He looked up and choked, covering himself with a cough. Brenda felt great, powerful. Essence had been right. It was attitude. As long as she looked the part she could pull it off. Wes stood and held her chair.

"I'd given up on you."

"I had a lot of work to do," she lied.

"You look gorgeous." His eyes roamed over her face and down to all the parts of her he could see without looking under the table. "Did you dress to impress me?"

It was on the tip of her tongue to say, *Not especially,* but she found she couldn't. "Did it work?"

"Brenda, you impress me by just being you."

Oh God, Brenda thought, *where did this guy come from?* She knew some things about him too. Glenn had been a fountain of information to her at the faculty parties. She knew Glenn was playing the unofficial Cupid, but she listened when he told her Wes hadn't spent much time dating until lately when he decided he wanted a wife. Yet he'd had all the bad luck in the world in finding one. He'd found all the incompatible females on the mountain. Glenn left it hanging that maybe she was the one he was looking for.

Brenda had adamantly told herself she didn't want to be around Wes. She'd gone the campus romance route and she didn't want to uproot herself again. Yet his looks were devastating, and he was kind and intelligent and easy to talk to. And he was pursuing her. Yet Reuben had been the same. What would happen when the bet was won?

"How do you feel about the hair and clothes?" Wes interrupted her thoughts.

She smiled. "I like them. I feel good in them."

"Then they're worth the trouble."

The ice was broken. The two of them fell into easy conversation and spent long hours over coffee and brandy. By the time Wes walked her to her compartment she was sleepy and content.

"Good night," he said. "Sleep well."

Brenda didn't move. They weren't touching, yet she could feel a connection. "I enjoyed myself."

Wes smiled. Brenda did something she hadn't planned and had never done before. She deliberately went into his arms, raising herself up on her toes, and hugged him. Wes's arms came around her a second later. He squeezed her to him as she sank down. She pressed her mouth onto his cheek.

"Good night," she whispered and slid back on her heels, touching the floor as if returning to the woman who lived on the outside. The one on the inside retreated from danger. Wes let her go without protest. But when she slipped inside and closed the door she remembered the dark look of passion in his eyes.

And wondered if she should have done anything about it.

A FAMILY AFFAIR

* * *

The ice between Brenda and Wes had clearly melted. From that dinner and her actions in the hallway they were friends. They spent all their time together. Like kids on an adventure they got off the train at stops and used the time to explore the area, run into gift shops, and buy magazines and books that they never read. Wes would hold her hand to keep track of her in a crowd. He would put his arm around her as he pointed out some historic landmark, but he never tried to kiss her again.

From Denver to Omaha to Chicago where they changed trains, Wes and she were companions. Chicago to Washington, D.C. where they had a four-hour layover and plenty of time to see the monuments in full light, they were never without each other. Brenda hated to see the trip end when they eventually reached Orlando. She knew all things must come to an end. Hers appeared to gain finality as the taxi inched through the morning rush-hour traffic to get to the hotel.

After a work week of travel she'd reached Orlando. She wouldn't have Wes's company anymore. He had his own problems to deal with. She needed to bone up on her information for her meeting with NASA.

They got out of the taxi and the bellman made a production of loading their stuff on a cart while she and Wes entered the lobby. After Brenda checked in and got her keys, she turned to Wes. It didn't seem appropriate to shake hands with him. Not after she'd been in his arms and after he'd seen her all the way to her hotel.

"Thank you, Wes. I enjoyed the trip." With her computer in one hand and her purse hanging on her arm, she tiptoed up to kiss his cheek. It was the first time in days they'd had any sexual contact. Immediately she felt the pull to press her mouth to his.

"I'll see you back at work," he said in a voice that seemed a bit strained to Brenda.

"Good luck with the investors."

"Thanks. You too, with NASA."

They both seemed a little reluctant to leave. "Would you like help with your luggage?"

Brenda looked around. The bellman had already taken her bags and headed for a freight elevator. In all likelihood they would arrive in her room before she did.

"Bye," she said again. She took a step back when Wes's arm went around her waist and pulled her close. He pressed a kiss on her mouth, hard and fast, then released her and smiled.

"I've wanted to do that for the last four thousand miles."

He turned then and left her, heading for the exit and his waiting taxi. Brenda watched him a moment; then as someone bumped into her she realized she was in the way and headed for the elevators.

Her suite was large and airy. On the top floor of the hotel, it had two bedrooms, one with a single king-size bed and one with two queens. The entire complex was appointed in dark woods, rose-colored walls, and thick gray carpeting. There was a huge living room-dining room combination that had a concert grand piano in one corner, along with a chandelier over a dining table, outfitted for eight. Three sofas provided a grouping in front of a big-screen television, and a lighted wall book rack complete with current novels stood against one wall. The coffee table held books on Orlando and Florida and one on the Kennedy Space Center at Cape Canaveral. Brenda would spend the next three days there.

Busying herself she unpacked, showered, and changed clothes. After an hour she had nothing else to do and she missed Wes. She wondered where he was staying. He hadn't said. She wondered when he would be returning to Meyers. In their week on the train the small details of their lives weren't discussed. Now she wished she knew.

A knock on the door had her going to answer it. She knew none of her family was in town yet so this could only be the maids checking to see if she needed more towels or a forgotten toothbrush. She peered through the hole in the door and saw Wes standing there. Gasping she opened the door.

"Wes!"

He stood there with his luggage, laptop, and suitcase in one hand. Brenda moved aside to let him in.

Wes sighed as he faced her.

"What's wrong?" she asked, closing the door and walking into the center of the room.

"You're not going to believe this." She waited. "I can't find a hotel room."

Brenda was almost relieved. She'd expected to hear something terrible about his investors.

"This city must have 100,000 hotel rooms."

"I know and every one of them is booked. I just spent so much change in the phone booth trying to find a room that I was too embarrassed to go to the cashier again and ask for more. Apparently this is the worst time to come to Orlando. Schools will be opening next week. People from the North are getting in the last holiday of the summer. There are conventions in town that have taken up several entire hotels and the tour group business is booming."

Brenda looked around her. She had enough space for

a large family. Wes looked worn out. She knew the investors were worrying him, and her heart softened.

"You came all the way to Orlando without a reservation?"

"I wasn't thinking clearly. I only got the call a day before I left and I was concerned about getting the research files and making the train."

"Train, not the plane?"

"Let's not go into that." Wes turned from her and faced the windows. The broad avenue below them glinted bright with traffic. It stretched as far as they could see before meeting the horizon and making the entire distance a part of the room she occupied. Brenda knew she shouldn't say it, but she knew she was going to. It was out of character for her, but Wes had become her friend and her friend was in trouble.

"Wes," she began. "You can either use the phone and find a room or you can use the other bedroom. I've already unpacked in this one." She indicated the room with the king-size bed. "The other is yours if you want it."

"Brenda, that's awfully nice of you, but I didn't come up here for that."

She honestly believed him. "I don't suppose you're a serial killer."

"I heard that the first time you said it." He looked at her with a smile.

The look in his eyes was tiring. Her heart went out to him. On the train he'd been happy-go-lucky, but she knew he was concerned that his entire project could go down the tubes.

"I believe you didn't come here for a room," she said. "You came for change."

He smiled and it warmed her heart. She loved to see

him smile. "Try the phone. If you don't find anything, the room's yours until you leave."

It was a lot like a train, she told herself. When they were on the train they were two cars away from each other. Here there was a lock on her door and she could enter the suite through her bedroom if she wished. The other room was on the opposite side of the living room. They didn't even need to contact each other if they didn't want to. It was safe.

And if she needed Wes he'd be nearby.

Wes nodded. She could tell he was upset. Here was a problem and he couldn't fix it. He sat down with the phone book and started calling hotels. She left him alone but could hear his deep baritone voice as he spoke into the receiver. Time after time he discovered there was no room in the inn. After an hour of trying and finding no success he came to the bedroom door and looked in.

"You sure you don't mind?" he asked.

She was lying on the bed watching the news on television. "I'm sure." Inside, something stirred in her. She was glad he couldn't find a room. She wanted him to, didn't want the train to arrive at the station. This setup gave her a reprieve. She could keep Wes close by for a few more days.

"Thanks. I'll take the room on condition that you let it be my treat."

Brenda nodded. She didn't care about paying for the room. Her heart was hammering. For the next few days, Wes would be with her. She had to spend time at NASA and she didn't know when he had to go to his investors, but for sure their evenings would be free. They could talk more and enjoy each other's company. Even if she did maintain her distance she liked knowing he was there.

***

Wes left to unpack.

"Are you hungry?" Brenda called from the living room.

"I'm starving. Why don't you order from room service?"

Brenda took his requests and called the order in. She heard the shower in Wes's bathroom and figured he'd felt the same as she did when she arrived. He must have unpacked quickly. Since he'd only decided to come on the spur of the moment he didn't have nearly the suitcases Brenda had for her three-week visit.

She waited for the meal to arrive and Wes to join her, passing the time by continuing to listen to the news. There were the usual stories about the weather, the unusual crowds of holiday travelers during this time of year, and an addition of another whale at Sea World. Brenda allowed the voices to mute into white noise. She barely heard any of it.

Wes came into the room wearing shorts and no shirt. His body was still damp and he brought the scent of soap with him. Brenda's throat went dry. She couldn't move, feeling riveted to her seat as he came toward her. She'd seen men before without shirts, but none of them exhibited the raw sexuality as the man advancing on her. Her body went into overdrive. She was hot and shivering at the same time. His shoulders were broad, with well-defined muscles blending into each other and forming his arms and chest as if some sculptor had drawn him to scale.

The knock on the door snapped the thread that had her gaping at him. "Perfect timing," she said and nearly raced to the door. She swung it open without looking through the peephole.

"Scottie!" Her Aunts Doris and Karen rushed into the room, both of them hugging her at once. The heat Brenda felt at seeing Wes without his shirt escalated into an inferno of fear.

Brenda couldn't see Wes, but she knew by the way her aunts stiffened that they had seen him. Both of them released her and stared at the man across the room, the man wearing shorts, the man *without* his shirt, without shoes, and apparently living in her rooms.

"Hello," Aunt Doris said as she released her. Brenda heard the slight elongation of the word. Aunt Doris's voice wasn't her usual southern drawl. It was surprise, pretification at seeing a healthy man with Brenda. She wasn't sure if the expression on her aunt's face was incredulity or shocked glee.

"Good afternoon," Wes said as if nothing out of the ordinary were occurring.

"We're Scottie's aunts," Aunt Karen said, moving toward Wes as if she were ready to protect her cub. The aunts had always done that. She, Shiri, and Essence could have come from all three mothers, since their aunts acted as one in certain circumstances. Protection of the family was one of them.

"Who might you be?" Aunt Doris asked.

"Aunt Doris, Aunt Karen, this is Doctor Wesley Cooper."

Brenda intended to explain that he worked with her and that he couldn't find a room, but her Aunt Karen got in first. "Young man, are you living here with my niece?"

Brenda prayed he'd say no. That he would let them

know the circumstances, but she saw her aunts swing their glances toward the two bedrooms.

"Aunt Doris, Aunt Karen, I can explain. This isn't what it looks like."

"Scottie, you never said a word about bringing a man to the reunion," Aunt Doris said, censuring her. Aunt Doris needed all the details nailed down or her world was off-cocked.

"Scottie?" Wes said, coming up next to her with that wretched raised eyebrow that said more than his words.

"Don't ask," she threw at him. She had no time to deal with him right now, and why didn't he go put a shirt on? It was hard enough to look at him without wanting to eat him alive when he was fully dressed. With him half naked she couldn't concentrate at all.

"It was a last-minute decision." Wes played right into their hands. Brenda knew he was doing it to throw her off balance. He'd told her she was too orderly, that she needed not only spice in her life, but adventure. Why did he pick this time to give her a lesson?

"Brenda could have sent word," Aunt Karen went on. "After all, they have cell phones."

"Aunt Karen—"

"It only happened recently," Wes said, interrupting.

"What?" Aunt Doris asked. "What happened recently?"

"We got engaged."

For an eternity it seemed no one said a thing. Her aunts stared dumbfounded. Brenda was stunned and so apparently were her two aunts. For a second she saw their expression before she whipped around to face Wes. Brenda looked at him as if she wanted to tear his eyes out. He looked at her with all the heat and passion of a man in love. He immediately embraced her, pulling her into contact with his naked skin. She felt his strong legs against hers. His soap was intoxicating, but not as intoxicating as the underlying smell that was all male, all him, all Wes. He bent and kissed her neck. She couldn't do anything. The kiss melted her muscles. Her knees turned to water and she had to hold on to him or fall.

"Does Pamela know?" Aunt Karen asked.

"No," she shouted, a little too quickly and too loudly. "It—it just happened," she stuttered and pushed herself away from Wes to face her aunts.

"Please, don't tell her." Wes came to stand behind Brenda. "We're saving it as a surprise. Brenda says her mother will be thrilled and she wanted to do it in person."

"We understand." The two women looked at each other with the knowlege of a lifetime of friendship and confidences.

"This is absolutely wonderful." Doris Rowlan pranced across the room and hugged Wes as if she were welcoming him into the fold. "We all said Scottie would be the last to marry, if she ever did. Apparently, she's going to surprise us."

"None of us thought she'd get her head out of the sky long enough." Karen Johnson replaced her sister and hugged Wes too. "You just don't know what a wonderful thing it is to know that she's finally found someone to love."

Wes glanced at her. He nodded in understanding. He knew how they'd treated her all her life and why she turned into herself.

"So tell me, Wes," Aunt Doris chimed in, "where did you two meet?"

"We both work at the university."

"What do you do there?" Doris asked.

"I'm in the genetics department."

"Brenda said you were a doctor."

"PhD. Doctorate in genetics."

"I was hoping for medicine." Doris spoke again. "We could use a good medical man in the family."

"I'll bet she snubbed you the first time she saw you," Aunt Karen added.

"She snubs everyone. If she chose to date you, you must be someone special." This from Aunt Doris. "I want to hear all about it." She moved around to take a seat. Brenda knew she was digging in for the long haul.

"Aunts!" Brenda gritted her teeth and tried to remain in control. She didn't want her aunts giving Wes a character study on her. Her world was spinning away from her and the three people in this room were all in a conspiracy to keep it going that way. She knew she'd get no help from Wes. He was enjoying her discomfort. Brenda took a deep breath and asked in a calmer voice, "Why are you here?"

"We had some arrangements to make with the hotel to make sure everything is set for the reunion. We had a few minutes and thought we'd drop by and see how you were doing."

"Have you talked to the hotel people yet?"

"We're meeting them for lunch." They both checked their watches. "We're already late." They started bustling around grabbing sweaters that had fallen when they hugged their nonexistent future nephew-in-law. "We've got to go, honey."

"I'll walk with you," Brenda said. "I have some explaining to do."

Both aunts headed for the door. They looked back at Wes again. The smiles on their faces couldn't have been wider if they'd won the Florida lottery. "We'll talk to you later," Aunt Karen said. "Pamela is going to be so happy."

At the door Brenda looked back. The two women were rushing down the hall toward the elevator. "Maybe while I'm gone," Brenda said, "you'll be able to find a shirt."

"Why, your aunts didn't seen to mind. And neither do you—*Scottie.*"

Brenda couldn't tell them. They were too happy being happy for her. She felt as if she'd let them down all her life and she'd finally done something for which they approved. She knew their opinion of her and her willingness to even look at a man, but to find a live one who wasn't old enough to be her grandfather in her room brought out the child in them. They were gay and laughing, enjoying the secret they had. Brenda found it impossible to burst their bubble. She only thanked the heavens her mother was not with them.

The hotel staff was late in arriving and she had a few minutes to talk to her aunts alone but they were falling over themselves with comments on Wes. Brenda wanted to explain something. She wanted to tell them about their living arrangements, but Aunt Karen cut her off each time with some licentious comment about Wes's chest or his long legs that had Brenda blushing.

"He's got a great body, darling," Aunt Karen said.

"Did you get a load of that stomach?" Aunt Doris asked Aunt Karen. "If I wasn't happily married . . ."

"Mmmm, mmmm, mmmm." Aunt Karen sounded like a Campbell soup song.

They were acting like a couple of teenagers over a new boy in class. Brenda had never seen them this way. A year ago none of their girls had married yet. Shiri had already made it to the to the altar. She didn't know about Essence, but Brenda was definitely not marrying Wesley Cooper. Why had he said that? Now she couldn't get out of it and her aunts were bound to tell her mother. Her life had been nothing but out of sorts since she met Wes.

"Honey, are you happy?" Karen interrupted her thoughts.

She hesitated, unsure how to answer. She liked being with Wes. He made her laugh and he made her hot. She didn't know if she was happy. All she was sure of was that she was scared.

"I've never seen you two act like this."

"We're so happy for you, Scottie. With Shiri marrying and you finding Wes, the family will be thrilled—"

"You won't tell them?" she pleaded. "We need some time and I want to be the one making the announcement." Brenda didn't know she could lie so readily. She'd never done it before. Her face would burn, her ears would turn hot, and her expression would give her away. This time the aunts looked as if they believed her. "With the reunion coming and Shiri married, I want it to be her time."

"We understand." Again the two women looked at each other. "You'll announce it during the reunion."

Brenda nodded quickly. She didn't know how she was going to get out of it, but for the moment she had deferred the rumor spreading further than this hotel. By the time she got to the reunion Wes would be back in California. She'd think of something.

"He is good looking," Aunt Karen said.

"And that voice," Aunt Doris chimed in. "Did you hear that voice?"

"Can you imagine hearing it in the dark?" They both looked at Brenda.

A FAMILY AFFAIR   139

"Stop it," Brenda said. "I am not ready for you two to act like this."

"Like what, honey? Don't you think we know what goes on?"

"Aunt Doris, please let me keep my myths."

Aunt Doris, sitting in the booth next to her, slipped her arm around her shoulders. "Sweetheart, I am so happy for you. Wes is really taken with you. I can see it in the way he looks at you. You deserve a man like that." She kissed her hair the way she'd done for as long as Brenda could remember.

Brenda loved her family and she'd never deceived them. Why had Wes put her in this position? And what did Aunt Doris see? She didn't get the chance to ask. At that time the people they were meeting arrived.

Brenda excused herself but asked if she could see them after the meeting. She still had doubts about their ability to keep quiet. She decided she'd have more courage to tell them the truth after the novelty wore off. And they'd be more willing to listen after their meeting. Brenda needed to clear up this misunderstanding before her aunts returned to Birmingham.

"This is going to take several hours," Aunt Karen said. "After that we have a car to take us back to the airport. We're not going to have much time."

"Don't worry, Scottie. They'll be plenty of time to talk at the reunion," Aunt Doris said.

Brenda must have looked shocked, or some other emotion was on her face. Her Aunt Doris walked her to the elevators while Aunt Karen sat down with the hotel personnel.

"This doesn't have anything to do with what we talked about a few minutes ago."

Brenda was confused. They hadn't been talking about

anything. She had been sitting there while they mentally raked their hands over Wes's unclothed form.

"Sex," she said, finally understanding what her aunt meant. After teasing her with bawdy comments about her pretend fiancée, she couldn't say the word *sex*.

Her aunt nodded.

"No, this has nothing to do with sex."

Relief was apparent on her aunt's face.

"I could ride to the airport with you," she suggested.

"With all the security we have these days it would be best if we didn't do anything but observe airport protocol. The hotel has offered us a car."

"All right. I'll see you at the reunion."

Brenda kissed her aunt on the cheek.

"Don't worry, Scottie. We won't tell Pamela. She's too busy planning another shopping center."

Brenda returned to the suite and Wes. She was sure they would keep her secret—at least for a while. She could only be thankful that her mother hadn't been with her two aunts. The three sisters together were hard to deal with once they found a subject that interested them.

Brenda felt terrible as she entered the suite. She'd seen them happy before, but this time they looked thrilled. It couldn't just be Wes. They had encouraged her to have dates in high school, not to spend so much time with her head in books, but Brenda never found any of the boys interesting when she was in high school. The first time she'd seen Wes she was bowled over. Bowled over and angry. She didn't want this man who pushed buttons she didn't know she had to be the man who bet the entire campus he could date her.

It was hard not to be interested in a man who looked like Wes, who talked like him, and who made her feel like a queen. He was intelligent and kind and attentive.

A FAMILY AFFAIR

She remembered the vineyard and her reaction to being in his arms. She remembered holding the train door, knowing she didn't want to spend days on the train without him. And that kiss in the lobby just before he left her. It was fast and unexpected, shocking and thrilling, and threw her completely off balance. Even if that had been his purpose she didn't care. She knew he rocked her world. He'd say it needed rocking. And she could find no reason to disagree with him.

The elevator opened on her floor. A red-patterned rug led the way to the suite at the end of the hall. It seemed to rush toward the cause of her dilemma. Brenda stared down it. She had to face him now. Anger flashed through her, replacing the dizzying feelings of a moment ago. What was she going to do? How was she going to explain this to Shiri and Essence? Brenda could just see her e-mail now. She hadn't set up her laptop. She didn't want to read any mail. Of course, it couldn't be there yet. Her aunts were still in the lobby. And they had promised to keep her secret.

Which she wouldn't need if Wes, good-looking Wes, Wes-to-my-friends had just kept his mouth shut. Brenda slammed the door to the common room. Wes sat at the dining room table eating.

"I ate your lunch," he said.

Brenda walked into the room, put her hands on her hips, and faced a man who sat as casually as if he were a model in a male magazine. He'd changed clothes, but it didn't matter. He wore slacks and an open-necked shirt. Yet they couldn't hide his body from her memory. Brenda knew that under that fabric was even brown skin. Bone and flesh defined the outline of arms, chest, and washboard stomach. The whole package had been carved from brown rock, down to the arrow of hair that disappeared below his waistband. As he was sitting, she couldn't see his legs, but the shirt outlined his form like a second skin. Brenda was determined to keep his body from distracting her.

"What were you thinking?" As loud as the door had been when she slammed it, her voice was low, lined with a tremor that harnessed her extreme anger.

"I was thinking your butt needed saving."

"But engaged! Why did you tell them we were engaged?"

"What should I have said? That I was some guy you picked up in the hotel gift shop?"

"I would never pick up anyone in a gift shop."

"Maybe you should."

Brenda turned away. She leaned on the bar where a tray held a bucket of ice and several bottles of water. Brenda opened one of them and poured some into a glass. She drank it.

"You could have told them the truth, Wes, or if you had to say something outrageous you could have said you were gay."

He stood up, looking at her as if she'd grown a second head. Wes came toward her. Brenda didn't know what to do. She'd overstepped her bounds. She wanted to run to her bedroom and lock the door, but she refused to move. She'd never let anyone know she was afraid and she wasn't about to start now. "No, I couldn't," he said when he stood in front of her. His voice held the same low quality hers had, yet there wasn't the tremor of anger in it. It was something far more menacing.

"Why not? It takes the same amount of air," she said.

"Because of later."

"Later? What happens later?"

"This."

A FAMILY AFFAIR

Brenda had no warning. She didn't know what he intended until it was too late. Like that of a basketball player faking a move, one hand went around her waist while the other gathered her loose hair in a knot and held her head still. His mouth took hers sure and hard. Brenda felt everything, every cord of his arms, every muscle in his legs, his chest to her chest, his mouth to her mouth. Wes held her tightly. Not even air separated the place where his body ended and hers began.

She tried to resist, tried to hold herself aloof, but she was no match for the sensation going through her, the explosion of feeling that fissured through her like an erupting volcano. His mouth brushed over hers. Then his tongue entered her mouth. Fire replaced the blood in her veins and shot through her system like an atomic attack.

She melted into him. Brenda could do nothing else. She'd never felt like this before. She'd been fighting with him, angrier with him than she'd ever been with anyone in her life, and now she couldn't get close enough to him. Her arms came up of their own volition and she gave up to the kiss, to the uproar that sapped her of strength for anything except Wes.

His head angled left and right in a duel as old as time, his mouth feeding off of hers. Brenda clung to him, bathing in emotions, drunk with a headiness that made her lighter than air. She couldn't get her body close enough to his. She'd never done this before, never felt as if she wanted to climb all over a man. And there was no doubting this. She did want to climb over him, inside him, find out what it was about him that made her forget she had bones in her body.

Brenda heard someone moan. She didn't know if it came from her or Wes. It didn't matter. It made her feel good. *He* made her feel good. She tightened her arms around him, felt his hands run the length of her back. Fire trailed where his hands touched her. Her body was hot, hot enough to burn, to fuse, but it was no contest to the liquefying encounter that generated from his mouth. Brenda didn't think she could stand much more of this assault. Yet she didn't want it to end. She wanted more of him and he was offering it. She could feel his body harden, imagine the feel of his weight on her. Again she moaned.

Wes raised his head, moving his mouth from hers, but keeping her close, folding her in his arms as if she were a baby who needed holding. She heard his breathing. It was as ragged as hers. She kept her arms around his neck, hanging from him as her legs wouldn't support her.

"You're right," she whispered as she pushed back. "You're definitely not gay."

"I've wanted to do that ever since I saw you standing under the light of President Langley's front porch."

President Langley. The name hit her like a bullet. She stumbled away from Wes. Her legs supported her weight, but she grabbed the bar anyway, feeling the need for reassurance. She had to return to her job. Meyers University. President Langley. *Both* of them had to return.

"Don't you ever kiss me again," she said, mustering all the anger she could. "I may be sharing my room with you, but not my bed."

Brenda made it to her bedroom before she collapsed on the king-size bed. She balled her long legs into the fetal position, holding her stomach. Wes had touched something deep inside her. She tried to reach it, tried to stop the shaking, but she couldn't. He'd had found her core and no matter how much she told him she didn't want him to touch her, it was too late. He'd found the faucet inside her and turned the fountain on. Unfortunately she was the one drowning. She wanted to rush through the door and back into his arms. She wanted him to kiss her again. She wanted to make love to him.

Never before had she thought of fantasies, *sexual* fantasies, and now she couldn't get them out of her mind. Wes without his shirt had sparked it. For a scientist he was built more like a long-distance runner. When her aunts had hugged him, Brenda wanted to do the same. She remembered how dry her mouth had been when he came into the living room wearing no shirt, no shoes, only shorts. She didn't know that a man could make her feel as if she could fly with only a look, only a touch, or that a kiss could sear her to the core of her existence. She didn't know that her imagination could undress him totally, that she would think of smearing his long body in warm honey and licking every inch of it off. Images of them naked in front of a roaring fire, him playfully feeding her ice cream and the two of them collapsing into another mind-blowing, insane, brain-crazed kiss before making savage love, crowded in her mind, activating the inner tingle inside her.

She couldn't stop the images. She knew she didn't want to. They were all she had of him, even if she wanted reality instead of fantasy. Fantasy was all she would get, all she would allow. Wes was more dangerous than Reuben had been. She'd need to be on her guard every moment. She'd told him not to bother her.

And she was going to have to live with that.

***

Never kiss her again. Wes wasn't capable of following that direction. He decided to take Brenda's statement as a guideline and not a command. The fact that she told him never to do it again was only a minor inconvenience, another challenge among the others she'd issued. He'd known kissing her would be a wild experience, but wild didn't even graze the truth of the matter. He had intended to kiss her, and kiss her passionately, but he hadn't thought it would be a fall-off-the-side-of-the-earth kiss. Yet it was and he was still falling. He had to repeat it. He needed Brenda Reid's body pressed against his again.

Then Wes remembered the bet. He sat down and poured a soft drink over his dwindling supply of ice. He wondered if Brenda had thought of the bet. Had the mention of President Langley's name brought Meyers University and all it meant back to her? Was that the reason she told him not to touch her again? He wished he'd never said it, never even thought to agree to Jerry's contest. It was turning out to be more trouble than it was worth, especially in the light of the reason he was here in Orlando.

Wes needed to talk to Brenda. He needed to apologize. The impulse to kiss her had been on his mind. The comment about being gay gave him a reason to put action to the challenges she sent. He hadn't planned what happened after his mouth met hers. That was something he had no control over. She couldn't control it either or she wouldn't have been such a willing participant in his arms. He was only slightly less shocked than she was. Now was not the time to say anything, however. She had stormed into her room. When she calmed down he would explain.

In the meantime he'd go for a swim. The exercise would help clear his head and possibly give Brenda some space, and the cold water would help the throb in more than one part of his body. The suite was large and the common room separated them, but for him the space wasn't enough to keep him from thinking it was only a room away from her.

He slipped a towel over his shoulders. He had no room key and as much as he hated interrupting Brenda he had to let her know he was going out. She was in the living room when he opened the door. There was a glass of wine in front of her.

"You haven't had anything to eat. You shouldn't drink that."

"Why not? It's my day for stepping out of character."

Wes didn't know what that meant. Family put pressure on you from all sorts of directions, but he didn't get the impression that that was what happened to her.

"You didn't tell them, did you?"

She lifted the glass and sipped. "I couldn't."

"Why not?"

"I don't really know why. They weren't the same. I never saw them act like that before. I thought I knew what they thought of me, but I had no clue it was this bad."

"What did they say?"

She swung around on the stool. She was still angry, but she didn't scream. "They never expected to find a man in my room. They never thought I even had the capability to entice a man, that no one would want to be with me."

"I'm sure you're wrong." Wes stood his ground. He

wanted to go to her and take away her pain, he wanted to tell how beautiful she was, but she thought of him as the cause of the situation and she'd surely push him away.

"And I lied to them. I let them go on believing I'm engaged to you." She took another drink. Wes went behind the wet bar and took the glass. "This is definitely not like me," she said.

"Maybe that is the reason," he said.

"What?"

"That it isn't like you and you want once in your life to be reckless." He set a cup of black coffee in front of her.

"I don't want to be reckless."

"We all do," he told her. "It's what keeps us alive. We all have dreams or fantasies of things we'd like to do, how we'd like people to see us, but we hide some of it, never letting anyone know. We worry about what they might think."

"You think I want to be reckless? With you?"

He shrugged one shoulder as if it didn't matter. "I'm convenient. I'm close and I'm willing."

"Don't hold your breath." She got up and went to her room.

"I don't think I'm going to have to," Wes said when she was out of earshot.

SEVEN

The conference room at the National Aeronautics and Space Administration was appointed to receive scientists from all over the world. The room had a long polished table with chairs designed to support comfort during long meetings. The lighting could be adjusted to any level. Carpeting on both the floor and walls kept the sound inside the room, and a computer station and LED wall displays could change the space into a command center instantly.

Brenda had been in and out of it for nearly eight hours. She'd met countless doctors, some of whom she knew by reputation. Others she met just today.

They were interested in the star maps she'd created while she worked at Connelley. There were some slight variations in the already chartered maps for that area, and in space a slight difference could be hundreds of thousands of miles. For space travel it could mean the difference between hitting the mark and being lost forever.

Brenda enjoyed engaging in active discussions with other astronomers. She found herself redefining her charts, using better systems and more sophisticated equipment to analyze results. The day wasn't like work, but fun. She knew Meyers had some state-of-the-art equipment, but none of it was as good as the telescopes and computers she had at her disposal in this facility. If she worked here it would be like going to heaven every day. Everything she needed was right at hand.

For three days she came and went. Each day was a different aspect of star mapping, predictions, and theories. Some of them she had encountered before; others were totally new but infinitely possible. She found herself in long debates with colleagues over vast patches of sky and what could be in them.

At first she was shy, awed by being in the company of men and women whose names filled textbooks and who held Nobel Prizes, but when she began to explain her work and they asked questions, she lost all shyness in her ability to defend her work. They admired her for it.

As she left the first night, Doctor Pruwinski, who'd spent fifty years in the business, stopped her. "I haven't enjoyed a day like this one in a very long time," he said. "I look forward to continuing tomorrow."

The daily routines and long nights of meetings kept her mind busy. After three days with rocket scientists and three nights of avoiding Wes and her feelings for him, she found the real reason the NASA executives had asked her to come in. They were interested in her theories and wanted her to continue her star-mapping research in northern California. They wanted to fund a program for her designed to reach deeper into the star charts.

When Brenda asked why, they were honest enough to tell her they couldn't give any more information. They would fund her program through a grant to the university.

Brenda couldn't have been happier. It was like having everything she ever wanted handed to her. And the university would be thrilled about the money. It would bring more students in, increase the interest in astronomy, and give her what she needed to work on something that really interested her and would have a far-reaching effect on the future.

Brenda left the facility floating on air. Now all she wanted to do was run to Wes and tell him.

Wes wasn't in the suite when she returned. Brenda got a bottle of water and opened it. The phone rang as she took the first swallow. She hoped it was him. It was six o'clock and she had wonderful news to tell him. Maybe they would go to dinner and celebrate all that had happened in the last three days.

Flopping down on the sofa, she picked up the receiver.

"You're not picking up your e-mail," Shiri started, without saying hello.

"Shiri!" Brenda was glad to hear her voice. Shiri could always raise her spirits or share in her happiness.

"What's up? I know you work day and night but you usually answer your mail once a month or so. And since you're in Orlando you're not stuck on a mountain and out of communication range."

"I've been a little distracted lately." Brenda thought of her laptop, still in the case in her room. She hadn't even opened it. With the computers at NASA her laptop seemed to work at Stone-Age speed. And then there was Wes.

"By a man?"

Brenda could almost see Shiri freeze in place at the thought.

"No, not by a man," she lied. "I had a meeting today with some NASA scientists."

"Any of them cute?"

Brenda opened her mouth to answer, then closed it. She had noticed the men. She hadn't thought of that before. In the past she was only interested in the work. But she had noticed for the last three days a sexual quality to those within her age group.

There were a couple of men old enough to be her father, a couple of women, and one man whom she'd taken more than one look at. He reminded her of Wes. She noticed he returned her glances and sat next to her at all of the lunches and group dinners.

"I wasn't there to check out the way they looked. And why are you asking? The last time I saw you, you only had eyes for J.D."

"J.D. is surely my Mr. Right. I just want you to be as happy as I am."

For a moment there was silence on the phone. Brenda checked the door to Wes's room. It was closed. Outside, the clouds were gathering for the afternoon downpour.

"Shiri, I want to ask you something. And I want an honest answer."

"Oh dear, let me sit down." Shiri's voice was serious. She wasn't mocking Brenda. She never would. They were too close for that. They joked and talked, but they could be compassionate and brutally honest with each other.

"When you think about me, what do you think?"

"Where did that come from?"

"I'll explain later. Just tell me."

"Well," she began. Brenda thought Shiri didn't want to answer. "You're definitely the smartest person I know. You never had to figure out how to build something or explain something. You just knew. And I might add that always ticked me off."

"Is that all?" Brenda was disappointed. There were many times her brain got in the way with people. She

An important message from the ARABESQUE Editor

Dear Arabesque Reader,

Because you've chosen to read one of our Arabesque romance novels, we'd like to say "thank you"! And, as a special way to thank you, we've selected four more of the books you love so well to send you for FREE!

Please enjoy them with our compliments, and thank you for continuing to enjoy Arabesque...the soul of romance.

Karen Thomas
Senior Editor,
Arabesque Romance Novels

Check out our website at
www.arabesquebooks.com

**SPECIAL OFFER!
4 FREE BOOKS**

ARABESQUE®
A PRODUCT OF
BET BOOKS

3 QUICK STEPS TO RECEIVE YOUR "THANK YOU" GIFT FROM THE EDITOR

Send this card back and you'll receive 4 FREE Arabesque novels! The introductory shipment of 4 Arabesque novels – a $23.96 value – is yours absolutely FREE!

There's no catch. You're under no obligation to buy anything. You'll receive your introductory shipment of 4 Arabesque novels absolutely FREE (plus $1.99 to offset the costs of shipping & handling). And you don't have to make any minimum number of purchases—not even one!

We hope that after receiving your books you'll want to remain an Arabesque subscriber. But the choice is yours to continue or cancel, anytime at all! So why not take us up on our invitation to receive 4 Arabesque Romance Novels, with no risk of any kind. You'll be glad you did!

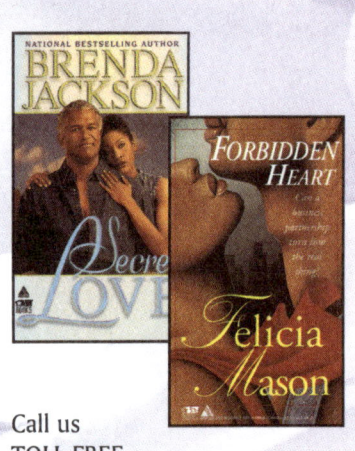

Call us
TOLL-FREE
at 1-800-770-1963

didn't ask for it. Why didn't they see it as something she got with birth, just like they did? It controlled body functions the same as anyone else's. But somehow her circuits weren't crossed the same way as Shiri's.

"Brenda, it would help if you told me what you were looking for."

"Why did you ask me if anyone at NASA was cute?"

She heard her cousin sigh. "Because of Reuben Sherwood."

"What's he got to do with NASA?"

"Nothing. It's you I'm worried about."

"Now you sound like Aunt Karen and Aunt Doris. It's over between Reuben and me. I know now I was never in love with him."

Wes had taught her that. She'd never felt for Reuben what she felt for Wes. Reuben's kisses had never burned her the way Wes's did, and long after he wasn't in the same room with her she was still thinking of him and wanting him.

"What about the rest of mankind?"

"I haven't sworn off men."

"Have you admitted they exist for more than discussing the formation of supernovas and even horizons?"

It was *event* horizon. Brenda ignored the mistake. After meeting Wes she couldn't help but think of things other than science, but she couldn't tell her cousin. She couldn't remember keeping anything from either Shiri or Essence, but she wasn't ready to talk about Wes.

There was nothing real between them. She was allowing him space rights to an empty bedroom. Not her heart. The two of them could be living in separate hotels—except for the kiss. The thought came without warning and her mouth tingled. Heat flashed through her body like a pain.

"Brenda, are you still there?"

"I'm here."

"Well?" Shiri wanted an answer to her question. "I'm talking mankind one at a time." She paused and her voice changed a little. It was lower, more compassionate. "I know your life will be complete and full without having a man in it, but don't discount them because of one bad one."

Brenda knew from Shiri's comment that she felt the same as her mother. Neither of them expected her to be involved with a man. She wasn't involved with Wes.

But she might want to be.

"I don't intend to," she told Shiri. Brenda thought the subject had already been wrested from her hands. She might have maintained it until a few days ago. The day Wes had gotten up from the table and branded her mouth with his. At that moment her world had exploded. A new world replaced it. The sky wasn't the limit. The limit was right here on earth diguised in the form of a chocolate-covered idol whom the mere thought of could reduce her body to liquid.

"Shiri, is there something in the e-mail I should read?"

"It's nothing important, only a note that says call me when you get to Orlando."

The door to the suite opened then. Wes came in. Brenda moved her feet from the coffee table and sat up. He glanced her way, but didn't look happy. Brenda knew he'd met with his investors today. It must have gone badly.

"Shiri, I have to go. I'll see you in a couple of weeks. Tell J.D. I'm looking forward to meeting him again."

Brenda stood up as she replaced the telephone receiver. Wes had closed his door. She wondered what had happened. She hadn't told Shiri about NASA. She wanted Wes to be the first to know. She wanted to share her happiness with him. But he hadn't looked much like celebrating.

Brenda stood outside his door. She'd never invaded his privacy before, but this was different. She knocked.

"Come in."

Brenda opened the door. Wes stood at the sliding glass door that led to the balcony. His hands were in the pockets of his slacks. His suit jacket lay on the bed along with his laptop case. The rain had just begun to fall. He stared off into the distance, not turning around to look at her. She advanced into the room.

"It didn't go well?"

"They're pulling the funding."

She gasped. Her hand came up to her chest. She hadn't expected this would happen. "They said that?"

"They might as well. There were three of them, and they weren't happy."

"Did you explain?"

"What I knew—" He stopped abruptly. "I showed them the research. I explained the progress." He turned back into the room. His hands came out of his pockets. "I told them everything I knew. I tried to find a reason for the failure; temperature, contamination, even sloppy record keeping. Nothing proved it. Glenn is meticulous. No one could ask for a better assistant."

Brenda took a step forward and stopped. Never had she thought there was a maternal instinct in her, but she wanted to go to him and hug him.

"Sit down," she said. He looked at her, then moved to a chair near the door. It swiveled around and faced another one across from it. The rain began in earnest. Huge drops plopped on the balcony floor and bounced into the room. Wes ignored it. Brenda backed up and sat on the bed.

"Tell me the real story," she said. "All of it."

"What do you mean?"

"I mean forget the charts and progress reports. Tell me what you really believe happened. The stuff you've been holding back, even from yourself."

"There isn't anything."

"Something you suspect?"

He didn't say anything.

"Sabotage?" she asked. He swiveled the chair around and looked at her. She could see confirmation in his eyes. The rain behind him pelted the window with a force strong enough to want entry into the room. The open doorway allowed the water to wet the rug. Wes stood up but did nothing to stop it. Brenda got up and went to the door. She pulled it closed and locked the rain outside. As she turned back, he was beside her. Without thinking she went into his arms. The gesture was purely for comfort.

"How did you know?"

She felt his voice in her hair and his arms snaked around her. "From what you said the night it happened, it appeared you'd done everything right. And if you had, the only explanation that made any sense was that someone tampered with it."

"I have no proof. I couldn't tell the Reeves Foundation that I think someone sabotaged my experiment."

Brenda was still in his arms. She moved back and looked up at him. She should have pulled free, totally disengaged herself from him, but she didn't. Warmth invaded her blood and that inner place that only Wes touched could spring to life.

"Have you mentioned this to Glenn?"

He kept her to him, but shook his head. "I have nothing to go on. It's only a hunch."

"Maybe he's feeling the same thing. Since he's there, he could start an investigation, check to see if he finds anything."

"There's nothing to be found. I would have found it if there was. I searched that lab up and down."

"Give Glenn a call. He might have seen something you didn't."

He nodded and they stood together watching the rain, holding each other. After a while Brenda asked, "How about after the rain we go out? Have dinner someplace nice? My treat."

"I don't feel much like going out."

"What about room service and a movie? We could eat it in front of the television like the kids at school do."

He smiled quickly. "Not very hungry at the moment."

"Would you like me to leave you alone?"

He looked down at her. "I think if you don't go I'm going to kiss you, and that didn't go off so well last time."

Brenda stepped back. Nervously she looked at the floor, then back at him. "Oh, I'm sorry. I didn't . . . I mean it felt so—"

"So natural," he finished for her.

"Something like that," she whispered, backing toward the door. She stopped before going through it. Wes hadn't moved from his place in front of the windows. The storm unleashed its fury, pounding against the window, running in sheets down the glass. Lightning flashed, turning them into surreal characters. Brenda couldn't see anything through the water. Yet inside the room was quiet, except for the charged electricity that rifled between them each time they got together.

It was natural being in his arms. Brenda had never

been more comfortable in her life. And while she wanted to move back toward him, he was really upset. He didn't even take her up on a date when she offered it.

"Do you have another meeting with them?"

"Tomorrow."

"What are you going to say?"

"I have no idea."

"Do you have any idea who ruined the experiment?"

He shook his head. Brenda felt he had an idea but didn't want to give voice to it. She understood he couldn't tell the Reese people his thoughts. Maybe he could convince them his research was worthwhile.

"Tomorrow will be different. Convince them of the merits of the research and try not to let the problem of last year weigh on you. You can deal with that when you get back to Meyers."

"Good idea." He nodded, but she wasn't fully sure he agreed with her.

Brenda left the door open. She had wanted to share her good news with him, but in the light of what happened to him, she couldn't. The rain shower was nearly over. The people in Disneyworld would remove their yellow slickers and resume their day of fun. The sun would remove all vestiges of rain and help to dry out the rides that would reopen. The shoppers would go back to malls. Dinner plans would be made. The people at Cape Canaveral would come out of the restaurants and pavilions like winter animals waking from hibernation. The day would begin anew.

The click of the computer keys was barely noticeable in Wes's room. Brenda sat in the common room. She could almost feel the momentum in the next room. Wes

A FAMILY AFFAIR

had begun typing on the keyboard almost as soon as she left him. He hadn't appeared in the doorway or called to her since she left, but he'd kept a steady rhythm of activity going. Often she heard the modem connecting and assumed he and Glenn were discussing the events of the day and possibly what had been on his mind since the night he discovered the sabotage.

At seven Brenda ordered dinner. She didn't ask Wes if he wanted to eat. He could eat when he was hungry. At eight it arrived. Brenda sat on the sofa and turned the television on low. She'd watch a movie while she ate.

"What are you watching?" Wes walked into the room as the credits came on the screen.

"I don't know. It's something just coming on."

He looked at the rolling cart that held dinner.

"Did you order something for me?"

She nodded as he lifted the silver cover and smelled the steak and potatoes. He took the plate and came to the sofa. He cut the meat and took a bite. "I don't remember telling you how I liked my steak."

"I'm very observant, haven't you noticed? Everything I see and hear I file away in my brain and keep for future reference."

He smiled at her, a kind of crooked turn of the lips. The old Wes was back.

"What were you doing in there?"

"Taking your advice mostly. I called Glenn and talked to him. You were right. He had the same thoughts. We know someone had to tamper with the experiment. We just don't know who. Or why."

"This research was very important to you?"

He nodded, taking another piece of steak and chewing it. Across the television screen Brenda saw a fight begin. She loved action-adventure movies, but she ignored the television. She'd put the sound on so low she could barely hear it.

"You told me your experiment helped victims of spina bifida. Did you ever know anyone who had it?"

Immediately Brenda realized she'd touched a nerve. Wes sat next to her. Not close enough to touch, but they both leaned forward to eat in an awkward position from the low coffee table. She could feel his body heat and it appeared to increase the moment she asked her question.

"I had a sister who died from it."

"Oh," Brenda said weakly.

Wes pushed his plate away and sat back. "She was only three years old when she died. It was three of the hardest years of our lives."

Brenda waited. She wanted him to tell her about it. She finished her food and poured coffee, offering a cup to Wes. He refused it. She turned off the television and sat turned toward him as she sipped.

"What was her name?"

"Eleanor. We called her Nori. She was the sweetest baby. She changed all our lives." He paused. "My mother had already had three children. She wasn't planning to have any more. When she got pregnant she didn't know it. It was a while before she realized what had happened and went to the doctor."

Brenda didn't say it, but she knew he was describing the scenario he'd outlined for her earlier about women who didn't plan their pregnancies.

"She was just under the age when tests are suggested for birth defects. She'd had three healthy pregnancies and no reason to believe this one would be any different. She was strong, healthy, and active."

"It often occurs in people who have no history of birth defects."

Wes looked at her as if she'd given knowledge of something she shouldn't know.

"I read a couple of articles after we cleaned the lab and you told me about your research."

"I see," he said. She wasn't sure what that meant.

"I don't know a lot about children with defects. There have been lots of babies in my family, but we've been lucky and they've all been healthy."

"That is lucky," Wes said. "The incidents of birth defects have been on the rise."

"Do you know why?"

He shook his head. "There are a lot of theories, but no one really knows. Planning and preparing with adequate medical advice are the best preventions. Without that children have defects that require entire families to help out."

"Is that what happened with Nori?"

He nodded. "She took up all my mother's time. She nursed her, hoping, denying, trying to keep her alive, doing everything humanly possible to save her."

"What about the other three of you?"

"We helped too. We tried to relieve her. She didn't want relief. Somehow she blamed herself, but it was nobody's fault. Finally, Nori died. We all felt so guilty that we hadn't done enough, hadn't helped enough."

"I'm sure you'd done everything possible."

"We had. We had counselors who told us that. Grief is hard to get over. My father solved it with camping trips and long talks to us kids. My mother changed jobs and went to the art gallery. Nori is never out of her mind. After her death my mother protected us more. She always had to know where we were."

"That's natural, don't you think? She'd lost a child. She cherished those that were left and wanted nothing to happen to you."

"I agree. When Nori died I decided to go into medicine. It was after I discovered that I could only treat a disease and not prevent it that I changed to research."

So it was personal, Brenda thought. He'd chosen this disease because it had changed his family and his life. There was a strong tie between him and his parents. He'd told her about his sister and brother. There was a tie there too. Brenda was tied to her family. She was glad they had no tragedy, no childhood death to change the course of their growing up. Brenda might not be an astronomer. She might well have gone into medicine or something else. And she might never have met Wes.

Wes's movement caught her attention. She looked at him as he got up and moved the dishes back to the cart covered with a white tablecloth. He filled a cup of coffee for himself and replenished her cup.

"You haven't mentioned NASA," he said, taking the same seat he'd left.

"We'll talk about it tomorrow."

"You've been gone for three days. What happened with your meetings?"

"Believe me, it's nothing you want to hear."

She turned away and got up. He put his cup down and followed her.

"Brenda, I shared mine with you. Share yours with me."

It was only fair, she told herself. She'd come into his room and he'd told her everything, even the fears he had of sabotage. But her story wasn't like that. It was the exact opposite of what had happened to him.

"I missed seeing you," he whispered. "I waited up, but you came in very late."

"I'm a night person," she joked. "You can only see the stars at night."

"You don't want to tell me?" His question was serious.

Brenda looked at him. "Can we talk about it tomorrow?"

Twenty-four hours meant a lifetime of difference. Wes stood on the steps of the Reese Foundation. The glass and steel building set on a major Orlando thoroughfare had never looked more distinctive. Traffic streaked by oblivious of the events that had changed Wes's existence. The meeting today in no way mirrored the high-tension discussion of the day before. He was sure it had to do with one director—and Brenda.

Doctor Claude Grace believed in him, believed in his work. "I've spent the entire night going over your files," he said after Wes had told his story simply, and straightforwardly, exactly as Brenda had told him to do. "I've been in genetics most of my life and I can find no flaw in your theory or your execution of it. Your notes are precise and appear accurate."

"I assure you they're accurate."

"I believe you." Doctor Claude Grace was renowned in the field. He was a short man with a round face and a bulbous nose that gave him a clown-like appearance, but he was all business. "I also believe you know something you haven't told us."

He raised his hand when Wes started to speak.

"Don't worry, we're not going to ask what it is. We think we already know."

Wes only watched the three unreadable faces. He

didn't know what they were getting at. They couldn't know anything about his thoughts, his belief that someone had tampered with his experiment. He'd given them his papers, all the notes, his computer files, and his personal log on his progress. He'd left nothing out except the feeling that the only truth he could come up with was tampering.

"So we've decided to reinstate your funding."

"What?" Wes didn't believe his ears.

"Claude convinced the two of us," Doctor Joseph Beers continued, glancing at the doubting Doctor Rayford Thomas. "He thinks your research is valuable enough that we should extend our funding."

"I admit he has a good argument," Doctor Thomas said. Wes had the feeling they weren't talking about the research itself, but the argument that it should have worked. Somehow he thought they knew about the sabotage or at least suspected it.

"Gentlemen, I don't know what to say."

"Don't say anything, Doctor Cooper." Claude Grace stood and extended his hand. "I'll look forward to success in the future."

"Thank you," Wes said.

"The university will receive funding by the end of September."

"Thank you, Doctors," Wes said. "Thank you very much."

Wes couldn't wait to tell Brenda. She'd told him to simply explain, to keep to himself the attitude that someone had destroyed his work , out of his voice and out of his being. He was sure that was part of the reason the review committee changed their minds. He didn't expect them to. He'd gone into the meeting without notes or excuses. He'd simply talked about his belief in the project and they'd believed him, at least enough to extend him additional funding.

Doctor Grace had walked with him to the door. As they shook hands, he said, "Doctor Thomas might not appear it, but he is very interested in your research."

Wes remembered his sour face. He looked as if he wanted to be someplace else. And he'd been very uncommunicative, except when he was grilling Wes on what went wrong.

"His grandson died last year. Leukemia. I'm afraid your program brought it all back to him."

Wes understood. "I had a sister who died of Spina bifida. I know what he's going through."

Doctor Grace looked at him with greater understanding. Wes didn't ask him to relay the information, but he was sure he would. He left the foundation knowing this time his research would help some unknown families who didn't have to go through grief over children.

He took the car and drove through the midday traffic. He hoped Brenda was in the suite when he got there. He wanted to find her, tell her that her advice had worked, hug and kiss her, make love to her.

Wes opened the suite door calling her name. Only the echo of his voice replied. He knew she didn't have to meet with NASA today. She'd met with them for three days. Three days when he'd hardly seen her. She was avoiding him. He'd waited up late but when she came in she went straight to bed, then was up and gone before he got up.

Yesterday she was on the phone when he'd come back. She'd had her final meeting and she didn't want to tell him about it. Had things gone well for her? She said they would discuss it today. He had good news. What if hers wasn't? Was that why she didn't want to tell him last night?

He went into the bedroom and opened the balcony door. Twenty-four hours ago he'd stood here feeling like there was nothing in the world that could lift his spirits, but Brenda had. He'd called Glenn and like Brenda said, Glenn had the same suspicions about sabotage. Glenn was quietly investigating. Neither Wes nor Glenn knew what happened but if they both had the same thoughts it was worth checking out.

Wes removed his jacket and tie and threw them on the bed. He stepped onto the balcony and looked at the panoramic view of the city and the distant Disneyworld Amusement Park. The balcony also overlooked the hotel pool. Wes spotted Brenda swimming laps. The pool had a few people in it, but she was the only one doing laps. He leaned over the balcony smiling as she moved through the water. After he watched her make several trips up and down the pool he was amazed that she could swim in perfectly straight lines. She'd swim the distance of the pool, then flip over and push off on her way back in the other direction. He counted thirty laps before deciding to join her.

Five minutes later Wes was standing by the pool. Brenda was still in the water and still swimming lap for lap. She looked tense as if she swam for exercise and not fun. He enjoyed the water and only wanted to have fun when he swam. He hadn't gone out for the team in high school or college. In Maine their summers were too short for anything except enjoying the water for the time they had it.

She must have seen him for when she reached the end of the pool where he stood she caught the edge and looked up.

"How many is that?"

"One hundred and ten."

Brenda climbed out of the pool. Wes handed her his towel. She was breathing hard. He wondered how often she did this.

"How was the meeting?" It was the first thing she asked about. She'd known he'd been apprehensive about it. Her eyes had concern in them and it showed in her voice.

"Better than I expected." They moved toward the hotel chaise longues that sat around the pool in an army of white. Brenda pulled her wrap from one of the seats and put it on. Wes wished she'd left it off. She had a great body and he loved looking at her. She had small breasts, a tight waist, and long, smooth legs. Water ran over them, down to her polished toenails. He was surprised she'd even use polish on her feet. He watched tiny droplets glistening over brown skin. The urge to bend over and lick each drop entered his mind and had him shifting on his seat.

"What happened?" she asked.

"They reinstated the funding."

She smiled. It was wide and beautiful. "Just like that?"

He remembered she'd hugged him yesterday. Today she looked at the bright water and the children who'd taken over the space in the water where she'd been swimming. "One member of the committee believed in the project. He convinced the others."

"I'm sure it wasn't only that. You had to have some influence."

"Maybe. But the funds are back and I can begin again as soon as I return."

"When will that be?"

They both seemed to understand the impact of her

words at the same time. Brenda sat still on the seat. Wes sat across from her and they both looked at each other.

"You're engaged to me. What will you tell your family?" he asked.

"Wes, we're not really engaged. When my family comes I'll think of something to tell them. Hopefully, the only people I have to explain anything to are Aunt Karen and Aunt Doris."

Wes could see she wanted to be rid of him. He wondered if it was because of his lie or her own feelings. He wasn't ignorant of them. Or his own.

"I have no commitments back at the university until fall."

"What about setting up for the new research?"

"I can do that from here. Everything I need is in the laptop. If there's anything missing I can dial into the network and download it or ask Glenn to e-mail it."

"And the investigation?"

"Glenn's handling it."

"I see," Brenda said.

"You say that like you mean the opposite."

She was looking out over the hotel grounds, but in a manner that said she wasn't seeing what was in front of her. Wes was surprised at how much he wanted to stay.

"I mean . . ." She linked her hands. "I believe things could get a little sticky in about a couple of weeks."

"Your aunts."

"Aunts, cousins, my parents, grandparents, the entire Johnson clan. I can't even be sure some of them won't arrive early like I did."

"They sound like a nice bunch of people. I'd like to meet them."

"Wes, that is not going to happen." She shifted

around on the chair. Her knees practically touched his. "I appreciate you trying to save my face—"

"It's an awfully pretty face."

She blushed, but went on as if he hadn't spoken.

". . . But I will explain to my aunts who you really are and what you were doing in my room."

He reached over and took her chin in his hand. Then he leaned forward and kissed her mouth, leaving her bottom lip wet. "They won't believe you."

"They will." Her voice was hoarse and breathy. "Are we back to the bet again?"

"No," he said. He hadn't thought of that.

"Yes, we are and I've told you it isn't going to work. So now that you have what you came for, I think you should leave."

Her voice wasn't convincing and he still held her face. He could feel her swallowing, see the accelerated pulse beat in her neck. He rubbed his knuckles along her jawline. She was having trouble concentrating. He watched her struggle, watched her eyes close and open.

"I can't leave."

"Why—why not?"

"You need me."

She stood up then. "I'm going back in the pool." She removed her wrap and rushed, diving cleanly into the water, immediately falling into swimming laps. Wes followed her and matched her pace. For him it was slow, but he didn't often swim laps. He'd rather play. He grabbed her leg and pulled her back. She went under the water, coming up spurting.

"Why did you do that?"

Wes answered her with his mouth. He put his hands in her wet hair and held her mouth to his. "I'm staying," he said and kissed her again. He heard the kids in the pool making noises behind him. Wes ignored them. He backed Brenda up against the wall and pinned her there. "Say I can stay." She squirmed in his arms. He put his mouth on hers again. "Say it." Gently he kept up the torture. He had to make her say he could stay. He wanted to stay.

"All right," she whispered. "Just until the reunion begins."

He smiled.

"Promise me, you'll go then."

Wes didn't promise. He leaned into her and kissed her. Her hands were behind her, gripping the edge of the blue-tiled pool. Wes put his arms around her and dragged her through the resistant water closer to him. He felt her arms move, tentatively as if she was making a decision. Her mouth was hot and seeking, but her head was ruling her. Wes pressed closer. Then he felt her hands, her fingernails. They lightly touched him, sliding up his arms and joining him in the kiss.

Wes leaned into it, but pulled back just before he lost all control. They were in a public pool and there were children nearby. He slid his mouth from hers and held her. He was definitely staying. Brenda lay in his arms for several moments. They she pushed off and started her regimental laps again. He stood watching, smiling at the kids who stared at him. One of them, a teenager, gave him the three-finger salute for okay.

Brenda passed him five or six times before he reached out and stopped her in midlap.

"I knew it," he said.

"You knew what?" She stood up, wiping the water from her face.

"Knew you'd make a job out of swimming."

She was beautiful in a one-piece blue-and-white suit.

Her hair was gathered into a ponytail and her face was free of any makeup. It took all his reserve not to touch her again.

"I do not."

"Don't you ever have any fun? You work all the time. Even when you play, you make it work."

"Thank you for the character assessment. It's exactly what I needed today." She struck out for the pool's edge and levered herself out of the water.

Picking up a towel she started to dry herself. Wes got out of the water. He hadn't intended to anger her, but he'd struck a nerve. She was more likely angry with herself. She wanted him to leave and he'd forced her to let him stay. He knew that she wanted him and whenever he touched her neither of them could resist.

Brenda had his towel and he waited for her to finish. Hers lay on the chaise longue but he didn't move to pick it up. Eventually she realized why he was standing still and pushed the towel at him. Tossing her wet hair she strode away, not bothering to put on her cover, but grabbing it and heading for the hotel entrance. Wes caught up with her as the elevator doors closed on him. He pushed them back and joined her inside.

"I apologize, Brenda. I shouldn't have said that. But you didn't come here three weeks early so you could go to the reunion as the same person they've always known?"

"I didn't?"

"No, you didn't." She dropped her chin and didn't answer.

"I suppose now that I've agreed to you staying for the next two weeks, you're going to be my teacher."

"If you need one."

They went inside the suite. Wes caught her arm and

turned her around. "That's it, isn't it? Your family looks at you as all work and no play. They don't expect you to do anything except count the stars and you want to change that?"

"What would you know about it?"

"Don't fight me, Brenda. I'm on your side."

She looked at the floor and back at him. Then she nodded, admitting the truth of his statement. "How do you plan to do that? Swimming laps and sightseeing isn't going to show them you've changed."

"I suppose you have a plan?"

"I have a plan." He rubbed his hands together as if he were about to embark on a new and wonderful adventure. "We're going to make you over."

"I've already had a makeover."

"Not the kind I have in mind."

A makeover in Wes's mind, as Brenda discovered, had nothing to do with wardrobe, makeup, or hairstyle. Learning to relax, he told her, was what she needed. So right after lunch the next day Wes ushered her into a rented car and off they went to places unknown.

"Where are we going?"

"To have fun."

"Is that a place?"

"Oh, yes."

"Should I ask where it is?"

"Not unless you really want to know."

She opted to let it pass. The look in his eyes said more than she wanted to know. Brenda knew she was falling into a pit. She wasn't sure how far she could go before there was no return. Wes mesmerized her. She felt comfortable with him and she wanted him to touch her, kiss her, take her to that place where time stood still. But she knew this wasn't real. They were in fantasyland and eventually they would both return to the real world.

The world of Meyers University.

Her family would arrive soon and she would like to change the opinion of her aunts and her cousins. She wanted them to think that she had a brain, but it wasn't the *only* thing she had. She had passion too and she wanted to marry and have children.

"NASA," Brenda said out loud. She recognized the road. She'd traveled it for three days. In the distance she could see spacecraft standing like spires ready for launching. They were the grandfathers of the space program. Almost props now, they invited millions of tourists each year to visit the Space Center.

"You've been there?" he teased, his brows raising.

She laughed.

"I've never seen it," he told her. "I thought you'd give me the tour."

"I thought this was my makeover, not yours."

"Don't worry, you'll have yours."

Wes parked but didn't move to leave the car. Brenda turned in her seat.

"Is this where you went in?" he asked.

"This is the tourist area. I went in over there." She pointed to an area behind some of the buildings. "You can't see the building from here. The car went in and drove around to the administration building."

She got out of the car. There was a breeze off the water and the smell of salt and fish. Brenda liked it. She turned to Wes, expecting him to join her. He got out of the car but didn't move from the closed door.

"Tell me how your meetings went. You said we'd discuss it today."

"Is that why we came here?"

"No, but before we go in, I want to know."

"They gave me a grant. They want me to continue my research into the star maps I created in Illinois, only now I'm going to do them in California."

She started to walk toward the entrance. Wes fell into step with her. "That was it?" he asked.

"That was it."

"Why didn't you say so? That's wonderful. The university will be thrilled and you'll be staying there."

She stopped. "Did you think I was leaving?"

"This is the government. They have more money than God. They could give you the lab of your desires. I figured if they offered you a job here it would be something too good to resist."

"And how would that affect you?" she teased.

"I suppose I'd have to find someone else to ride the train with."

Brenda started walking. She felt as if a knife had been stuck into her. She didn't want him riding the train with anyone but her. She didn't want him with anyone but her.

They went into the Space Museum. Under the special lighting of the cavernous building that highlighted the relatively short amount of space-years the United States had catalogued, they read all the plaques and watched the films of space travel's triumphs and tragedies.

Brenda realized she wasn't going to be able to hold on to Wes. She'd set the rule herself, told him that she wasn't falling into the trap of a campus romance. She had a job to do and now she had funding for a special project. She would do that at Meyers and she couldn't afford the distraction of him.

She reminded herself this was part of her fantasy vacation. The two of them together for fun. Fun, he'd said. She'd keep it at that. For when she returned to northern California it would be back to business. Back to being colleagues, not lovers.

She moved from panel to panel in the room, reading the signs and staring at the beginnings of space travel.

"Is this part of the makeover technique?" she asked, feeling the heat of Wes's arm above her head. Each time she looked into one of the small glass panels his arms enclosed them. He'd rest one on the side of the display above her head or stand behind her with his hands on either side of her.

"It's called relaxation. You need to be comfortable around me. You wouldn't want to give away the truth of our relationship."

"Oh, no, I wouldn't want to do that," she agreed with him playfully.

Wes didn't know what was happening to her. The truth was each time he got near her her blood shot through her system with as much thrust as one of the rockets that took off from this field. Each time he kissed her, she wanted to fall into his arms and never leave them. Comfort around him wasn't the problem; remembering to keep hold of herself, bracing her knees to support her posture, allowing fantasies of the two of them making love to invade her mind—these were the things she needed to guard against. Comfort was the least of them.

Outside they circled the ground, watching the sunlight pass through the Space Mirror, a huge square inscribed with the names of those astronauts who have died while on duty. From a distance the panel looked as if it were only a black panel with nothing on it.

They read the inscription on a glassed-in board, discussing the first African-American astronaut, Robert H.

Lawrence, Jr., to die on duty. Although Guion Bluford was the first black astronaut to fly in space, Robert Lawrence was the first admitted into the space program as an astronaut. Somewhere between the museum and the panel Wes had taken hold of her hand, and he still held it.

Brenda looked up at the sky. "When I was thirteen I wanted to go to Space Camp," she told Wes.

"From an early age you were already reaching for the stars."

"I guess you could say that. My aunts always do."

Wes stopped and looked directly at her. "Your aunts and your cousins. It bothers you, doesn't it?"

She had never been read so clearly by anyone other than Shiri and Essence. The three of them had a special bond.

"I don't really let it."

"I think you do."

She looked up at him. "I don't really dislike the words so much as what they mean."

"And that is?"

She hesitated a moment. The man she was looking at was someone she worked with. He wasn't a friend, someone she had known all her life, someone she could confide in. She hadn't known Wesley Cooper more than three months and most of that was in passing, saying hello as they crossed the same campus, meeting at faculty parties. They weren't confidants or even close friends. But they weren't strangers either. They were merely colleagues thrown together by time and circumstance.

Their time together would end. This trip would end. They would both return to California. She didn't know if she wanted him to know her secrets. Secrets changed people. They either brought people closer together or acted as a wedge that widened and eventually broke their friendship. Yet she wanted to tell him.

"I promise you, anything you tell me will stay with me," he said as if he could read her thoughts. When she didn't move he stepped closer to her. "I promise. Do you want me to do the Scouts' honor?" He raised the three fingers on his right hand.

She couldn't help but laugh. He had the ability to make her laugh every time she retreated into herself. Other than her Aunt Rosie, no one had ever been able to do that.

"If I ever hear—" She started speaking, but Wes stepped forward and stopped her with a kiss. She instantly froze. The first clap of thunder broke overhead and Brenda felt it pass through her like a violent inner shake.

"I won't," he said when he raised his head. His voice was low, quiet and dripping with some indefinable sincerity. "Now, what do your aunts mean that you wish they wouldn't think?"

She looked at the open collar of his shirt, her hands holding on to his arms where she'd grabbed when he kissed her. "That I have nothing in my life except the stars."

"What more do you want?"

She stepped back. It was difficult to think straight when he held her. And she couldn't understand the jolting images she saw in her mind when his mouth was only a kiss away from hers.

"I want what every woman wants."

She walked away. The clouds were darker now and the wind flattened her clothes against her body like an outline.

"Go on, don't keep me in suspense." Wes came up behind her.

"I want marriage and children. I want a man who'll cherish the ground I walk on." She turned to fully face him. "And I want to cherish him too. I want to love him better than anyone else ever could. I want to do new things, things neither of us have ever done, experience things we hadn't thought of."

Wes swallowed and Brenda wondered if she'd gone too far. She hadn't intended to rush so passionately into speech.

"I don't want much," she continued with less passion. "Only the moon and the stars."

EIGHT

"May I have your attention please . . ." The announcement regarding the rain began. All visitors had to go inside during the rain. The standing metal rockets acted as lightning rods to the unrelenting storm. It was dangerous to be outdoors and ungrounded during the storm. Yet the storm had nothing on Brenda's racing heart. Wes looked down at her as if she were the only person on earth, as if this space were an island populated with two. She watched his head lower and knew he was about to kiss her. Her throat went dry in anticipation. His hands cupped her face as the first drop of water plopped against her cheek. Brenda didn't even blink. Her eyes were fixed on the man sharing breath with her.

"All visitors must take shelter during the rainstorm. Please . . ." Brenda didn't hear anything more, not the flash of lightning or the clap of thunder that sounded as if it were ripping the fabric of the sky apart. The sound of her heart overrode the elements.

She stared at Wes. He looked different, his eyes darker than the gathering clouds.

"You're nervous," she told him. "I've never seen you nervous before."

"Yes, you have."

For a moment he just stared at her as she stared at

him. It had been between them from almost the beginning. Here it was now. And it must be dealt with: the tension, the unspoken glances, unasked questions. The pool had only been a prelude. This was the real deal. The area around them become a sea of heat, thick with tense emotions, radiant of their own personal auras that expanded, each reaching toward the other as they moved forward. Not even the sweeping winds could dispel it. Their legs didn't seem to have purpose as much as their hearts, the inner secrets that were as visible now as if they'd been Sunday-dressed and put on display.

He reached for her, his hands touching her face and up into her hair. She tilted her head. His eyes on her mouth, his breath shallow and controlled. She could feel his hunger, knew it in the tenderness with which his hands caressed her while the muscles of his chest and arms were taut and tight.

He drew her into his world. She went willingly. The sweep of Wes's head blocked out the heavens. His mouth touched hers with the tenderness of a father kissing his firstborn child. His lips moved back and forth over hers in a caress so sweet, so achingly sensitive that she could feel the birth of a new dimension of her identity. She was someone new, an emerging life-form, an embryotic entity that prior to now had not existed.

Like a star being born, a magical dust gathered around them, colliding with itself and weaving a spell around them, insulating them from the rain that washed their clothes, plastered their hair to their heads. Brenda collapsed into Wes and he into her as the kiss changed, deepened, grew with them, became part of the new being that was growing between them. Her arms circled his neck as his hands moved to her waist and gathered her closer, forcing out the rain as if he were a press intent on drying her soaked clothing.

Oblivious of the downpour, ignoring the warnings of the metallic voice that insisted they take cover, they went on, joined to each other, renewing and inventing the entity that their bobbing and insistent heads created. Water pounded her back and legs, tenacious as a petulant child being ignored by its parents. His mouth on her mouth, his tongue dancing with hers. Fire washed down her body, creating rivulets of hot passion that melded her to him. It should have been drying, totally consuming. Yet Brenda could only feel the wetness of Wes's mouth, the sweep of his tongue as it tangled with hers, devoured hers. She drowned in the sensation created by uncultivated emotions crashing inside her and bursting to life in an event that rivaled the raw brilliance of a supernova. Need swelled inside her like a teenager with raging hormones. Brenda wanted him.

Here.

In the rain.

Outside.

Now.

Wes wrenched his mouth from hers. The coldness of wind and water replaced the furnace that had warmed her. Her eyes snapped open. Water rained down his face. His mouth was moving. He was saying something. She couldn't hear him for the rushing blood in her ears. The kiss ended. The torrential storm in her bloodstream hadn't caught up with her newfound status.

Wes took her arm and pushed her toward shelter. She ran along to keep from falling. He shouldered a door open as both lightning and thunder struck simultaneously. The heads of spectators turned to stare at them as they burst through the opening. Brenda turned her head, lowering it to keep them from seeing what she knew was apparent on her face. She'd been kissed, solidly, thoroughly and she hadn't had time to conceal the truth, hadn't been able to crawl back into her cocoon of safety before she was displayed, like a moving picture, in front of a pavilion of strangers.

Wes found a support pole and sat down in front of it. Another lightning strike sent the curious stares in another direction and Brenda felt less exposed. Wes pulled her down to sit in front of him.

"You're cold," he said, positioning her back to his chest. She shivered in her wet clothes. He wrapped his arms around her. Brenda felt protected but couldn't stop the shivering. "Relax," Wes whispered in her ear. Her hair was straight and dripping water onto her shoulders. She wanted to stop shivering but the impact of Wes's kiss was rebounding through her system. She pulled a tissue from her purse and wiped at her face. It crumbled to pieces under the onslaught of water.

"Tissues aren't any good with this much water," she said.

"Just a minute." Wes levered himself up and went across the room. She watched him walk, laden down by his wet clothes. The man had a great butt and long, strong legs. Returning he handed her a handful of paper towels, then took up his position behind her. As she tried to dry her face and chest he soaked the water from her hair and neck. Brenda's concentration went right back to the kiss in the rain and she heated up immediately. She was surprised not to find steam rising from her skin.

As Wes repositioned her Brenda stopped fighting her feelings. She relaxed against him and tried to cover her emotions with the first thing that came to mind.

"We're back to comfort, yes?"

'Comfort, yes," he confirmed.

"Don't think I don't know what you're doing."

"What am I doing?"

"You're using the rain and these circumstances to have your way."

He kissed her shoulder. "Am I having my way?"

"Not exactly." Although she felt his kiss all the way to her toes. She shivered and sat up straight. "It won't work, you know."

"What won't work?"

She let her head fall back against him.

"Look around you," he told her. "It must be the summer rain."

Couples were sitting all over the floor, most of them in the same position as the two of them. They were giggling and laughing and glad to be with each other. Brenda sagged when she saw them. Even the rain was against her and her convictions.

"While we're waiting, why don't you explain why it rains every day at this time?"

"Don't you know?"

"I'm a geneticist. I deal in cell generation and the prevention of mutations in the human species. Rain comes from the sky. I believe that's your territory."

"Actually my territory is way above the rain." She looked at the roof of the pavilion listening to the wetness drumming on the surface. "But the rain has to do with rising heat and moisture." She tried to turn to face him. He kept her in place with his hands on her shoulders. Then they slipped down her arms and around her waist.

"You were saying."

"I—I was saying," she stammered, "that the warm moisture from the West Coast rises and meets the cold moisture from the East. About four o'clock every day they battle, creating thunder and lightning and causing a thunderstorm."

Brenda was having a hard time speaking. The rain wouldn't last long and she would just be still until it was time to go. She'd allow the warm feelings to wash over her.

"You know people do strange things in thunderstorms," she started.

Wes reached up and ran his hand down her hair all the way to the tip of her ponytail. "What kind of strange things?"

"Some fight, some make love, some get engaged, some do therapy."

Nothing she said caused a ripple of change in him. He continued to nibble on her as if she were a sweet candy bar. "Will you marry me?"

"No," she whispered. "I won't even date you."

"I suppose I'm going to have to work on that."

Wes woke the next morning clutching his pillow, his body as hard as a rock, his dreams erotic and filled with armloads of Brenda Reid. He cursed when he opened his eyes and discovered he was alone. She was across the space of one room. And he wanted to go there. Here and now. He turned over, closing his eyes against the bright rising sun, trying to recapture the illusion of having Brenda in his bed.

He'd only known Brenda a short time, yet he thought of her all the time. He liked being around her, liked holding her. She was intelligent, but didn't talk a lot. He wasn't often physically affectionate in public, yet yesterday and the day before he'd kissed her passionately in front of anyone who cared to look. And he didn't care.

With her he wanted to claim possession. He wanted the world to know they were a couple.

He'd been playing when he asked her to marry him. It was only part of the banter they'd developed, but if she'd said yes he wasn't sure he wouldn't have rushed her off to a chapel.

Wes got up, tossing the pillow onto the floor. He was getting nowhere thinking about her. He needed her in his arms, in his bed, beneath him. He went into the shower and turned on the cold water.

Twenty minutes later he was in control of his body if not his mind. He ordered room service for two, dressed, and stood looking out the massive windows of the suite's common room as he waited for it to arrive. It was only eight o'clock and they hadn't returned last night until well past midnight. Wes glanced at Brenda's door. He wondered if she was awake yet. He couldn't hear anything coming from her room. He imagined her sprawled under the sheets, naked, hot, and waiting for him.

He was glad when the knock came on the door so it would give his lustful mind something else think about. He supposed life was getting back at him. He didn't do the adolescent things when he was a teenager. Now at thirty-two he was discovering you couldn't cheat nature. If you tried to skip part of your growing cycle, it only waited for a while and snuck up on you when you were not expecting it.

The waiter set up breakfast on the table overlooking the roads leading to the vast Disney complex. When he left, Wes went to Brenda's door. He knocked quickly. He thought of trying the knob, but thought better of it. After a moment he heard no movement. He listened for the shower, but heard nothing there either. Knocking again, harder this time, he still got no response.

"Brenda," he called.

Brenda did not respond.

"Brenda, are you in there?"

He heard a moan. She was inside.

"Brenda, wake up."

'Go away," she said, although he barely heard it.

"Brenda, wake up." He knocked again.

'I don't want to wake up."

"Grouchy in the mornings," he remarked to himself. "I have your breakfast ready. It's getting cold."

"You eat it."

"I have a full day planned of things to do. We need to get started."

"Later," she said.

"If you don't get up and come out here, I'm coming in."

Wes could almost see her sitting up in bed, her eyes wide open.

"Are you awake?"

"Yes," she said.

"I'm leaving a cup of coffee outside your door. And remember your breakfast is getting cold."

Five minutes later Brenda's door opened. Wes was sitting at the table. She picked up the cup of coffee and drained the contents. While he was fully dressed for the day in shorts and a shirt, completely showered and groomed, she staggered to the table wearing a short pink robe that draped down one arm and ended at midthigh. Beneath it the strap of her gown hung over her shoulder. Wes grinned. He'd only imagined her fully dressed or absolutely naked. This was more refreshing than he thought, than he'd hoped. On her head was the blue baseball cap with *NASA* stitched into the crown.

He'd bought her the hat yesterday after the rain. She

said her hair was ruined. Wes never thought she'd looked better, but she'd worn the hat for the rest of the day. He wondered if she'd slept in it, although her hair fell over her shoulders and down her back this morning, instead of being caught in the ponytail that she'd threaded through the back opening of the hat as it had been yesterday.

She grabbed a piece of toast and bit into it.

"So you're a grouch in the mornings."

"I warned you. I'm a night person. I don't do mornings well." She snapped a smile at him and reached for the coffeepot. Slipping into a chair next to him she leaned sideways and looked at his legs. For a moment she hung in the chair as if her center of gravity would push her over the side. "Did you sleep like that?"

"Like what?"

"Like you have an appointment with *GQ* this morning." She looked at his legs again.

He couldn't tell her how he'd slept. He'd had her in his arms most of the night and even if she wasn't a morning person he wasn't sure how she'd react if he told her the truth.

"Stop that," Wes said.

"What? Looking at your legs?" She sat up straight. She looked more awake after her encounter. In fact, the slight upturned corners of her mouth made her look like she had a secret. "Don't you like women looking at your legs?"

"Did you sleep in the hat?"

The smile widened, but she allowed the subject change. "Yes, and nothing else."

Wes didn't get the reaction he wanted. His body went hard again. He thought he'd tease her. Instead she'd turned the tables.

"You'd better eat. Obviously, your inhibitions come with food."

She laughed out loud. "I got you."

He smiled too. "You got me."

"All right. I'll be good." She buttered her cold toast and started to eat. "What's on for today?"

"Swimming."

"Water. I thought we had enough water yesterday."

He couldn't stop his mind from rushing back to yesterday. Back to the Astronaut's Memorial, to Brenda warm and pliant in his arms, to the drenching rain and the kiss that seemed to go on and on.

He leaned on his elbows and looked directly at her. "You know, you're a lot different this morning."

"Different good or different bad?" She pulled the sleeve of her robe up and reached for a slice of bacon.

"Different . . . more. Sexier. More relaxed."

"I thought that was the purpose of the makeover."

"Am I uncovering Madame Frankenstein?"

She stopped and gave him a look that could dissolve metal. "Do I look like Frankenstein to you?"

She was trying to seduce him. The knowledge surprised him and he wanted to let it go there, but somewhere he suddenly had a moment of consciousness. He knew her views and he knew his. He did want something from her, but seduction was not the way to get it.

"Are you finished?"

"No," she said.

"I meant with breakfast."

Brenda lifted a glass of orange juice and keeping her eyes on him she drank from the glass.

"I thought you grew up sheltered."

"You opened the door yesterday. All I did was walk

through it." She paused. "Do you want me to go back in?"

Both yes and no came to his mind simultaneously. This was a huge suite, but with these newfound feelings for her the space wasn't large enough. If she continued in her seductress role, he didn't have a chance of keeping his hands to himself. He compromised with himself; he wouldn't touch her while she was in the suite. When they were within view of other people he could control his feelings, but here there was no chaperone. Here there was only the two of them and while he wanted her more than he'd ever wanted a woman, he needed her to realize all the consequences that entailed a relationship between them. Right now she was playacting. Dangerous though it was, it had to do with her family. With the aunts and cousins who didn't expect her to be more than a career-oriented machine, not a soft, warm woman.

Wes was glad he realized that before he pulled her out of that chair and ran his hands under that hot-pink robe so he could feel the naked flesh under it.

"I said we were going swimming. Get a suit and be prepared to stay out all day."

He pushed his chair back and stood up.

"Aren't we going to swim in the pool?" Her head was turned up at him. Her mouth looked so inviting, but he didn't bend down. He couldn't resist touching her. He put his hand on the NASA hat and shook his head.

"Where are we going?"

"Be ready in twenty minutes," he said and went to his room.

Running from the bathroom to the bedroom Brenda tried to complete her entire morning ritual in twenty minutes. She let the makeup go and settled for eyeshadow and lipstick. The rest of the creams and powders would only come off in the water, she told herself.

When she was ready to join Wes she took a final look in the mirror. Her cheeks were flushed from rushing back and forth. Her hair totally pulled back left her face free. She thought of breakfast. Wes looked a little nervous when she'd come out of the bedroom only half dressed. She'd been nervous too. She'd never tried seduction before and she wasn't sure if it worked. He hadn't touched her. Was that her purpose in doing it? Did she want him to kiss her again? He'd kissed her yesterday in the rain like she'd never been kissed before. Throughout the day they had been in constant contact, hands clasped, arms around each other's waists, never moving more than a few feet out of touching range.

It seemed natural to continue it this morning, to take it to the next level. Wes hadn't taken the mantle. He hadn't rejected her, but refused to join her in the game. Looking at herself she was glad of that. Suppose he had?

"Brenda?"

"Ready," she called, grabbing her beach bag and going to join him.

"Why didn't you go to Space Camp?" Wes asked the question as they drove across the state toward the Gulf of Mexico. While every hotel in the known Floridian universe had a pool, he wanted to swim in the warm waters of the gulf.

"What?" she asked.

"Yesterday, you said you wanted to go to Space Camp when you were twelve. Why didn't you go? There is a camp right in your hometown."

Birmingham did have a facility and thousands of kids went through there every year. They learned with hands-on experience exactly what was involved in training to be an astronaut.

"I actually never told anyone I wanted to do it."

"Why not?"

"I was *twelve.*"

"At that age you ask for the moon."

Heat burned her ears. She kept her eyes on the flat road in front of them. His comment brought back memories of yesterday afternoon. Her request for the stars and the moon had caused him to take her in his arms. She could still feel her body pressed to his and his mouth sealed to her own.

"I didn't. I was a little more conservative."

"So your parents never knew you wanted to go?"

She shook her head.

"They have programs for adults. You can still go."

"I know. Maybe one summer I'll enroll."

Wes pulled into a parking lot that bordered a beach. Brenda smelled the water and the fish. She could see the gulls gliding in the sky above and the water lapping up to the sand.

"What about next summer?"

Brenda stopped in the action of getting out of the car. She suddenly remembered she was supposed to be engaged to Wes. Something that needed to be resolved in the next couple of weeks. She wasn't engaged to him, yet they acted as if they were. "Wes, this is not a long-term relationship. In fact, this is not a relationship at all."

"I guess you forgot that during breakfast?"

She had been teasing at breakfast. She made him nervous and she liked it. She also had never tried anything like that before, but seeing him sitting there completely dressed while she was wearing nearly nothing made her deflect the attention. It was fun. She never realized how much power seduction released in a person. She wanted to go on teasing, even though she knew the danger. It was like a narcotic in her blood, forcing her to push Wes until he kissed her.

But he hadn't.

She got out of the car. The wind brushed her skin. She felt tiny particles of sand against her exposed arms and legs.

"Maybe I did forget it earlier, but I won't again."

"Now that sounds like a challenge. I believe you've issued them before."

Wes grabbed the basket and blankets from the backseat. Brenda had no idea what was in the basket. It was already in the car when the hotel doorman opened her door. Together Brenda and Wes went toward the sand and water.

"Why couldn't we go to the pool?" she asked after they'd spread out the blanket and got settled. And Wes had taken off his shirt and shorts. He had a magnificent body. She openly stared at him.

"Too many people," he said. "And no boundaries."

"What do you mean no boundaries?"

"You swim laps. Here there are no pool walls, no beginning, no end. You can't swim to Texas so you have to relax in the water instead of using it as a flotation device."

Brenda had a comeback but she kept it to herself. She was thinking of him and how sexy he looked, how even his skin color was and how tightly his skin covered his frame.

The water was warm. She'd often swum in the gulf on family vacations, visits to Aunt Rosie, a few outings with friends and her cousins.

She lay out in the water on her back. She didn't want to spoil Wes's illusion that she only swam laps. She loved this position. Water covered her ears and made a strange whirring sound as she bobbed up and down. Her hair had both a weightless and weighted pull as the water lapped about her. The two of them were at one with each other.

"What are you doing?"

"Oh." She forgot to keep her back arched as Wes came up next to her. She went under the water. As she tried to speak when she went under, her mouth filled with water. She came up spurting, and Wes caught her arms.

"You shouldn't scare me like that." She coughed, as they both treaded water.

"You forget yourself."

"What are you talking about?"

"Boundaries. Look how far out you are."

She hadn't been thinking of swimming or the shore. She'd been lost in her own world. And she really wasn't out that far. While she hadn't excelled in activities that required teams, she had learned to swim. She was a strong swimmer and this was only a short spurt for her. It made her feel good that Wes was looking out for her, keeping her in sight, and being concerned over her safety.

They spent the morning playing, as Wes described it, in the water. The two of them would dive under the surface and look at the wonderful world hidden from view there. Brenda found it fascinating that the world she always thought of was above the earth and right beneath her feet was an entire community of living things that thrived with their own life cycles.

The beach filled with families, couples enjoying the

sun and sea. Wes and Brenda walked along the shore, collected colored stones and the relics of seashells, ate lunch from the picnic basket he'd brought with them, and lazed in the afternoon heat.

She was lying on the blanket, drowsy after the meal and the morning's activities. The clouds in the sky were high and it would be hours before the rains came. At this moment it was hard to believe that there would be a thunderstorm.

"Wes?" He lay on his stomach next to her. She turned to look at him. "I'm enjoying myself."

He smiled slowly as if he hadn't expected her to say anything like that.

"What would you be doing if I hadn't come along?"

"I don't know."

"Spending the day in Disneyworld?"

"No, the family reunion will go there. I'd wait for that."

"Then what would you do with two weeks alone?"

Brenda could barely conceive of being alone. He'd only been with her a few short days, yet they seemed to have connected so completely to each other.

"Swim, read. I brought some work—"

"Work," he said, interrupting.

"Don't tell me you're not working. I've heard you typing on your laptop."

"Wasn't that at your suggestion? I have to keep in touch with Glenn. Most of what I do is e-mail. After the meeting with the Reeves Foundation, I haven't even thought about work."

She turned her gaze to the cawing seagulls. The way he'd said it told her she had replaced any thoughts of work. Her body burned and not from the sun. She felt relaxed, peaceful, and content. She wondered if married people had this kind of contentment. Her parents were always laughing and joking. Even after thirty years of marriage and four children they had a great affection for each other.

"Well, I might have stayed on a few more days at NASA. I was caught up in the interesting projects they have on the drawing board."

"More work. You work all the time."

"I consider it fun." She was hurt that the tone of his censure was the same as her family's. She'd derived her work ethic from them. Both her parents worked and they were proud of their accomplishments.

"What happened at NASA?"

"I told you. They asked me to head up a project."

"You said it so matter-of-factly." There was a frown around his eyes and lines in his forehead. "Why didn't you tell me the other day?"

"Your world was falling apart that day. How could I tell you NASA had offered me carte blanc to continue something I love doing? The news wouldn't have sat well with you."

"Brenda." He sat up. "Don't you think I would have been thrilled for you?"

"Would you?" She hadn't been sure. She only had one relationship on which to base things, and Reuben had been self-centered and interested in only his accomplishments.

"Of course I would have. We should have been out that night celebrat—" He stopped. "That's why you wanted to go out last night. You should have told me."

"We can do it tonight," she suggested.

"Congratulations." The frown left his face and he relaxed. "We'll do it tonight." Brenda noticed a change in his expression. It was so minute she almost missed it. She wondered what it meant.

"So both of us had successful work going for us." Wes lay back on the blanket. "Other than working, what else would you have done?"

Alone, she thought. She'd been with him so constantly that the thought of being alone now was foreign. "I'd spend a few days relaxing by the pool, possibly go scuba diving. I have tickets to a piano concert next week. I'd planned to drive up the coast and visit an old friend from college. So you see, I can relax on occasion."

"Did I spoil of any of that?"

She looked back. His eyes were dark with concern. Brenda should have been used to this tightness that overcame her when Wes looked at her, when that note entered his voice that was almost like a catch, or when he touched her. But she wasn't.

She reached up and touched his cheek. "You didn't." Then she pushed herself up and kissed him. His lips were soft and tender and she felt as if he wanted to take more from her, but restrained himself. He didn't put his arm around her or touch her in any way except on the mouth. He let her control the amount of contact. Let her take the kiss where she wanted it to go. She wanted it to go further, but from her position on her elbow she could only fall back on the blanket if she moved her arm.

She pulled back, but rested against him. Both of them were breathing hard, harder than the soft kiss indicated they should. Brenda's heartbeat was thundering. She didn't understand it. Her experience was too limited to know if this was normal or not. It felt good. That was her only guide.

It was just a few days ago she'd told him never to kiss

her again and now she was drunk with the need of him. Her body was aroused almost at the thought of him.

"Brenda." Wes's voice hadn't quite returned to normal. "I want you. I want to make love to you more than I thought it was possible. So we'd better go for a swim. Otherwise the people on this beach are going to get a show they hadn't planned on."

He got up and pulled her with him. They turned toward the water, but the kiss she initiated set the tone for the day. Swimming wasn't the same. Playing now had sexual overtones. When they walked through a local marketplace that sold more T-shirts than vegetables it was the looks and non-looks that caused electricity to shoot between them. Brenda thought she'd burn up whenever she accidentally bumped into him. Each time their eyes met it was like some bond drew them together.

By the time they returned to the hotel parking garage Brenda didn't think she could stand being near him without incinerating. Wes parked the car in the silent garage. Neither of them moved or looked at each other. They stared ahead listening to the ticking of the cooling engine, each seeming to wait for the other to make a move or utter a word.

Then Wes got out and came around to open her door. Brenda turned with her eyes on the ground. She stood up. He didn't step back to give her room, but stood there until she raised her eyes. The lighting was low and his face was in shadow, but Brenda could see what was there. It was what was reflected in her own face, in the lines of her body and the movement of her head, her arms, every part of her.

They'd been trying to avoid it all day, the same as they wanted to avoid touching. But it was too late. They both came to the realization in the same moment. Brenda flew into his arms, knowing she couldn't live one more moment without his touch. Without his mouth on hers. She turned her head seeking his kiss with the same fierceness as she felt in him. Frantically they sought and found each other. With a force more powerful than the two of them, their mouths melded. Brenda felt as if her soul had fused with Wes's, as if she had been seeking him her entire life and not known it. Finally she'd found him and knew that life would not be the same without him.

She didn't know how long the kiss went on, how long Wes's hand massaged her back, how long her hands raked over every part of him. Everything within her had liquefied until she was a writhing, formless mass of feelings.

Wes wrenched his mouth from hers. He grabbed her hand, slamming the car door at the same time. The two of them headed for the garage elevator. Brenda didn't ask where they were going. She knew they were headed for the suite. All her thoughts about keeping their relationship professional and not getting involved with someone she worked with were lost in the numbing insistence of the blood rocketing through her system. She wanted to make love with this man more than she wanted to take her next breath.

The elevator doors slid silently open on the lobby level and the two of them rushed out. The elevators to rooms were on the other side of the ornate hotel entrance. Wes had her hand and was bent on reaching them when Brenda stopped short.

"What's wrong?" he asked, turning to her.

Brenda couldn't speak. She felt as if a typhoon of ice-cold water had been poured over her. She stared directly in front of her. Wes looked from her to the woman she stared at.

A FAMILY AFFAIR

"Who is she?" he asked.

The woman looked up then and recognized Brenda. The last person she expected to find in the lobby stood up and started toward her.

"Mom."

NINE

Brenda had read in numerous books that regardless of the age of children their parents could reduce them to adolescence with a look. Never had she known the depth of this genius, until now. She felt like a sixteen-year-old, caught coming in after curfew with the boy her parents disapproved of, but from whom she couldn't stay away. The fact that she never missed a curfew or even had one did nothing to assuage the sense of dread washing over her, removing the arousal she felt only seconds before and replacing it with guilt.

Wes was less able to remove the signs of his arousal. He stood behind her. Brenda could feel the heat of him and his erection, which she wanted to press herself against.

"Mom, I wasn't expecting you for another week." Brenda attempted to smile. She hugged her mother and kissed her on the cheek.

"When I have to find out about a future son-in-law from my sisters, I think it's time to come and see for myself." She looked up at Wes. "I suppose you're the fiancée?"

"Yes." Wes didn't hesitate. Brenda wanted the floor to open up so she could sink into it, carrying all her lies and guilt with her. "Wesley Cooper," he said, introducing himself.

"Wes, this is my mother, Pamela Reid."

He shook hands with her, keeping one hand on Brenda's shoulder and leaning around her. Brenda could see the approval in her mother's eyes. Wes was handsome. They'd been out all day. He no longer had the pressed *GQ* look, but one of rugged adventurism. She knew that appealed to her mother. Brenda had often heard her mother's remarks on actors. She went for the rough-and-tough type, the bad boys. And right now Wes looked every bit the role.

"So when were you going to tell me about him?"

"I—I wanted to save it for a surprise," she squeezed out.

"From your own mother?"

"With Shiri married and the family reunion coming up I didn't want to take anything away from the festivities."

"Scottie, you know—"

"It's very new too, Mrs. Reid." Wes tried to help her out of the situation.

"Call me Pamela, please."

"And I'm Wes, Pamela. The engagement is new. Brenda wanted to wait a while and get used to the idea."

"Mom, you know you and your sisters can't resist organizing everything. If I'd told you about Wes, you'd all be planning the engagement dinner and then the wedding." She couldn't believe these words were coming out of her mouth. "I just thought we should let Shiri and J.D. have the spotlight." She tried to appeal to her mother's sense of fairness.

"I suppose one wedding at a time is enough to deal with," Pamela Reid admitted.

A FAMILY AFFAIR

Brenda spotted her mother's suitcase sitting near the chair she'd been seated in. "Are you alone?" she asked, hoping she didn't have to deal with the entire Johnson sisterhood.

"Right after Doris and Karen let out the secret, they were both too busy to come with me. And a good thing too. I haven't been able to find a room. I'm going to have to stay the night with you."

Brenda felt her world spinning out of control. Her aunts had told her mother about her engagement, but obviously had failed to let her know she and Wes were sharing the same suite.

"You must be tired, Mrs. Reid," Wes said. "I'll get your suitcase and we'll go upstairs."

There were times Brenda wanted to strangle Wesley Cooper. This was one of them. He obviously was able to move now without the world seeing what he'd been hiding only moments ago. He picked up her bag and led them to the elevator.

"Wesley, where are you from? I can hear someplace in New England in your voice."

Brenda expected to hear the familiar Wes-to-my-friends speech, but he didn't say it.

"Maine originally," he said. Brenda watched him turn the charm on for her mother. "I live in California now."

"You two work at the same university?"

He nodded.

She kept up the interrogation all the way to the room. Brenda's thoughts were in such chaos that she didn't think to get her key out. Wes opened the door with his own key and showed them all into the common room. The raised eyebrows of her mother's expression was not lost on her.

"I must say I didn't expect this," Pamela Reid said.

"It is a nice suite," Brenda said, intentionally misunderstanding her. She knew she'd pay for it later, but for the time being she needed to buy herself some time. "Why don't you put her bag in my room?" she told Wes, slightly emphasizing "my room" and looking at the open door that led to the place where she slept.

"I'll take it," her mother said. "I need to get out of these shoes and comb my hair."

Brenda pointed the way. Her mother took the rolling suitcase handle and walked toward the open door.

"What are you doing?" She turned on Wes the moment her mother was out of earshot.

"Playing the role," he told her.

"This had gone too far. I never intended to lie to my mother. It was bad enough with my aunts."

He walked directly up to her. "Do you want to tell her the truth?"

Why didn't she say yes? She was confused and Brenda Reid was never confused. She always knew what she wanted. And often she went and got it, without help, without relying on anyone else. She'd find the path necessary and simply work toward it. But she couldn't do that now.

"Brenda?"

Her eyes focused on Wes's face. "I don't know what to do." She'd seen the look on her mother's face. It was the same look her aunts had. No wonder they couldn't keep her secret. "If I tell her the truth I'll have to explain my deception and if I don't the deception just gets more and more compounded."

"I'm sorry," he said. He hugged her to him. "I should never have lied to your aunts."

Brenda put her arms around him. She loved being there. When Wes hugged her there were no problems,

A FAMILY AFFAIR

but when he released her the outside world filled in all the crevices of her life. And right now one crevice held her mother.

"She only brought a small suitcase," he told her. "We should be able to keep the secret for a day or two. After all, you're a lot more comfortable with me now."

Brenda laughed. Her belly rocked against his. She looked up. "I suppose those lessons of the past few days had to pay off sooner or later."

Wes kissed her forehead. Pamela Reid chose that moment to rejoin them. Brenda turned to her mother.

Wes kept hold of her hand. "Pamela, we're celebrating tonight. We have plans to go to dinner. We hope you'll come with us."

Her mother smiled. "I'd love to. What are you celebrating?"

Wes looked at Brenda, giving her the opportunity to tell her mother what had happened.

"I met with NASA this week," she started. Pamela Reid's smile widened. She told her mother the story. How she'd met with them and they had given her a grant.

"To work here in Florida?" Brenda heard the hopeful note in her voice. She knew her mother would love to have her closer to home. Since Brenda didn't fly, her visits home were few.

"It's for the university in California. But I'll be doing what I want. They'll be providing the money."

"Wonderful, darling." Her mother approached her with open arms. "I know this is something that will make you happy." Brenda went into her mother's arms. Her mother supported all her children in what they wanted to do. She never tried to talk any of them out of anything they wanted to try. Brenda was consistent in her wants. She chose astronomy and never wavered. Her brother and sisters had tried a hundred different things and they had an attic full of discarded instruments, various sporting apparatus, woodworking kits, macrame projects, lopsided volcanoes, and a menagerie of other things that one or another of them wanted to try.

"Wes also received a renewal of his grant," Brenda said when her mother released her.

"Congratulations to you too, Wes. It seems both of you are starting off well."

Her mother moved to Wes and took his hand. Brenda heard it even if Wes didn't. That note of approval in her mother's voice. Pamela Reid wanted to make sure her daughter would be cared for. It didn't matter that Brenda had a well-paying job. Pamela needed to assure herself that Wes could support her daughter. Brenda reminded herself that she and Wes were not really engaged.

"Why don't you two sleep in my room?"

Brenda blinked at Wes's comment.

"I have two beds in my room and there's only one in there. Why don't we switch while your mother is here so you'll be more comfortable?"

"It's only for tonight," Pamela said to Wes. "I have to go home tomorrow." She switched her attention to her daughter. "Your father has been away on a business trip. He returns tomorrow. And I think you should call him."

"I will," Brenda promised, hearing the censure. How could she tell her father she was engaged to Wes? This was getting very complicated.

"Where are we eating?" Pamela asked.

Wes named a restaurant Brenda had never heard of. She had no idea what to wear. Except for her meetings with NASA where she'd worn a suit, she'd been in shorts and bathing suits the entire time.

"It's a seafood place not far from here. The service is

unhurried and the waiters unobtrusive. While your sisters were here, they were pressed for time. We'll be able to really get to know each other."

That was Wes's method of saying the dress was more than casual and that her mother would have all the time necessary to ask her subtle questions. Brenda found herself shaking at the disaster that was surely to come.

"What an absolutely beautiful dress, Scottie. Where did you get it?" Pamela Reid twirled around in front of the full-length mirror like a debutante on her way to her first party. The yellow chiffon cocktail dress looked great on her mother. The two of them were the same size and height. She'd been told most of her life that she looked like her mother. Seeing her dressed in something Brenda had bought for herself made her look younger, and Brenda could see the resemblance.

"The train stopped in Denver for several hours. There's a wonderful mall very close to it. I went shopping." She and Wes had gone shopping. She hadn't been without him since the day they left northern California.

Brenda admired her mother. The dress could have been made for her. It fit her to the waist, and then multilayers of fabric flounced out to her knees. Her long legs extended from the upturned hem to her high heels. Never had Brenda thought the day would come when her mother would approve of her clothes or when she wasn't being the parent. Looking at her, Brenda found it hard to believe that this woman was fifty-one years old, or that she could be a grandmother. She wished she could spend the night alone with her mother. She suddenly wanted to talk to her. She wanted to ask all kinds of questions about men and women, about life in general. But they had to go to dinner and she had to deceive the woman she loved.

"Mom, you look wonderful."

"And so do you." Brenda's mother came to hug her. "I was so angry when Karen dropped the comment about your engagement, but I like Wes already. He seems taken by you."

Brenda was sure she was wrong. Wes wanted her. He'd told her that and she wanted him, but he wasn't taken by her. The bet entered her mind. She pushed the thought aside. There was no need to remember it while she was here and no need to let her mother learn of it.

Pamela pushed back. "You're beautiful, honey." Tears were in her mother's eyes. "I can't wait to see you in a wedding gown."

Tears brimmed in Brenda's eyes. She would never please her mother that way. And she knew that as soon as the reunion began she'd hurt her more than she ever thought she would. She decided she couldn't lie. She'd have to tell everyone the truth.

Dinner wasn't that bad. Brenda found herself laughing at Wes's jokes. He bewitched her mother with the back-and-forth banter she'd become used to hearing and participating in. Pamela Reid lapped it up. Between the salad and the crème brûlée she got in all the questions about his family background, his work, and his future goals. Wes answered her honestly and without any irritation. Brenda sat on pins and needles thinking that something would go wrong. Yet it didn't.

Not until her last question.

"Wes, you've been very nice in answering all my questions. I just want to make sure my daughter is happy." Pamela looked at her then and smiled. Brenda smiled back although her smile was a little watery.

A FAMILY AFFAIR

Wes took her hand. His was warm against her ice-cold fingers. He didn't give away the fact that he noticed.

"Are you in love with my daughter?"

Her hand clenched. His completely covered it. He squeezed it, reassuring her. Neither movement was noticed by her mother. His head turned and he looked at Brenda. She held her breath. She wanted him to say yes. She wanted it to be true. The knowledge almost knocked her over. The moment stretched on. Brenda held her breath. She knew she was holding it. She couldn't let it out, couldn't let it go until he said something.

Wes gazed into her eyes. Nothing about him looked nervous. She wished she could look as comfortable as he did.

"I can see—" her mother began.

"Yes," Wes said, interrupting.

Brenda paced back and forth over the same area of carpet. The common room was dark. The curtains were open, adding the shimmering lights of the night to the room's dimensions. They hadn't celebrated her NASA success or Wes's triumph with his sponsors. Both areas had been completely blotted out by her mother's sudden appearance and her constant interrogation of Wes.

Pamela was taking a shower. Wes was in her room. Brenda had no place to go. Nervous energy wasn't going to let her sleep. Why did Wes say that? She knew he couldn't have said anything else. He couldn't have told her mother he wasn't in love with her. He was holding her hand, looking in her eyes. The way he said it. Did he mean it? He couldn't have meant it.

She sat down at the piano and raised the lid. She hadn't played in years. Lightly she ran her hands across the keys, but made no sound. She remembered her mother taking her to lessons and seeing that she practiced every day when she was twelve. She pressed middle C and heard the rich tone. Her hands went to the keys naturally. She didn't depress them. She could hear the sound in her head. She wanted to fill the room with it. But she knew that the woman in the shower, in Wes's room, a room that had all of Wes ingrained in it as if he'd personally embedded his personality into the walls, would know that there was something wrong. Her quality of piano playing was always emotional. Her mother had commented on it after her first recital. After she sat home during the junior prom her brother told her she should never play the piano when she was sad.

Brenda closed the cover and went to look out the window. She stood at the edge where her vertigo gave the sensation of falling and the glass protected her from any mishap. She stiffened as she heard the bedroom door open. It was her door. Wes's room for the night. He came up behind her.

Brenda turned around. "You shouldn't have told my mother that?"

"What?"

"You know what. How could you let her think that you love me?" Then she realized it wasn't his fault. There was nothing else he could have said. She was the one on edge. She was the one who had the dilemma. Wes had caused it, but she didn't clear it up when she could have and now it was out of control. "I'm sorry," she apologized, wiping a single tear from her eye and moving into his arms. She needed him to hold her. "It's that no matter what, I keep getting deeper and deeper into this engagement."

"I should never have told your aunts we were engaged."

Brenda laid her head on his shoulder. "I didn't tell the truth either. Now we're stuck."

"It'll be all right. We'll work it out."

Her mother opened the door. "Scottie, the shower is free. Oh." She stopped when the two of them separated. "Excuse me."

"I'll be right in, Mom."

"Good night, Wes," Pamela said. She went back into the room but left the door slightly open.

They both smiled.

"Feel better?" he asked in a whisper.

"A little."

"You'd better go in. She left the door open so she could hear us."

"I know," Brenda told him. "She's being discreet. She thinks you're kissing me good night."

"I have a rule about that."

Brenda stared at him. His features were somewhat shadowed in the darkness, but she could see his handsome face.

"You know I want you." He took her hands and pulled her closer. "If your mother hadn't shown up tonight we'd have made love."

She couldn't deny that. They'd been headed for the bedroom when they discovered Pamela Reid sitting in the lobby.

"I know it's something you didn't want to happen. So it was good that she came."

Brenda wasn't sure of that anymore. Even now she wanted Wes to make love to her.

"You see, with an audience around, with your mother, there is no way we can make love."

Brenda dropped her head so he couldn't see her face. "But I can handle a kiss good night."

He raised her chin and kissed her quickly. Brenda didn't move when he broke away. She stared at him through half-closed eyes. She heard the catch in his throat and the groan that told her he was holding himself under the tightest control. His mouth took hers.

His arms slipped around her waist and he pulled her into him. Brenda felt an almost desperation in the way he held her. His kiss was different, but it was different each time he touched her. Passion flared between them and Wes deepened the kiss until her arms were just as tightly around him as his were around her. She clung to him as if she were part of his body, his being, the essence of him. In a flash the world receded, her mother receded, the hotel room disappeared, some wizard transformed them from here until there was nothing around them except a realm of ghostly mist. Together they supported each other in this netherworld.

Brenda felt weightless, full of sensation. Wes's arms around her the only anchor in an alternate universe. She wanted to stay here. She never wanted to return. She only wanted to keep her mouth melded to his, to go on and on until time ended with her blood pumping double time, the musky scent of him filling her nostrils, and her heart full to the point of bursting.

Her hands moved over him with practiced familiarity. She touched everywhere, his back, his arms, his tight buttocks, feeling the inward draft of air that came at his surprise. She loved it, loved doing things that took him by surprise, took them both by surprise. Brenda raised her leg along his. He trembled. It passed through her like a fiery arrow. She wanted to climb onto him, join, become one.

A FAMILY AFFAIR   213

It was there in her mouth, in her kiss, the ultimate communication vehicle. He knew it and she knew he knew it. Gently he slid his mouth from hers, keeping her in his arms, holding her until the two of them could return to the world at large, until the room solidified into walls with floors and furniture. His breathing was ragged against her neck where he scorched her with hot, wet kisses that hardened the tips of her breasts and forced her to breathe through her mouth.

"We've got to stop, Brenda," Wes said.

"I don't want to." Her voice was as close to purring as she'd ever heard it.

"Your mother," he whispered in a voice she'd never heard before, one deep with emotion and regretful that a room away from them was her mother. Brenda's arms stopped moving. Her legs went still. Yet she was drenched with emotion. It rained over her like a waterfall.

She looked up at him. "I love my mother," she told him. "But her timing stinks."

A card was keeping Wes awake. A card that Brenda had conspicuously stuck inside the cover of the Orlando Visitors Guide. A hardcover coffee-table-size book outlining the sights of the city of Orlando that was left in every hotel room for the use of the guests.

This was disturbing his sleep.

The card instructed the maid service to only change the bedding if it was left on the bed. Wes was sleeping with her around him.

Brenda was in this room. Her presence was here as surely as if she were standing in the middle of the floor. Her clothes were in the closet. Her toothbrush and cosmetics in the bathroom. The NASA hat sat on the television stand in the space next to the screen.

But that wasn't the worst of it.

He could smell her on the pillowcase. Her scent surrounded him as surely as if he had her here in his arms, in this bed. She wasn't here and that was keeping him awake and wanting her.

He'd given himself a rule earlier. He was going to steer clear of her. Keep his hands to himself. That hadn't lasted long. Each time he looked at her he couldn't remember any rules. They didn't exist when the two of them were together. He'd thought he could handle a kiss because her mother was within twenty feet of them. Yet the moment her warm body made contact with his, his mind went on vacation.

He turned again, hugged her pillow to him, and inhaled deeply. Like a sadist, he couldn't not do it.

The room wasn't totally dark. Light filtered from the outside somewhere. He could see the white logo on the hat. He concentrated on it. They'd kissed in the rain and when the two of them left the pavilion he'd bought her the hat because he said her hair was ruined. Her hair was perfect. He wanted to run his hands through it and the only way he could stop himself was to have her cover it. Yet when she put it on she only looked more desirable.

Wes tossed and turned for another hour, reviewing their trip to the beach, which now seemed like years ago. Finally he turned his mind to his project. He was thankful for the grant, thankful that the foundation would continue to fund his research; but he needed to find out what had happened to the first experiment. Next time he intended to have more security. The need hadn't been there before, or so he thought, but now he knew there was someone who didn't want him to succeed.

It was too early to call Glenn. He hadn't heard from him since he decided to launch his own investigation. Wes wondered if anything had turned up.

He thought of the people most closely associated with the experiment or those who had access to his lab when he wasn't there. Glenn was closest, but he couldn't believe he would do anything to jeopardize it. He stood as much to gain as Wes with publication and the fruits of success, if they were successful, which Wes had every reason to believe they would be.

Wes thought of returning, going back to California to see if he could find anything. The campus would be deserted now. With very few exceptions everyone was gone unless there were scientists with projects that required careful tending. Had he not lost his he would be at the school.

Gerald Cusack was there. Tate Levy, who never left the mountain except for an occasion wedding or funeral, was there. Professor Olivia Harris, who always traveled with her brother to the Isle of Man during this time, mentioned that they would not be going this year. Instead she would be staying on at the school to complete a book she'd been working on, which was due to her publisher at the end of the summer.

Wes was glad he wasn't there. Doctor Harris could be a little overbearing at times. Gerald made no pretense about wanting Wes's experiment, but Wes didn't think him dishonest enough to sabotage his work. And what would that prove? Without the experiment there was no grant and nothing to take over. Wes realized he was getting nowhere.

As the sun chased away the dark sky turning the horizon to a soft pink he finally fell asleep. He didn't sleep long, however. He woke with the scent of Brenda in his nostrils and remembered he was in her bed with only her pillow and not the real woman.

Giving up on trying to fight his body and the imaginary person of Brenda, he rose, showered, and dressed. In the common room he found Brenda and her mother already finishing breakfast. The previous morning Brenda had come to the table in a short nightgown and robe. This morning she was dressed in a white dress that had wide straps that went over her shoulders. Her legs and feet were bare.

"Good morning, Wes," Pamela said.

"Good morning." He approached Brenda, remembering they were supposed to be engaged. She remembered too from the look she gave him and the way she raised her head for the light kiss he dropped on her lips. "I didn't think you two would be up." He glanced from mother to daughter, allowing his gaze to linger on Brenda.

"I have to get back. My plane leaves early this morning." She drank from her coffee cup. Wes slipped into a chair and poured a cup for himself. He drank it black, needing the infusion of caffeine to counteract his night.

"Did you order for me?" he asked Brenda. She nodded. He lifted the silver cover to find a full breakfast. He was hungry despite his night of wrestling with the sheets.

Brenda looked as tired as he felt. He knew the reason. Or thought he did. He was just as environmentally conscious as she was and if the bed she chose last night was his, then she had as much of an issue with a pillow partner as he'd had.

"Wes, I believe you're having a positive influence on my daughter."

A FAMILY AFFAIR 217

Both he and Brenda looked at her mother. Brenda's head came up in surprise.

"She's always had her head in a book, always trying to learn the next thing, in control of everything. Yet I find she's thinking only of you."

"Mother!"

Since they'd discovered Pamela Reid yesterday, Brenda had only called her Mom. "Mother" must mean she was a little perturbed.

"That's all right, Scottie. You're supposed to be off balanced when you're in love."

"Tell me what Scottie means."

"It's just a nickname," Brenda rushed on. "Nicknames are just something that someone starts calling you and suddenly it sticks like a second skin."

"When Scottie was in high school—"

"Mom, please."

"I want to hear." Wes looked at her. "I want to know everything, even see that picture of you bald and totally naked at six months old."

"I was never bald."

"She wasn't," her mother said, backing her up. "Scottie was born with a full head of hair and it's been her best feature since."

Wes could debate that. He considered the total package worthy of study.

"Back to the name," he prompted.

"When Scottie was twelve she discovered astronomy. Her head was always in the stars. My two sisters, you've already met them," she reminded Wes. "They were great fans of a television series called *Star Trek*."

Wes knew the show. He'd enjoyed later versions of the original series.

Brenda sat silently nibbling on a piece of toast.

"We always had to call Scottie more than once when she was lost in the stars. Doris used to say 'Beam me up, Scottie' mimicking one of the television characters on the popular science fiction program."

"Doris dubbed her Scottie for a character on that show. Scottie loved watching the reruns and understood all the science that this character had to work with."

Wes looked at Brenda.

"The name stuck," Pamela said. "Only the family uses it. She won't answer to anyone else, not even her cousins."

"Stop smiling," she said. "I could have been called Beam."

He burst out laughing at that. When he started to speak, she interrupted him, saying, "Don't you even consider calling me that. I am not having the entire campus at Meyers calling me by a nickname."

"I won't," he said, nodding. To her mother Wes said, "She seems very earthbound when I'm around her."

For a charged moment he and Brenda looked at each other. Every sexual innuendo he could think of went through his mind.

Pamela glanced at her watch. "Well, I have a few more things to put in my suitcase. Then I'll be ready." Pamela Reid stood up and started for the bedroom. Wes was amazed how much mother and daughter resembled each other. Pamela was dressed in a sleeveless white blouse and green Bermuda shorts. Her jacket, of the same green as the shorts, completed her outfit and augmented the deep russet coloring of her skin tone. Her legs were as long and shapely as her daughter's. The two women could easily be mistaken for one another from a distance. Only Brenda's face was dotted with freckles.

Wes could see both his parents in himself when he

looked in the mirror. Brenda had been right when she told him her mother and his were the same kind of people. Pamela Reid's ensemble was perfect. She was the type who'd look perfectly cool in the middle of a heat wave. Yet Wes liked her. She was real. She was family oriented and concerned about her daughter, concerned enough to come several hundred miles to make sure her bookish daughter had brought her head out of the clouds for a good reason. Wes felt as if she approved of him and that made him feel good. He wanted her approval.

"I like her," he said.

"I think the feeling is mutual."

He smiled.

"I'd better go and see if she's ready." Brenda stood. Wes joined her.

"Would you like me to go with you?"

"No, I need to talk to my mother alone." She moved toward the bedroom. Wes stopped her.

"Are you going to tell her the truth about our engagement?"

She didn't answer, looking as if she were weighing the question, not sure whether she'd made up her mind yet. Wes found himself wanting her to say no. He wanted her to make the same decision she'd made with her aunts.

"I don't think so," she said and Wes let go of his breath. He wanted to be engaged to her. A real engagement. Did he want to marry her or was he riding this new experience without being able to see consequences?

"I've got everything." Pamela Reid came out of the bedroom pulling her suitcase. Brenda was still standing with him. "All right, kiss good-bye so we can go."

Brenda looked up and him. Her eyes were filled with something like fear. He closed the small distance and touched his mouth to hers in a reassuring way. He wanted to tell her everything would be all right.

When they separated, Pamela said, "Wes, it was a pleasure to meet you." She came forward and hugged him. "I'll be glad to welcome you into the family."

Moments later they were gone. The shocked look on Brenda's face haunted him after the door closed. She looked tired and he could only wonder what bed she had slept in last night.

He picked up the phone and dialed a two-digit number.

"Housekeeping," a voice said.

"This is Doctor Cooper in Suite 1228. Please have the maids change the linen on all the beds today."

TEN

The streets of Orlando were never free and clear. Traffic flowed from every direction in an unending quest to reach Never-Never Land or any of the other tourist sites in and around the city. There was no good way to go. While dwarf palm trees set off shopping centers and regular palms swayed in the gentle breeze along the avenues, the nightmare of traffic made the normal thirty-five-minute trip to the airport an hour long.

Pamela Reid sat next to her like the queen of all she surveyed. She checked her watch several times, but made no comment on the time. She mentioned Wes and each time she did something inside Brenda pinched. By the time they got to the terminal and were seated in a restaurant near the security area with cold drinks in front of them, Brenda's mind was back at the hotel.

Things were out of hand. Now the thought ate at her that her mother believed Wes and she would make an announcement at the family reunion. She was basically an honest person. She should tell her mother the truth. She looked at her perfectly coiffed mother. While Brenda's hair was long, her mother had cut hers years ago and it fell into the same chic style that was as up to date today as it had been ten years ago.

She looked happy, even radiant as she spoke about

Wes. She started on plans for a big wedding as soon as they set the date, maybe next June as soon as school ended for the two of them.

Brenda knew there would be no wedding. As much as the fantasy now entered her conscious mind, she knew it would never happen. She and Wes would part in little over a week. When she returned to Meyers, she'd make a point of avoiding him. Thank God she'd never slept with him.

"What is it, honey?"

Brenda's attention snapped back to her mother. "I'm sorry, Mom, what did you say?"

"You're a little tense, Scottie. Is anything wrong?"

"No, I'm fine." Brenda lifted her drink and sipped some of the watery liquid.

"Is it Wes?"

She shook her head. "It's not him." Each time her mother spoke his name she heard that litany of their first meeting, when he lounged in the doorway saying, Wes-to-my-friends. She wanted to talk to her mother, but she couldn't tell her the truth.

"Don't worry about me. I really like him." She smiled at her daughter, giving her hand a slight shake. "I know you didn't tell me first, but I'm over that. And your father will love him. He's smart and obviously in love with you."

"You really like Wes?"

"I think he's perfect for you." She paused. "Are you having second thoughts?" When Brenda didn't answer, she went on. "When he kisses you, what do you feel?"

"Mother!" Brenda's eyes opened wide.

"Scottie, grow up. You think I never kissed a man?"

"No, I just never expected to discuss it with you."

"Well, pretend I'm Shiri or Essence." She waited, expectant. "Well?"

A FAMILY AFFAIR

Brenda remembered being in Wes's arms, his mouth on hers. It was heaven. It was like having all the wishes she'd ever wanted rolled into one. Quickly she threw water on the memory or she'd be too hot to be sitting in a restaurant with her mother.

"Is it like fire? Your entire body tingles? You feel everything, even your blood rushing through your veins?"

Brenda looked at her mother as if the older woman had somehow gotten inside her head and viewed her memory. Pamela Reid only smiled.

"It does, doesn't it?"

Brenda nodded, dropping her chin.

"Honey, don't look so shocked. It's supposed to be that way. What about when you make love?"

"I am not doing this." Brenda got up and walked away from her mother. Pamela followed her, pulling her suitcase behind her. "It's important, Scottie," her mother said. "If you don't like the way he makes love, marriage will never work."

"Mom, can we talk about something else?"

Brenda looked about for direction. They left the restaurant and outside she suddenly couldn't think where she'd planned to go. She walked toward security keeping close to the wall and out of the flowing stream of travelers who were rushing.

"You two *have* made love?"

Brenda stopped and stared at the woman who'd given birth to her.

A second later her mother laughed. "You haven't." She hugged her daughter.

"Mom."

"Come over here and sit down." They went to the windows in a section of the terminal where no one could hear them. Brenda sat down on a small lip in front of the floor-to-ceiling windows. Her mother kneeled in front of her, resting back on her legs. Even in this position she still managed to look as if she were on her way to a modeling assignment. Leaning forward with her elbows on her thighs, Brenda stared at her hands.

"Remember when you were little and we used to talk about everything?" Her mother paused. "You'd come home from school and tell me all the things that had happened during the day, right down to Shiri throwing her shoe at Jason Holt. Or after your first date when we sat up half the night over hot chocolate?"

"Mom, I was crying over that date and this isn't like that. I was sixteen then."

"I know you're an adult, Scottie. You can talk to me as an adult. I'm not too old that I won't understand."

"I'm in love with him, Mom." Tears filled her eyes. "I never thought I'd feel like this. I never knew you *could* feel like this."

"That's wonderful, darling. With the way he looks at you, the two of you are well suited for each other. So what's the problem?"

The way he looks at you. Brenda hadn't noticed Wes looking at her in any special way. She could see passion and want in his eyes, but love? It wasn't there. He was compassionate, trying to help her in a dilemma he caused, but they weren't in love with each other. The love was all on her side.

Then she thought of his kisses. The way she melted in his arms. The way she longed to talk to him and how frantic she was at the idea of making love with him.

"I'm not sure there is a problem. I'm a little nervous. Nothing like this has ever happened to me." She didn't know what else to say. Looking at the light that practically shone from her mother's face at the prospect of her

A FAMILY AFFAIR 225

daughter being in love took the thought of pouring out her heart to her mother away from her. How could she tell the truth? She knew continuing to lie would only postpone the hurt, but right now she was taking the coward's way out.

Pamela Reid's laugher filled the tiny space. She gathered her daughter and rocked her in her arms as if she were a small child.

"That's the best kind of love, sweetheart. A first love."

The woman who returned to the hotel was different than the one who'd left it three hours earlier. Brenda Reid couldn't return to who she'd been before she met Wesley Cooper. There was no going back to that person. She'd died quietly and without fanfare. But she also wasn't the person her mother thought her to be and she wasn't who Wes thought she was either, although there was an area of unknown for both of them. She was someone else. Someone newly emerging, being born full-grown at twenty-nine.

Could her mother be right? Did Wes look at her with something special in his eyes? She wanted to believe he did, but then remembered he was acting for her benefit. He was putting on a show for her mother. She needed to find out who she was and what she wanted. With Wes in the room she had a hard time thinking.

At the reception desk she inquired about a separate room only to discover the hotel still had no space available. She couldn't throw Wes out with no place to sleep. She did like him. She felt more than like for him, she'd fallen in love, but he was going to break her heart, had already broken it.

Brenda thought of her mother's story about her nickname. How she wished she'd let her head remain in the stars. Coming down to earth was scary, dangerous, and the consequences to her heart were overwhelming. Above the clouds, outside the troposphere, stratosphere, and the ionosphere in the cosmic regions of the universe was where she belonged, where she was safe from the entanglements of the heart.

But was she happy?

The question came unbidden. She hadn't thought of happiness or unhappiness before Wes. The sky was a place she loved. It was her work, her fulfillment. Not even Reuben had removed that place from her life.

Then she'd met Wes.

And change was not only rapid and wild, it was cataclysmic and irrevocable.

The suite was empty when she got to it. She let out a breathy sigh. For a while longer she didn't have to deal with the inevitable. But she was going to have to deal with it. Brenda went to her room and closed the door in case Wes returned to the suite. She sat down in the chair near the balcony. What had happened to her?

Where was the woman she used to be? She was intelligent, called a genius by educational psychologists since she was first tested in grade school. She knew logic, could conceptualize an expanding and contracting universe, the curvature of time, and the existence of black holes. Yet with Wes she was a mass of confusion. When she was with him, she only wanted to be in his arms. Yet when she was away she knew the folly of her actions.

Falling in love with him was the worst thing that could happen to her. It confused her. She didn't live by emotions. She lived under principles, physical laws, things that could be mathematically calculated. Love didn't fit any of her formulas. She relied on them. They hadn't failed her in the past.

But they were failing her now.

Was this what Essence and Shiri went through? They were the normal ones. Brenda knew what it was to feel abnormal. Special schools, grades skipped, boys ostracizing her because she "spoke like an encyclopedia." She'd cultivated the ability to keep her comments to herself, to not explain everything that someone asked.

With Wes it wasn't like that. She didn't have to edit her speech when she was with him. She could be herself, say what she wanted, do what she wanted. He accepted her for exactly who she was.

Brenda curled her legs under her and stared unseeingly out the window. She realized she'd just enumerated all the reasons why she should fall in love with Wes. The problem was him. She wasn't sure he was sincere in his feelings for her. Their association began over a bet and as far as she knew it was still standing. All he had to do was get back to campus and prove to the brotherhood that he was top dog. Another conquest. A promised fulfilled. Brenda felt like a notch on the bedpost. Only there was no bedpost and there wasn't going to be one. It was time she took her life back. She had to go back to that balance she had before this new person came out. It was safe back there.

But safety no longer seemed like the haven she'd once felt comfortable in. Comfort now had another name.

When Wes came in she was waiting for him. The moment she saw him she knew it wasn't going to be easy. He'd been in the pool. The smell of chlorine, which should have been irritating, wafted across the room like an erotic fragrance. Brenda, like most women, would have worn a wrap over her suit. Wes didn't. He had on trunks, a towel around his neck, and his feet encased in deck shoes. Otherwise he was naked. Water still rolled down his chest and legs. She forced herself to keep her eyes away from the trails of water and the paths to which they led.

"Did your mother get off all right?"

She nodded, unable to trust her voice. Wes quickly understood that something was wrong. Something had happened between breakfast and the airport that changed her. He didn't have to say it. The two of them had begun to communicate without words. Yet he couldn't read her mind. He didn't know the upheaval that had taken place while her mother held her in front of a window in the airport.

He came toward her. Brenda knew he planned to put his arms around her. It was his method of taking everything away, the hurt, confusion, logic. And she wanted to go there . . . but she couldn't go there.

She stepped aside. Wes stopped as surely as if she'd slapped him.

"Are you all right?"

"No," she snapped.

"What happened? Did you tell her?"

"No, I couldn't tell her. She's thrilled. It's like she thinks I've discovered the cure for cancer or something."

"Sit down, Brenda."

"I don't want to sit down."

"Sit down anyway. We need to talk." His voice was calm. Brenda wanted to fight. She wanted to scream and shout and even break something, but Wes wasn't giving her the opportunity. He was going to be civil, probably logical, and explain to her how all her fears were ungrounded. She didn't want to hear that. It wasn't true. He'd come into her world and turned it upside down. She had to get it back on track.

Brenda stood her ground. She faced him on her level. Her heart was thudding so fast she was sure Wes could see her shirt moving back and forth. "I lied to my mother."

He said nothing. She understood the predicament. What could he say?

"I've never lied to her before. I don't like the feeling."

He took a step. Brenda matched it, keeping the distance between them the same.

"Wes, this can't go on. I know it started as a harmless little joke, but it's affecting me and my family. I don't like who I'm turning into."

"Who are you turning into?"

She hadn't expected that question. She was turning into a woman in love and it was scaring her to death. She didn't have experience. She hadn't taken on the experience a little at a time. She'd been thrust into it all at once, not knowing she was unprepared to handle it.

"Where did you sleep last night?"

"What are you talking about? You know where I slept."

"Which bed?"

"What does that have to do with anything?"

"You slept in my bed, didn't you? On my pillow. With my scent on it. With me on it."

She turned away from him. She had. How had he known?

"Is that what's eating you? This isn't about your family. Yes, it was a lie and it's a little more than I thought of when I made the comment, but all this can be explained. You've had one failed engagement. Your parents got over that. So this has nothing to do with the white lie."

Brenda groped for something to say. She hadn't admitted it to herself, but he was right.

"Look at me." He took her arm and held her so she looked at him. "Your eyes are full of hunger. Even in anger there a raw sexuality that's there whenever you look at me. You look and you wonder. You wonder what it would be like. You and me together and if we don't get interrupted by your family we're going to find out. And that scares you, doesn't it?"

"Stop it!"

"I won't stop it. And your mouth won't lie for you. When I touch you, when I kiss you, you're with me. The two of us could be one person. You want to know what making love is like. You want to see if the stars fall, the moon rises, and the world explodes."

"So I want to know. What does it matter? Nothing will come of it."

She wrenched her arm free.

"Nothing!"

Brenda restlessly walked between the bed and the windows of her room. The day had been miserable. She'd passed it alone after her fight with Wes. She walked the beach for hours listening to the gulls and allowing the wind to pull her hair into straight lines. She thought about her situation, tried to reason with it, but nothing made sense. Her feelings didn't make sense. She was angry with Wes, yet he was the only person she wanted to be around.

For the second night in a row Brenda couldn't sleep. She expected to find the remnants of Wes on her pillow, but only the starchy smell of laundry soap was on the linen. The sheets had been changed. Wes must have ordered it. He'd mentioned the sheets. Didn't she wonder what it would be like? She'd slept in his space, hugged his pillow, with the essence of him on it, breathed it in as if it were a healing tonic, and wondered. Wanted to know what it would be like to slip into the silky reserves of his strength, learn the nocturnal lessons of making love to a man she burned for.

She pulled the pillow under her head and closed her eyes, but she didn't sleep. She tossed and turned for hours unable to get him out of her mind. Throwing the covers off she got up. Her throat was dry and she was hot. Checking the room temperature, she lowered it a degree and headed to the connecting door. There was cold water in the refrigerator in the bar area of the common room.

Her door had been locked since early afternoon. She opened it and found the inside door to the common room already open, in the same position she had left it when she slammed her own on Wes. Wearing a long pink gown that Essence had given her when she came to console her after Reuben Sherwood, she stepped into the room. Could a pink robe help after she and Wes returned to their lives?

Brenda was halfway across the room when she heard the sound. She stopped, turning toward it. Expecting the room to be empty she was startled to see Wes sitting on the sofa using his laptop computer. The whirring sound of a modem connecting one computer to another sounded as loud as a scream. She eyed his laptop, lying casually across his knees. Only one lamp burned near the position where he sat. Brenda thought nothing of the light. They often left it on in case one of them went to the refrigerator before sunrise. Her own laptop was in her room. She'd yet to take it out of its case.

"I thought you'd be asleep," she said, feeling inadequate and finding their last conversation clear in her mind.

"I had some work to do."

"I won't disturb you. I needed something to drink." Realizing he could interpret that comment in many ways, she amended it. "Some water."

Wes nodded, but remained where he was. His back was against the sofa, his feet propped up on the coffee table, and the laptop throwing a bluish light across his chest.

Brenda went to the refrigerator and took out a bottle of water. She opened it and poured it into a glass. Then she drank it as if her throat were parched from years in the Sahara. Taking her glass and a second bottle, she headed back to her room. Wes's eyes were on her as she crossed in front of him. She stopped and suddenly sat down. She hadn't intended to, but that was how Wes affected her. She did things she didn't expect to do and she thrilled in the doing.

"I apologize for this afternoon," she started. "It seems there are a lot of things that are happening and I just don't know how to handle them."

Wes moved the laptop to the sofa and sat up straight.

"I didn't intend to cause you strife with your family."

"I believe you," she told him honestly. She truly believed he'd just been displaying his usual Wes-to-my-friends attitude. "My mother went home today and by now the entire family thinks there's truth to something that isn't the case."

She curled up in the chair facing him, pulling her long legs up to her chin. Her gown slipped over her legs and slid like a pink waterfall down the side of the chair.

"What do you suggest we do?"

A FAMILY AFFAIR

"I think we should drop the deception. I will tell my family the truth and whatever happens, happens."

He stared at her for a moment. "They're going to be disappointed."

"I know." Both her aunts and her mother had been taken by Wes's charm. Brenda was taken by it too, but they had to stop. It was time to return to reality. "I'll wait until they arrive for the reunion. So much is going on then. Trips to Disneyworld. Meeting and greeting. Reacquainting ourselves with each other, discovering what everyone has been doing."

"What will you tell them?"

"That we thought better of the engagement." She reached for her water and drank most of the glass. "We're still friends, but we haven't known each other long enough to be engaged."

"I won't have to pretend to be your fiancé. You can tell them our relationship was fast and fiery and burned out quickly."

Her head snapped up to stare at him. His tone was derisive as if she had somehow struck a nerve.

"Something like that," she said. She felt guilty for no reason. "I hate lying to them, but at least I can put closure to this. We're in too deep as it is. I don't want to go any deeper."

"Would you like me to leave?"

Brenda hadn't expected the question and she had no ready answer for it. Her heart screamed no. Her mind told her yes. The best thing she could do was go cold turkey. Wes wasn't part of her life and he wasn't likely to be. She admitted to the chemistry between them. But when they were both back at Meyers and school was in session, she would have her work with classes, the observatory, and the NASA contract she'd accepted. Wes would have his research. He'd been more involved in it since his last attempt had been disastrous. There was no need for the two of them to see much of each other. Brenda could avoid the faculty parties using her schedule as the reason.

"Brenda?" Wes waited for her answer.

She nodded.

He stood up. "I'll leave in the morning."

Wes moved toward his room. Brenda felt disappointment. Disappointment in herself and in what she thought she saw in Wes. Was he disappointed?

"Wes?"

He was nearly to his door when she called and he stopped. He turned back to her.

Brenda got up and faced him. "Thank you." Her voice was a soft whisper. She appreciated what he'd done for her. He'd changed her more than he knew or would ever know.

Wes came back toward her. Brenda felt her body warming. She'd never get used to the excitement he caused in her. She should have stepped back. She shouldn't have let him get close to her. But she didn't move a centimeter. Unless she counted the layers of skin that dissolved into heat-seeking missiles and exploded in her erogenous zones.

Wes took her face in his hands. He stared at her as if he were counting her freckles. His hands were warm. He tilted her face up to his and looked at her lips. Brenda forced herself to control her breathing. Yet she knew he could feel her breath. She felt his. He wanted to kiss her. She knew it. She wanted it too. After staring down at her until she thought the scream in her throat would erupt, he bent down and placed his lips on her forehead.

Brenda's hands slid up his shirt and over his shoulders.

He breathed hard, wanting to take her now. He knew he had to stop. He should never have moved from the room's geography, never come back to this island of carpet, never put his hands on her, and never kissed her forehead.

He lifted his head and looked at her. Her eyes were barely open, heavy with passion and asking for more. But not on these terms. If he made love to her, she'd have to be fully aware that this was no game.

"Brenda." He called her name. Her eyes opened a little wider and she looked at him. "I want you. I want to make love to you. This is a warning. Move your arms from around my neck and back away. You can go to your room with your character and your body intact. Or you can kiss me again. If you do, there'll be nothing to stop me. I won't have time to make it to either of the bedrooms. I'll take you right here on the floor, make love to you until you scream. Now what's it to be? What do you want? Your bed? Or the floor?"

Brenda stared at him. He was so close to her she could see the tiny indentations in her skin. He wanted to kiss each of them, slowly, with care, raising her level of anticipation until she was on the brink of pain. Then he wanted to make love to her fast and hard, make love until she couldn't keep her mouth shut, until she screamed to the high heavens. And he was only a half second from making his thoughts reality.

Brenda's hands slid down his chest the same way they had ridden up it. She took a step backward and stopped. Several heartbeats passed between them, loud, thudding heartbeats, before she took another step. Then she turned and walked away.

Wes watched. He didn't move as she retraced her steps. As her door closed she looked up at him. He couldn't see her eyes, but the hesitation of her decision was evident. Still she closed her door. A door in his heart closed at the same time.

"Good night, Scottie." He spoke to the closed door, remembering how her skin felt under his mouth. For a while he lingered in the doorway, closing his eyes, savoring the sensations that fissured through him like inner rockets. Then he released the image and went to his room.

Brenda opened her door and peered into the common room. The lamp still burned next to the sofa. Wes's laptop was still there. Moonlight filtered across the dining room table. Wes wasn't there. His door was closed.

Brenda couldn't sleep. Wes was on her mind and her body craved him to the point of refusing to let her relax. She'd tossed and turned for three hours. She couldn't do it anymore.

Throwing back the covers she got up and made a decision. She went into the common room, unhurried, her heart banging loudly in her head.

The room seemed to expand as she walked across it, Wes's door seemingly getting farther and farther away. Finally she reached it, her heart in her throat. Taking a deep breath she raised her fist and wrapped on the polished wood. She didn't wait for him to answer. She opened the door. He sat up in bed, the sheets falling to his waist. His chest was bare. Moonlight washed over him. She caught her breath and stared. Wes remained silent. Her eyes traveled upward to his face, which was indefinable in the gloom.

"I want to scream."

* * *

The knock was soft. At first Wes was unsure if he'd heard it for real or if he'd just wanted to hear it so badly it was a sound inside his head. Then the door opened. He watched it swing inward slowly, as if some ghostly apparition had released the lock.

He waited, watching, hoping Brenda would be standing there in her pink gown with passion in her eyes.

"Oh God," he groaned as the door finished arcing into the room.

"I know it's crazy," Brenda said. Her voice was hesitant and low. "I know this doesn't make sense after everything I've said."

Wes didn't move. He wanted to sprint across the floor and crush her to him, yet the tremors running through him kept him in place. For a long moment they stared at each other across the space of the bedroom, anticipation as palpable as heavy fog. Slowly Brenda began to move. He watched the shimmer of her gown as she glided across the carpet, coming toward him like some ethereal queen. "I don't want to imagine what it would be like." Her voice low, sexy, and disturbing to his libido. "I want to know."

Wes didn't know he could move so fast. In a flash he was in front of her. He remembered to stop before his hands acted like clamps and he ground her to him. Standing in front of her he took her face in his hands and bent down and kissed her cheek. Her skin was heated under his mouth and he wanted to slide his mouth over her face and take hers, but he knew it would be a desperate kiss if he did any more than what he was doing right now. For a second longer he held her face, not touching any other part of her body, but feeling the heat of her presence from neck to toe.

Her open palms slid up his chest and connected

around his neck. Her mouth sought his and kissed it. His opened to her seeking tongue. Heat flooded his loins. He held back, allowing her to lead, and she took the sword by the hilt and drove it home. Her mouth was hot and sweet and devastating on his. He rested his hands on her waist, giving up, joining her in the kiss, taking control, dragging her closer to him, melding her into his body. Her imprint fit into his, her softness like a hot mold carving into him and seeking her own shape, her own place in his being.

She was soft and smelled of soap and roses. It reminded him of the gown she wore, rose pink and soft. Her mouth was soft too. He liked her taste. He swept his tongue inside and his arms crushed her tightly to him. His hand swept up and down her back, tracing the shape of her, memorizing the long line of her back, the curve of her spine, and the shape of her buttocks.

He angled his head and repositioned his mouth. Her arms wrapped around him. She went up on her toes and rubbed her body against his. Wes groaned into her mouth feeling his body stiffen, feeling himself growing harder and harder the more she moved. As in a dance she raised one leg and shifted it up and down his bare one. He wore shorts, but the silkiness of her gown and the warm leg beneath the fabric as it moved across the coarseness of his had his body burning for hers.

He lifted her, carried her to the bed, and gently set her on her feet. He stared down at her. Her face was bright, her eyes radiant in the half-light filtering through the doorway. He bent and kissed her shoulder, slipping the strap of her gown down as he replaced it with his mouth. She moaned, throwing her head back and allowing him access to her neck. Wes switched to the other side and the second strap followed the first. He felt her

A FAMILY AFFAIR

breathing accelerating and watched her trying to control it, but the rise and fall of her breasts betrayed her effort.

Brenda slipped her arms out of the gown. For a moment her breasts held it in place. Then it fell. Wes gasped at the sight of her. She was beautiful, evenly brown, her skin glowing in the light. Then he was touching her. His mouth on her, his hands all over her, his mouth seeking, tasting.

Her fingers skirted around the top of his boxers. He felt her bare hand against his skin. Heat poured over him as she caressed his back. Her hands raked over his skin and she kissed him with openmouthed wetness.

Wes lowered her to the bed and joined her there. He pulled her close, kissing her, listening to the night sounds that came from her, loving the sweetness of her taste and the feel of softness next to his hardness. He rolled away from her, taking off his shorts and grabbing a condom from his pocket. Quickly he put it on and rolled back to the warmth he missed in so short a period.

Brenda came to him, meeting his body as if the two of them were old lovers. Wes knew they weren't. He had an unfamiliar anticipation that something wonderful was about to happen. He didn't have a past as experienced as most men his age, but he knew he'd never burned for a woman before, never had the fire in his loins like he had now. He felt as if he'd die without her.

Quickly he raised himself. She was waiting. Her legs opened and he settled between them. Entering her wasn't easy and he thought he might be hurting her, but the look on her face was pure rapture. The rhythm between them came quickly, as if they knew it, had experienced it in some past life. Wes was overwhelmed with feeling. He'd never felt so much pleasure. Never made love with anyone who did this to him. Yet he wanted to give her pleasure. For the first time in his life he wanted to make sure someone else enjoyed sex.

Brenda's legs wrapped around him and the groan that escaped his throat had all the pleasure he was feeling rolled into it. She knew where to touch him, what to do to drive him crazy, and he was about to go over the edge any moment. He gathered her to him, his body joined to hers. But they were joined in other ways. His spirit knew hers, his aura was combined with hers. There was nothing about them that was separate, nothing that didn't join and mesh.

Wes clenched his teeth as the pleasure he was feeling drove him higher and higher into a realm of consciousness that was akin to nonexistence. He knew in a moment the two of them would burst into flame. They would ignite and in a flash of fire cease to be.

He heard her moans. They came faster and faster lifted by her staccato breathing, making it faster and faster. He felt the clench in her, felt the moan in her throat, and heard the bursting scream that arced from her as their climax came together and they collapsed onto each other like a dying star.

ELEVEN

The fireworks were bright, beautiful. Lights burst in multicolors, brightening the sky. Brenda soared above the amusement park, floating among the greens and reds of bursting light. She followed the dying tails of starbursts, the rotating sparks of pinwheels, the radiating fire of two lovers, and the jangling of a telephone.

Telephone!

Brenda sat up. Her leg hit something warm. She turned and stared. She was in bed with Wes. The night came back to her with radiant clarity. She heard the phone again. It was a real phone ringing, not some remnant of a dream. She looked at the instrument next to the bed. It was silent. Then she remembered each room of the suite had a different number. Her phone was ringing.

Throwing the covers aside she rushed to her room, grabbing the phone. She pulled her short robe from the drawer and held the robe up to herself as she spoke into the receiver.

"Hello."

"Brenda, are you asleep?"

"Essence?"

"Of course, it's Essence. I talked to your mother yesterday and she told me the news."

"News?"

"About your engagement. Brenda, this is wonderful."

Essence's voice was excited. Brenda was trying to clear her head. Visions of her dream lingered. The lovers she'd identified, floating in the sky of her dream, were herself and Wes. Then she'd awakened to find him next to her, stretched out and relaxed. All her senses cried out to him, to repeat their night of lovemaking, but the phone was ringing.

"Brenda, are you there?"

"I'm here."

"Well, give me the details."

Brenda looked up. Wes stood in the doorway. He'd pulled on his boxers, but nothing more. She wore only the drape of her robe, which she held with one free hand. Her breath died in her throat. He was the best-looking man she'd ever seen. His body had been exercised to defined precision, his arms and shoulders sculptured, his legs proportionally balanced for strength and agility. Summing the parts of his body made each of her counterparts spring to life. Combining them into a single person had her neck burning and heat stealing up her ears. She was aroused.

"Details, Brenda, details."

Essence was talking in her ear. Wes started toward her. She scrunched the phone between her neck and shoulder and raised one hand, palm out, to ward him off.

"Essence, what did you say?"

Wes ignored her and kept coming.

"I said give me some details. Did you two set a date? You should hear how your mother described him. He sounds absolutely delicious. I can't wait to meet him."

Brenda could hardly listen. Wes kept coming, even though she was shaking her head vigorously.

A FAMILY AFFAIR

"We haven't set a date," Brenda said.

"Who is that?" Wes asked.

Both of them spoke at the same time.

"My cousin." Brenda mouthed the words without sound. Wes passed her and went to the opposite side of the bed.

"When did all this happen?"

"Not long ago."

"I'm thrilled for you. . . ."

Brenda shivered. She didn't hear anything else Essence said. Wes kneeled on the mattress and leaned down to kiss her bare back.

"Will he be at the reunion?"

"No!" she shouted. Her message was intended for Wes, but Essence took it as an answer to her question.

"Why not?"

"He's . . . got . . ." She closed her eyes as Wes's hands smoothed down her back. "Got to go back to work."

"Brenda, you can't keep him hidden."

"Hidden . . ." She could only repeat her cousin. Her head fell back on Wes's shoulder as his mouth worked its way across her shoulder and onto her neck.

"After the way your mother talked. She is just beside herself with glee."

Brenda gasped. Wes's hands came around her, sliding under the held-up robe, and cupped her breasts. His thumbs rubbed back and forth over her nipples. She moaned, nearly dropping the phone.

"I know," Brenda said, unsure if she was talking to Essence or answering some question inside her own head.

Wes pulled the robe out of her hands and threw it across the room, out of her reach. A tightness stole over her, moving with an erogenous sensitivity over her entire body.

"So what's this work that's more important than him meeting your family?"

"Ahhh," Brenda moaned. She had no idea what Essence had asked. She was lost in sensation and losing the battle she was fighting with herself. "Essence, I'll . . . call you . . . back. I have to do something right . . . now."

Wes took the phone and replaced it in its cradle. Then he turned her around and kissed her mouth. The kiss was strong, desperate, as if they had been separated for a thousand years and felt making up lost time was as essential as breathing. His hands roamed over her naked body, bestowing praise, worship, adulation as his mouth slanted across hers, his tongue dipping deep into her mouth, dueling with hers, their heads bobbing this way and that and their bodies joined at the mouth.

Wes slid his mouth to her neck and down her shoulders and chest to her breasts. Brenda arched into him when the wetness of his tongue touched her sensitized nipples. She gasped as rapture scissored through her system. His mouth immortalized her taut nipples, giving each one equal attention. Brenda felt her breath heaving as if she'd run up a mountain. She held on to Wes's head, keeping him pinned to her breasts, giving the sensations running through her free rein. Her blood was singing. She could feel every corpuscle as they bumped into each other, trying to get through her veins, excited with feeling and racing in an portentous attempt to complete the circle and begin the race again.

Brenda felt herself being pushed back against the floral pattern of the bedspread. Wes's mouth worked its way back to hers, where he renewed his assault. Brenda was burning up. She was sure this was as close to combustion

A FAMILY AFFAIR

as she'd ever been. His body stretched out on hers, his knee opening her legs as he joined with her for the primal dance of life. When he entered her this time, it was like a first. She couldn't keep the ecstasy from escaping her throat. The sound she made had no description. It embodied everything that was her, was them. It was sweet and innocent, carnal and promiscuous. It was daring, needy, dangerous, and exciting. It was the only act that she'd ever participated in where she wasn't herself. She was someone else, someone that only Wes could bring to life. When they joined they became one. Brenda had no past memory of this. She wanted more. She wanted it to continue. This was life, she thought. This was what she was born for, what they were on earth for. This was their path, their road. From here there was no other direction, no back, only a forward, only a togetherness, a oneness, a joining that required them both, in heart, mind, and body.

She was going to burst into flame soon. Her body was heated, overheated. No one could survive this much heat, this much passion, this much raw sex. Her body took Wes inside it. Each thrust made her more and more his, raised her erotic barometer to a new high. Grunts filled the room, sex filled the room, smoke and flame would soon fill the room as the two of them created fire. They would burn in this passionate embrace, holding each other, riding each other, loving each other. The pitch increased to frenzy, then went up. Brenda had never felt anything so wonderful, so erotically pleasurable, so fervidly physical that her entire body felt weightless and weighed down at the same time.

Her arms went up, her back arched, her fists drifting under Wes's as they glided over the bedspread. He pushed her hands open, entwined his with hers as the two of them reached the chasm over which only lovers go. For interminable moments they hung there, pleasure invading every cell of their bodies. Where need reached its zenith and where worlds collide. Brenda reached them all. Wes along with her.

And then she screamed.

The mirrored closet door slid back silently. Brenda's image, flushed from her shower and shimmering with the afterglow of frenzied lovemaking, disappeared as the clothes hanging there came into view. She didn't dwell on her image. She was in love and this was the way it looked.

She and Wes were going out. They were going to be children. She felt like a child, a pampered and well-loved little girl who had everything she could ever hope for in the world. They were going to Disneyworld. She could see herself playing with the Mickey Mouse figures, taking pictures, and standing in line to ride Dumbo. And tonight. Tonight they'd dress up and go dancing. She loved to dance and she loved being in Wes's arms. Maybe they could go shopping before tonight and she could buy a new dress, something slinky and form-fitting, something that said "touch me."

Brenda pulled out a pair of tennis shoes, then went to the drawers below the television stand and found a red sleeveless shirt and a pair of white Bermuda shorts. She dressed quickly, leaving her hair loose, but setting the NASA hat atop her head. She applied a small amount of makeup and went into the common room.

Wes was still in his bedroom. She thought of going to the door again, but stopped herself. She knew if she went there they'd make love again. The thought dimpled her

A FAMILY AFFAIR

cheeks. She moved toward the sofa where Wes's forgotten laptop sat open and abandoned. She perched on the arm of the sofa, looking through gauzy curtains hanging at the windows. The city and the world lay at her feet and she felt ready for it. Beyond anything she'd ever thought possible she'd found Wesley Cooper.

She remembered their first meeting with a laugh. And the trip on the train. The time when he'd nearly kissed her at the door of her stateroom. Brenda stretched, a huge smile covering her face. She leaned back and slipped onto the seat coming up against the laptop. Something sounded. She moved realizing the mouse wasn't part of the machine. Wes used a separate mouse and her fall wedged it between the cushions, pushing the button that activated something on the screen.

She looked at it, hearing the whirring modem connection. She reached for the cord, then decided against it. Her eye caught something on the screen.

Her name.

A hundred clichés ran through her head. The legality of reading someone else's mail spiked in her consciousness. Resistance ebbed away like the moon's gravity pulling water back from the shore. She told herself she shouldn't open the mail and she might have let it end there if another message hadn't arrived when the modem ended its call.

Brenda stared at the screen. *Get the eggs and win the bet* was reflected in the subject area. The bet. She'd forgotten about the bet in the light of falling in love with Wes. Meyers and the bet seemed as if it had happened in another galaxy, but here it was, staring at her, bringing her back to the real world. Brenda moved the mouse over the message and opened it.

Dear Wesley, it began. For a moment Brenda thought

of her mother. He was Wes-to-his-friends. Could she assume this woman was not a friend? The message was short and signed by *JoAnne*.

Congratulations on winning the bet. My physical is complete and I've been approved by the doctor. I've cleared my travel schedule for the next few months. Just bring me Brenda's eggs and your sperm and let the pregnancy begin.

Brenda didn't need a mirror to know her eyes had grown as large as dinner plates. The more she read, the greater her incredulity. She couldn't believe what she saw. And there was a postscript.

P.S. This will by my fifth surrogate pregnancy.

Anger boiled up inside her. She had never imagined anyone could be so callous. She thought Wes wanted a date. At the most he wanted sex with her. But this. *This!* . . . She groped for words. With her vast knowledge of the English language, she could think of nothing bad enough to call him. Her entire body shook with a burning anger so livid she could almost see it.

Brenda hit REPLY. The screen came up with a blinking cursor. It seemed to point at her, accusing her of being a fool. *NO EGGS, EVER!* She punched the keys as if they were the enemy. She signed it with her full name and hit the send key. She listened, making sure the machine dialed out, that the whirring connoted connection and that the *message sent* window appeared on the screen.

Each step of the short note made her angrier and angrier. Her blood pumped like battleship engines in full-battle mode. Hammers pounded on dynamite inside her head. Her hands shook as if she'd instantly developed a nerve disorder.

Brenda got up and crossed her arms, trying to keep them steady. She stared at Wes's door. Her eyes narrowed and a growl came from her throat. That was what the

A FAMILY AFFAIR

bet really was. It wasn't for a date or even to have sex with her. He was really after the family jewels. He wanted her to give him her eggs so he could have a baby with another woman! *Her baby*. She squeezed her hands together, digging her fingernails into her palms. How could he do this to her? How could he think she would agree to something like this? And she let him make love to her?

The thought sent shivers along her arms. She was suddenly cold, yet her skin felt clammy and hot. She grabbed the television cabinet to steady herself. She wasn't going to cry, she told herself. There was nothing to cry about. She was too angry to cry. She took deep breaths trying to gain control of herself.

She should have known something like this would happen. Hadn't it happened before? She'd been deceived before by someone who wanted more from her than was apparent and he had used her. Why hadn't she learned the first time?

"Oh God," Brenda moaned. They'd made love, wild, maddening love. She held her stomach as her knees weakened. She reached for the coffee table and sat down on it, rocking herself.

They had used a condom the first time.

Only the first time.

Brenda jumped up as if propelled from behind when she heard Wes's door open. She swung around and faced him. Her head pounded. Her heart beat fast and she felt as if there were a hole in her heart.

"Ready?" There was a wide smile on his handsome face. It galled her that he could stand in front of her as if nothing had happened. Then he must have seen the anger on her face. He knew something was wrong. The air between them crackled with venom. "What's wrong?"

"Wrong?" Brenda screamed. "Maybe you should ask JoAnne that question."

"JoAnne?" He looked confused. "JoAnne who?"

Brenda looked around. She went to the laptop, snapped the computer lid closed and picked up the unit without bothering to disconnect the cords. She threw it at Wes. Instinctively he put his hands up and like a wide receiver he caught the machine as it was propelled across the room.

"JoAnne, the surrogate mother." The silence after her pronouncement was solid, malleable, but no filter for her anger. "I want you out of my suite in ten minutes."

"Brenda—"

"You might not think so, because my experience is limited, but I have seen some low-down things in my time, but you . . . you give new meaning to the word. I thought you followed me across the country for a date. I was flattered. Even sex would be acceptable. But eggs!"

He rolled his eyes skyward. "Brenda—"

"Don't Brenda me," she said, interrupting. "Get your bags and find yourself some other place to live and I hope it's on the street."

"Brenda, let me explain."

"You can explain this? You can explain that you're not here because you find me so attractive that you'd follow me all the way across the country? And on a train? You can explain that you had sex with me for one purpose only? To get me to fall for you. At least enough to volunteer to have my eggs donated. You can explain that you want my eggs so another woman can carry a child that you and I parent? Get out of here, Doctor Cooper. I never want to see you again as long as I live."

He tried to say something, but Brenda wouldn't listen to him. She had never been so angry before in her life. All she could say was get out and point to the door. Wes packed faster than she'd ever seen anyone pack. In minutes the door closed and he was gone. His exit reverberated about the suite like a music hall with perfect acoustics.

Brenda slid to the floor. Clasping her arms around her drawn-up legs, she dissolved into tears. She loved him. She'd never loved anyone as much as she loved him. She knew she never would again. She couldn't believe it. How could this have happened so quickly? How could she fall for a man who could lie to her, deceive her with such horror? If he wanted to have a baby, what was so wrong with the old-fashioned way? What was wrong with asking her out, dating her, wooing and winning her? He was already past second base. Why did he assume that he could get her to give up her eggs without the least bit of sentimentality, and how could he assume that children weren't cherished in her family?

He was from Maine. Didn't they do things the same way as people from Birmingham? Didn't they love and cherish children and want to keep them close for all their lives? How could she be in love with a man who didn't share her values on the lives of children? On family?

Family! The thought halted her tears. Her mother, Essence, everyone believed Wes was her fiancé. She would have to tell her parents and her other relations that she discovered they were incompatible. Even with the click of the door still resounding in her memory, she couldn't believe that Wes had perpetrated such a deception. She felt as if the entire campus back at Meyers were in on the joke. It was an initiation. She was the new pledgee and they were the fraternity brothers. In order to gain acceptance she had to pass the test.

And there was the family. She'd been looking for something to tell them. Something plausible that they would believe without too many questions. She'd secretly hoped she wasn't going to have to concoct anything. She'd really wanted to be engaged to Wes. She'd hoped he'd fall in love with her. Then she could confess how she felt and they could go to the reunion and be really engaged.

Brenda thought he was the one. If there was only one soul in the universe that was compatible with hers, why did it have to belong to a schemer? Why did it have to come from a man who only pretended to understand her?

Wes had provided her with a reason for a broken engagement. And she wouldn't have to lie. She could tell the truth. The two of them didn't believe in the same things. The only lie in the mix was that they weren't engaged and had never been.

The reunion was only days away. After last night Brenda had thought of asking Wes to attend, to pretend to be her fiancé. Pretending with him would be no problem since on her side there would be little pretense. She was in love with him. Her family would believe her.

As if to remind her of family the phone rang.

The road was going nowhere. Wes was going nowhere. He pulled the car over at the side of the road and cut the engine. He didn't know where he was. He hadn't looked for a room when he left Brenda. He'd gotten in the car and started driving. He wanted to be alone. There was too much traffic in the city. Too many people heading for amusement, Disneyworld, Sea World, Universal Studios. They were all excited, happily anticipating a day of fun and exhilaration. For him they were just a long line of cars in his way.

He skirted in and out of lanes, around cars, trucks, SUVs, and minivans. His direction wasn't apparent. After the traffic thinned out he took to the open road with zeal. Wes couldn't remember how long he'd been driving. There were no buildings around him when he took notice. He must have gone a good ways from the hotel, from Brenda.

She drove him crazy. From the moment they met she'd consumed his every thought and now he'd blown the best deal he'd ever had. He thought losing the experiment was bad, but if he lost Brenda it would be like cutting out his heart.

Wesley Anderson Cooper, you've really screwed up this time. Wes heard his sister's voice echoing across the miles. That's exactly what she would have said to him. Then she would help him figure a way to fix what he'd done. He opened the computer and waited for it to boot up. Several messages had come in since he'd last looked. One was from Glenn, but he looked for what Brenda had seen. Finding it, he read, groaning over every word. No wonder Brenda had been so angry. He needed to explain to her what that message really meant.

Frustrated over the circumstances, he was seized by anger. Banging his hands on the steering wheel, he wanted to kill Glenn for telling JoAnne that story. The fact that JoAnne had jumped to an impossible conclusion did nothing to help the situation. He'd forgotten the bet. When he was with Brenda he thought of nothing other than being with her. He wanted to be with her all the time. He was in love with her.

Wes sat back and stared through the windshield. He was in love with her. The thought astounded him. This was why he forgot everything in her presence, why making love with her was like nothing his history could explain. He wanted Brenda more than anything. He'd wanted a wife and a family, in that order, but had given up the search for a woman and walked into the bet as if he were voluntarily accepting a sucker punch. Now it had come full circle. This bet could keep them apart if he couldn't make her listen to him.

They'd started out wrong. He should have told her about the bet right away. He knew she didn't have the details right. No one did. Initially he needed to find someone with his requirements. When she came onto the campus, somehow she'd gotten involved as the woman he was seeking. He'd let it go on, not explaining things to Glenn the way he saw them and not clearing up the misunderstanding. Now the bet had come back to haunt him and to hurt him. Hurt both of them. He knew Brenda was going to cry when he left her. She was barely holding the tears back as she ordered him out. He'd heard her through the door as he paused to shift the suitcase and laptop.

He hated that he'd caused her pain. Hadn't Brenda told him that lying was not the answer? That combining one lie with another only enmeshed them in a mire in which they'd be forever anchored? When he announced their engagement to her aunts more family came, her mother, her cousins on the phone, and in a few days she'd have to lie about their breakup. Lying was not the answer. He needed to find her and tell the truth.

He'd wanted a child of his own and he'd thought he had given up on the wife. That was until the first time he'd kissed Brenda Reid. It must have been in his mind all the time. What else could make him impulsively take a train ride across the United States just because he knew she was on it? And once here, there was no reason for him to force himself into her suite. He could have traveled a little farther afield and taken a room in a nearby town. After meeting with the Reeves Foundation he could have flown back to the university and put his efforts into discovering if there was a real sabotage to his experiment.

Yet he'd chosen none of those options. He'd followed Brenda as if she were the only woman in the world. Now he knew she was. He wanted her, could think of nothing else except making her his wife and having a family with her. But he'd misconceived the situation with monumental calamity. He'd sent the e-mail last night and told JoAnne the scheme was off, but their messages had crossed in the transom and she commented on something Glenn had said. That's what Brenda saw.

Wes glanced back at the machine. He hit the escape key and the message disappeared. The list of read and unread messages reappeared. There was an unread message from Glenn that had *sabotage* as the subject. Wes wasn't even interested in finding out what it said. He only wanted to straighten things out with Brenda.

What he wouldn't give to relive this morning! He didn't want to forget them making love. Their encounter had been like nothing he'd ever thought he'd experience in his life, like an uncontrollable battle in which there was no loser, only radiant satisfaction. With Brenda he'd discovered paradise. He'd searched for her all his life. He couldn't walk away from what they'd had together even if she didn't understand it. He had to convince her that together they had all the magic necessary for a long and wonderful marriage.

She valued family. It was important to her and having

her in his life was important to him. The two of them bonded to each other. Having a family they could grow with and love. That was important to him too.

Wes started the engine and turned the car around. He didn't know how he was going to make her understand, but he had to try.

Brenda sat at the shoreline. She'd swum until she was tired. Her suit had dried completely while she watched the water lapping against the sand. She didn't know any other place to go. Staying in the hotel room, keeping her tears to herself, was not to be. The maids had to clean the rooms and they needed cleaning. She wanted Wes of out her life, and the rooms were the first order of business.

She'd gone to the beach, back to the place Wes had taken her along the Gulf of Mexico. Overhead, the gulls sang their incessant song, but her eyes were trained on the horizon, the distant location of sky blending into sea. She remembered their day, the sun shining brightly on their world, their frolicking in the water. She'd felt happy. Whenever she was with Wes she *was* happy. She should have known it wouldn't last. It never lasted. Not for her.

But he'd lied to her. Tears dried on her face as she remembered reading the e-mail. The question of how could he do such a thing, even conceive of such a plan ran through her mind like a train on a continuous loop. She had no answer. Her feelings for him, her love for him crowded in on her and she was confused about everything that had happened in the last few months.

Finally she went back in the water and started swimming again. Wes had said there were no barriers, no boundaries since it wasn't a pool. Brenda swam parallel to the beach using sand dunes as bases. She counted three hundred laps before dragging herself out of the water and returning to her blanket on the gritty sand.

She knew it wasn't good to stay in the sun too long, but as she lay on the blanket, trying to empty her mind of all activity involving herself and Wesley Cooper, she closed her eyes against the brightness and fell asleep.

She woke to the sound of a child laughing. Brenda thought the sound was in her mind, but when she opened her eyes there was a small boy looking down at her. He giggled in the tone that only a three-year-old could. Sitting up she looked around for his parents. Close to the water she saw a man with his pants legs rolled midway up his legs and a woman whose hair blew in the breeze. They were holding hands.

"Bobby, come on," the woman called to the child. He smiled and waved at Brenda, then ran off to his mother. The couple dropped hands and both of them took hold of their son's hands and swung him in the air. Man, woman, and child, Brenda thought as fresh tears rushed to her eyes. She held them back, refusing to let herself cry. Through her mind she saw herself and Wes as the parents and the child as theirs, a happy little boy who was the best of them.

Brenda followed the progress of the family as they walked along the water. She wondered where they lived; were they here as vacationers or did they call Florida home? She wondered where the parents had met. Did they have the same problems before getting married that she and Wes were having? She discarded the thought. She doubted this kind of crisis had ever happened to any couple on earth.

She wished she could talk to Essence and Shiri. They were as close to sisters as she could get, but there was no way she could explain this. No way could she tell them about the sham of an engagement, the fact that even though she told him she wouldn't even date him, she'd fallen in love with him, or about the ultimate deception of his bet that turned out to require her harvesting eggs for him. And through all this, she'd fallen in love with him. How was this all be possible? It was like some out-of-control soap opera with her in the starring role, a role she never auditioned for and one she couldn't quit.

Well, she would. She got up and pulled her blanket with her. She couldn't continue in this story. She had a family reunion coming up and she would withstand the stares and answer the questions about a failed engagement that didn't get as far as her family meeting the man they thought she intended to marry.

Brenda shivered as she stepped off the elevator. After the heat of the outside, the air-conditioned hotel was cold to her overheated skin. With her beach bag over her shoulder and her purse in hand she found the key as she headed for her door at the end of the hall. She wasn't looking forward to opening that door. Since she'd arrived in Florida she hadn't been alone. Wes had always been there, across the room, ready to talk or spend time with her. She slipped the electronic key card in the slot and heard the sound of the lock releasing.

She already missed Wes. Instead of using the common room door that she always used to enter the suite, she came in through the bedroom where Wes had slept. It was dark, the curtains drawn against the blinding brilliance of the afternoon sun. The dresser, where he'd had his travel kit and hairbrush, was clear. The desk where he'd kept the damning laptop had nothing on it except the hotel books detailing the attraction of Orlando. The bed was made and the room had been cleaned. There was no trace that Wes had ever been there, but Brenda knew better. He was here in the walls, in the fabric of the room, and in her heart.

She ran her hand over the desk wondering where he was. Where had he gone when he left her? Did he find another room? Or . . . Her heart clutched when she thought that he might have gone to the airport and taken a flight back to California. Could he have left her for good?

"Brenda."

Brenda thought she heard Wes's voice. It was all in her head. She was just thinking of him. She really did want to hear his voice, but she knew better than to think that was possible.

"Brenda." It came again. This time closer and louder. She whirled around. Dropping her bag and purse she saw Wes.

"What are you doing here?"

"I need to talk to you. I thought you'd be calm enough to listen to me."

"Get out," she said. "I don't want to hear anything you have to say."

He took a step toward her. She backed up. She should have thought to get the keys changed, but she hadn't. She didn't think clearly around Wes and she'd been distraught to learn his true motives. Consequently, he stood before her. He looked miserable. She hardened herself to his looks. It was probably a ploy anyway. She'd found out what he wanted and he'd put a lot of time into grooming her. To lose her now would set him back. And

JoAnne was ready. Brenda didn't care. She wanted him out of her life.

"Leave," she told him. "I never want to see you again."

"Brenda, it's not what you think."

"You told me yourself there was a bet."

"There was a bet."

"And what were the terms?"

He sighed. "I was to find someone with specific qualifications who was willing to donate her eggs and a surrogate mother who was willing to carry the child and deliver it to me."

"And you picked me?"

"No."

"No!"

"Glenn picked you."

"Get out of here, Wes. I already told you I am not willing to play your game. You're all little boys who play with laboratory cells and think you can cross over into people's lives."

"I don't want to play with your life."

"No, you want my child. A good DNA match to combine with your own. Someone who's highly intelligent, the right age, good hair, good teeth, what else is it you require?"

"Would you just let me explain?"

"Would you get out of here?"

He looked down and his shoulders dropped. A second later he headed for the door. Brenda wanted to move as he got near her, but stood her ground. He was the one at fault. Why did she feel guilty?

When Wes reached her she expected him to keep going. She forgot he never did what she expected. He reached for her and in a second he'd turned her into

A FAMILY AFFAIR

his arms and had his mouth on hers. Instinctively she struggled, pushing at him, her fists beating at his shoulders. Her mind screamed for him to stop, but all that came forth were grunting sounds.

Wes was strong and he knew if he held her long enough she'd give in. She fought valiantly, but lost. His mouth on hers and his arms holding her against him melted her resolve. She stopped struggling, allowing her arms to fall listlessly to her sides. She tried not to respond, not to let him know that his machinations were having any effect on her, but he was good. His level of resistance was lower than hers. She gave up even the silent struggle and joined him in the kiss. She'd missed him. Missed his mouth on hers, his body bringing hers to life.

Brenda was standing against the bed. She was ready to slip down on it, taking Wes with her.

He raised his head. "Thank God your body remembers me," he said.

Brenda pushed him away. She couldn't believe the gall. Like a frustrated schoolgirl she resorted to angry swipes at him, which he dodged with ease. "My body might remember you, but my head does too. Now get out of here and never come back."

"Stop, I'll explain." He caught her arms and pinned them behind her, bringing her body close to his. "Promise you'll listen."

"Why? You have nothing to say that I want to hear."

"Then just let me talk to myself."

She didn't answer. He stared closely into her eyes and taking her silence for assent, he released her. Brenda sat down on the bed. She couldn't remain standing any longer. She had no strength and Wes's kiss was still fresh on her mind and her mouth.

Wes took the chair at the desk. He couldn't really see her face. The room was dark with the curtains drawn. Outside, the storm was gathering, the darkening sky adding to the room's gloom.

"I grew up a lot like you did. I studied a lot and didn't do much else. But I wanted a family. I don't know how I supposed it would happen. I thought finding a wife would be easy, but it never seemed to happen. Finally I was over thirty, no wife, no children, working at a remote university in the California mountains without any prospects."

"You didn't have to stay at Meyers. With your reputation you could work anywhere. According to campus scuttlebutt you're a sought-after commodity. I know the experiment was a setback, but I've heard about the breakthroughs in genetic research you've already made." Actually she had asked. She'd read some of his papers in the library and was impressed by what he had accomplished. "Many people are using the Internet to meet people. You could have tried that."

"I did. I've been on more blind dates, computer dates, and dating service setups than you can imagine."

"And you never found anyone compatible." She found that hard to believe. "Your standards must be sky high." She should have been flattered that she fit whatever those standards were.

"After my last blind date, which happened a few months before you appeared on campus, I joined our weekly card game. The usual bull session was in progress and my presence added fuel to an already burning fire. They all knew I wanted to marry. There was friendly banter when I first arrived, but it turned serious and the gauntlet was thrown."

"Naturally, you had to accept it." Brenda thought he

had more intelligence than that. She'd seen his records, accessed them on the Internet. There was no need for her to hack into the registrar's office or to look over the shoulder of the office staff. Everything she needed to know was there for the searching.

"It's a guy thing," he said.

Brenda rolled her eyes.

"I was fed up with trying to find Mrs. Right. So as a geneticist I thought of going for the family."

"Is this where I come in?"

"Not exactly. I did nothing for three months to find a subject. Glenn was more upset about it than I was. He looked for me."

"You asked him to do that?"

Wes shook his head. "He did it on his own. We shared the same research and if I lost the bet he had no job."

"Why?"

"If I lost, my research went to Gerald Cusack. The point became moot when Glenn's own research grant came through, but he didn't stop. He thought he was helping me. I admit I didn't stop him."

"What do you get if you win?"

"Other than the family I wanted, Jerry's promise that he'd treat everyone who worked in the sciences with the respect they deserved."

Brenda tried to give it some credence, enough weight to stake his career on. She wasn't sure she could do it. It had to be a guy thing. Maybe she should have left it at that.

"Glenn didn't stop his crusade to find me the woman who fit my qualifications. He thought you had it all. Then I met you and you did."

Brenda stared at him. Her heartbeat increased. She'd wanted to hear those words.

"I forgot the bet. Never did I think of it when I thought of you. I just wanted to be with you."

She wanted to reply with the same words. But she kept quiet.

"The first time we kissed I knew you were the woman I'd been looking for, not for a bet, but as my wife. Brenda, I want to marry you."

TWELVE

The room was too gloomy. Brenda got up and snapped on the lamps over the beds. She then turned on the lamps on the desk and the one next to the chair where Wes sat. She needed light to make sure Wes understood her.

Moving back from him she stared directly in the eyes. "That was precious, Wes," Brenda said, sarcasm evident in her tone. "Did you spend the afternoon coming up with that?"

"Don't you believe me?" He stood up.

"Not for a minute. And the marriage proposal." She looked at the ceiling with a laugh. "That was priceless. You can't get me to donate my . . . my . . ." She stuttered, unable to say it. ". . . to your project so you go to plan B. You'll marry me. This way you don't need the surrogate mother. I can serve in both capacities."

"Brenda, why are you acting like this?"

"Me! You come up with the proposition of the century and I'm the one who's acting crazy? I think I get that right. Now you get out of my suite and leave the key."

"Brenda, can't we talk about this? I promise you I never thought of that bet when I was with you."

"So what was that e-mail message?"

"It was a huge misunderstanding. Glenn said something to JoAnne and she jumped to conclusions."

"And this morning?"

"This morning?"

"That little episode in my bedroom. Was that part of the backup plan?"

"What plan?"

"You must have guessed by now that I'd never agree to your plan; otherwise you'd have told me about it. Even suggested I participate. But you didn't. So you knew it wouldn't sit well."

"It didn't cross my mind."

"And I suppose it didn't cross your mind that we didn't use protection either?"

The way his eyes opened, she almost believed this was the first time he'd thought of it. Brenda was determined not to let that get to her. He'd deceived her from the beginning. He'd only been interested in her because of what he wanted from her, not because he wanted her.

"Get out, Wes." She turned around and went to the desk. She couldn't look at him anymore. He looked vulnerable and she didn't want that to sway her. Wes had kissed her and she was as pliable as wax in his arms. She wasn't going to let that influence her now.

She knew he hadn't moved. He stood behind her somewhere on the other side of the room. The silence stretched between them as wide as outer space. She wouldn't turn around. She wouldn't look at him again. She'd placed her heart in his hands and he'd trampled over it. There was nothing left for them. Brenda knew she should have kept to herself. When she found him on her train she should have insisted on another table. She shouldn't have been concerned about him having a room or spending time with him. It was all a comedy of manipulation. He'd planned it every step of the way and she'd fallen into the deceptive plan like a naive mark.

Well, she was done with that and with Wesley Cooper. She heard the door open and close. He'd left without another word. Brenda turned to the empty room and sank down on the chair.

He was lying. Brenda didn't believe a word he'd said. It was all part of some elaborate lie to get out of a bad situation. And the proposal was perfect. He couldn't get her to donate her eggs so now he was willing to marry her to get the perfect baby. Well, he could go to hell.

Hot tears burned down her cheeks. What if his plan was already working? They hadn't used protection. What if she was already pregnant with the perfect child?

Ten miles from downtown Orlando the rains began. Within minutes it was impossible to see the road. Wes had to pull over on the side and wait for the storm to pass. He wasn't driving anywhere in particular. He figured he'd find a place to stay the night and return to California in the morning. But he'd turned the car away from the tourist centers and sought a place farther out.

Water pounded on the roof of the rented car. Inside, Wes rested his head on the steering wheel. It seemed to take forever. He wanted to get moving. He could still hear Brenda telling him to get out and while he wanted her to understand, she refused. There was nothing more he could do. Maybe by the time she returned to California they could talk, but she was in no mood to listen to him now.

He pulled his cell phone out and dialed Glenn's number in the lab.

"Doctor Steuben," he answered on the first ring.

"Glenn, Wes here."

"Wes, did you get my message?"

"I haven't read it yet."

Glenn was an ambitious scientist and a take-charge guy. He'd been looking forward to coauthoring his first paper with Wes on the experiment in which they had worked together. As soon as Wes mentioned his suspicion of sabotage to him, he'd launched a quiet investigation.

"Pay dirt, Wes. We got her."

"Her?"

"Yeah, you'll never guess who came up dirty."

"Who?" Wes was in no mood for games. Brenda was still on his mind. He didn't need Glenn playing Clue.

"Doctor Harris."

"Olivia Harris?" He couldn't believe it. Olivia Harris had sabotaged his experiment.

"One and the same. I kept some of the experiment."

"Glenn!" Wes shouted. "We were supposed to destroy everything."

"We are allowed to keep a sample for study as long as it poses no risk. I took precautions and made sure it was properly stored. I didn't do anything against the law."

Wes knew the law. He'd also kept a sample. It was under lock and key in his lab and not even Glenn had access to it.

"What did you find?"

"I tested it for everything known to man, and nothing produced the results that the computers gave. I analyzed samples and got trace quantities of something I couldn't identify. But the new equipment we ordered last spring arrived. I tried the sample in that and found minute traces of several alcohols, water, and blue, red, and violet dye."

"Alchohol and dye? How could it have gotten there?"

"Perfume bottle. She sprayed it." Glenn paused. "After I found the compounds I went over to biochemistry and asked Tate Levy if he could tell me what they were. He came back with a bottle of perfume. Said his wife uses it."

"How did you discover it was Doctor Harris?"

"As I was leaving, Tate mentioned Doctor Harris used to use the same scent, but stopped about a year ago."

"Did he say why?"

"No."

"Then how do you know she did it?"

"She confessed," Glenn said as if he'd wrung the confession out of her.

"Just out of the blue she told you she did it?"

"Not exactly. When Tate confirmed there was a contaminant in the sample I went to Doctor Eaglemen and gave him the findings."

Doctor Eaglemen was head of the genetics department at the university. Wes had discussed the loss of the experiment with him. He was upset at the loss and the funding from the Reeves Foundation. He'd also assured Wes there would be an investigation. Wes hadn't thought that would happen. There was nothing left of the experiment except the sample he'd kept. He didn't know about Glenn's keeping one. If there was any investigation Wes was sure he was the only one to do it.

"He asked me who had access to the lab," Glenn was saying. "The only females who'd been in it during the time frame before we noticed the cell destruction was Doctor Harris. She stayed here over the summer and Doctor Eaglemen called her in to ask if she knew anything about the contamination. He only wanted to ask if she knew anyone who used this kind of perfume. And she confessed."

"I can't believe it. What reason could she have?"

"You, apparently."

"Me!"

"She's been throwing herself at you for three years and you've been ignoring her."

"What?"

"That's what she said. After the story about the bet got out and Doctor Reid came on campus she could see you were interested in her. She was a little teed off. So one night she went into the lab with an empty perfume bottle. She filled it with water and aerated the room. She assumed it would be enough to contaminate or kill some of the cells. She said she didn't think it would completely obliterate the project."

"What did Doctor Eaglemen do?"

"He read her the riot act. Before the day ended she'd tendered her resignation. But the final decision on prosecution is being left up to you."

Wes wished he had found Olivia attractive. She had a nice smile. He supposed things would have been a lot less distorted if he had. Wes should have been happy to discover that his suspicions were correct, but the knowledge did nothing to overcome the problem of Brenda.

"Glenn, when you see Doctor Eaglemen next, tell him the Reeves Foundation is going to continue funding the research."

"Wow! That's great. When are you coming back? I have some time. I can help you set the lab up again."

"I was thinking of flying back tomorrow."

"Thinking?"

"Brenda," he said as if that answered all questions.

"How are you two getting along? Is there a wedding coming?"

"The furthest thing from. She's not even talking to me."

"What did you do?"

"Why do you think I did something?"

"Because every time something goes wrong at our house, I did it. Whether I did it or not."

Glenn was perceptive too. Only this time he had done it. "It's too long a story to tell over the phone."

"I'll see you day after tomorrow then," Glenn said.

Wes rang off. The rain was still coming down. He thought of Brenda. How had things gotten so complicated? Wes asked himself that question for the fifth time since he'd left Brenda in the room where he'd slept the last two weeks. Now he sat in the car, parked along the side of the road waiting for the storm to end. The rain pounded down on the rooftop hard enough to dent the metal.

Brenda had been right. He should have told her. He didn't know why he hadn't. She wasn't really the person he thought of as the mother of the child. In his mind the baby had no mother. He had planned to contact a bank, fill out forms, discover someone with all the attributes he required. He had never thought of meeting and dating a woman and asking her to be part of his project. Glenn and the guys were the ones who assumed that was what he meant when he accepted Jerry's bet.

It was purely coincidental that Brenda took a job at Meyers three months after the bet was made and that Glenn was afraid of losing him and having to work with Jerry instead. If Wes could go back and reconstruct the last few months, he would. But he didn't have that option. He'd made a mess of his relationship with Brenda. He was in love with her.

He wasn't even interested in creating a child unless he had one with her. And he no longer wanted the sterile surrogate birth. He wanted to be part of the loving, part of the creation and all that it entailed. He didn't want some sterile scientific laboratory to create his child. He wanted to do it the old-fashioned way, with all the magic that the two of them pioneered when they joined. He'd wanted that. He wanted her. He loved her, but she wouldn't even talk to him. He needed help and there were only two people Brenda trusted.

Her cousins.

If she went to anyone, it would be Shiri and Essence. He needed to get them on his side.

The rain stopped almost as abruptly as it had begun. The sun came out and Wes saw the rainbow in the distance. He took it as an omen. Everything would be fine.

Then her turned the car on and headed it north. He wasn't going to California. He was going to Birmingham.

Brenda survived the week alone. She made herself get up each day and go out. She spent hours at tourist attractions she was sure to visit with family in the coming week, but she needed something to occupy her mind. Keep her sane.

The trips almost worked except that most of the places were family events: Sea World, Epcot Center, Disneyworld. She saw so many man, woman, and child groups that they began to wear on her mind. She shopped, bought clothes she didn't need and had no room for in her suitcase to take back to Meyers. She had a makeover

A FAMILY AFFAIR

in a department store, had her hair braided in microbraids and designed into an elaborate style that changed her entire appearance. Yet under all of this she was still Brenda Reid. And she was miserable.

A week later when her family arrived she awaited them with a large smile and a ready story. She hugged and kissed aunts, uncles, cousins, her parents, grandparents, and great-grandparents. She found it strange that none of them mentioned Wes. Not even her mother, who had met him and been charmed by him, said a word.

Brenda felt as if she were in some virtual game program where there was a penalty if someone mentioned Wes's name. She wondered what the consolation was for uttering it first.

She stopped her mother in the midst of several arrivals.

Pamela Reid kissed her cheek. "Your hair looks gorgeous," Pamela commented, raising her hands but never actually touching the braids that were swept up. The front was woven into a basket weave pattern that fell down Brenda's back in a myriad of curling braids.

"Mom, you didn't mention Wes."

"I know, dear." She smiled and waved at someone across the lobby.

"Don't you want to know where he is?"

"I know all about it, dear." She patted Brenda's hand as if she were a four-year-old. "There's Aunt Rosie." She left Brenda and rushed across to welcome her aunt.

Brenda was in a daze after that. What was going on? Everyone hugged and kissed and welcomed each other the same as they had done all the years she had come to these family gatherings. They all acted the same. But something was different.

Brenda got a headache trying to understand what was happening. Even Aunt Rosie, who never held her tongue, said nothing about her having a fiancé. Finally, Brenda went to her suite. She'd rest for an hour, then dress for the first event, a cocktail party.

She hadn't been inside more than five minutes before someone was knocking at the door. Brenda padded barefoot to the door. She was sure it would be her mother come to ask why Wes wasn't at her side. But when she looked through the peephole she yanked the door inward.

"Shiri! Essence!" she called. They ran into each other's arms as they backed into the room. "I thought you weren't coming until tomorrow." She addressed Shiri. "And, Essence, I'm so glad you decided to come after all."

She led them to the common room and they all sat down.

"Anyone want something to drink? There's water, juice, and soda in the fridge. I can make some coffee, and there's a bottle of chilled wine."

"Water for me," Essence said.

"Me, too," Shiri followed.

Brenda went to the small bar area. She was stooping to the floor, getting the bottled water, when Shiri's question nearly made her sit down. "So tell us what happened with Wes?"

Brenda got up slowly. Her head came up an inch at a time as if some sniper might be pointing a rifle at her. "You know about Wes?"

"Sure, we've met him." Essence threw the comment over her shoulder as if she were throwing out three-day-old fish.

A FAMILY AFFAIR

Brenda stared back, then remembered the water. She took three bottles and passed them out.

Shiri sat in the corner of the sofa, the place where Wes usually sat. Essence was in the armchair next to her. Brenda sat down on the coffee table in front of them.

"What do you mean you've met him?"

"He came to see us last week. We've spent the last five days with him."

"What?"

Essence opened her bottle of water and drank. "He's really in love with you, you know."

"Did he say that?"

"In three little words," Shiri said.

"You believe him?"

"That's not the point," Essence said. "Do you love him?"

Brenda got up and walked around the table. She stood in front of the television and faced them. "I thought I was."

"Thought?"

"Tell us the truth," Shiri said.

"He was everything I thought I ever wanted in a man." She looked at her cousins' faces, unable to read anything there. "I know you two never thought I had any feelings for romance. My head was in the stars. Isn't that what you always told me? But I thought Wes was different."

"What happened to change your mind?" Essence asked.

"He lied to me. He's not interested in me. He only wants—" She stopped. It was hard even to think of it, much less say it.

"To have a baby."

Brenda gasped.

"He told us."

"Everything?" she asked.

"He told us about the bet, the train trip, the two of you sharing this suite, you swimming in the ocean, and the NASA hat."

"He told you about that?"

"Even the rainstorm," Essence said.

"He said all he wants now is to marry you," Shiri said.

"I don't believe him." Anger came with the volatility of dynamite. "He only wants to marry me, does he? He only really wants a child. And he's invested a lot in me. Did he tell you that? I have all the attributes he requires for the mother of his child. I can't believe he did this."

"Did what?"

"Went to my family. He knows how much you guys mean to me. How close our family is. So he's appealing to you. Getting you to fight his battle. When all he really wants is for me to have a child. Then he'll be on his way. I hate him."

"Brenda," Essence said, "I've seen some rats in my time. If Wes is not telling the truth, then he should give up genetics and go into screen acting."

Shiri leaned forward and set her now empty bottle on the table. "It's hard to convince us of sincerity when it's not there." Brenda looked from Essence to her and back. "Especially when it involves one of the family," Shiri continued. "I believe he's in love with you. How do you feel about him?"

Brenda dropped down in the chair opposite her two cousins.

"Are you running scared?" Essence asked.

"What?"

"Is this retaliation against Reuben Sherwood?"

"I don't think Reuben has anything to do with this."

"He hurt you. And you're afraid Wes will do the same."

He'd already done it. Brenda was miserable. She'd fought to forget him for a week and all she thought of *was* him. At Sea World she thought of going there with him. When they brought out the baby whale that was born only last year, she thought of herself and Wes having a baby. At the shopping center she thought of the two of them shopping. He occupied her thoughts day and night. In every crevice of her room there was something that reminded her of Wes and now her cousins were here talking about him.

"Brenda?" Essence prompted. Brenda knew she wanted an answer to her question.

"I'm terrified, Essence. I know all the things he said. He asked me to marry him, but he doesn't want me. Even if there was no bet, he still wants a child."

"Don't you want one too?" Shiri asked quietly.

Brenda looked at her and nodded.

"Brenda, he's a good man. He's miserable without you."

"He is?" Her voice was small like a little girl's.

"You are in love with him," Essence stated.

"More than I thought it possible. But it's too late. He left over a week ago. He's probably back in California by now."

"No, he's here," Shiri said. Her gaze went to the door. Brenda followed it.

Wes pushed the door open. It hadn't closed all the way. He'd been there all the time. His eyes were dark. He face, although clean shaven, looked tight and strained. Brenda felt as if she were holding his life in her hands. He had her heart. Did she have his? If she told him to go away would she shatter him?

For a long moment, no one said anything. Then Wes

opened his arms. Brenda didn't take time to think. She was out of the chair racing across the small space. His arms closed around her and she felt as if something inside her had just been completed.

"I love you," she said.

She heard Wes expel a long breath. "I love you too. I'll love you forever."

"Excuse us," Shiri said, but Brenda hardly noticed her. "We'll be leaving now."

As Wes's mouth settled on hers she heard the lock on the door engage. Wes folded her into his arms. She felt as if she were the most important woman on earth. As if Wes were the most important man. She was in love. Nothing was more wonderful. She felt as if life glowed, that the two of them, entwined in each other's arms, intimately sharing their love, without restraint, had found the greatest that life had to offer.

"I have something to say." Wes raised his head. "If there had never been a bet and if we never have children, I want to spend the rest of my life with you."

"I want to marry you. More than I every wanted anything."

"Even the stars?"

She laughed. "Even the moon and the stars."

Wes pulled a small package from his pocket. He handed it to her. There was no wrapping paper to cover it. It was a small globe with a scene in water. There was the moon and the stars over a small house. When she shook it snow filled the scene.

"Where did you find this?"

"At a shop in Birmingham where your mother took me. I told them what I wanted and they made it."

Brenda hugged him. "I want to have a lot of children and I want them all to have you as their father."

Wes kissed her tenderly. He held her with such fragility that she could have been made of sugar lace. Brenda had missed him, missed the sensations that went through her when he kissed her, held her. She molded herself to him, fitting her body to his in the way they had become familiar with as they had learned each other's needs. The kiss changed. He pulled her closer, held her tighter, his mouth took hers with greater force. Her hands smoothed over his arms and around his neck. Her legs rubbed against his. She heard his groans and was quite surprised when he reached down and lifted her. He carried her into the bedroom and placed her on the king-size, bed where he undressed her in slow stages, kissing her body as he exposed it.

"I can't tell you how much I missed you." His voice was scratchy and more sexy than she'd ever heard. It raced along her skin, igniting tiny nerve endings and calling them to life.

"Me too," she rasped, her hands moving to release his clothes. Pants joined blouse, and socks joined underwear on the floor of the suite. His hands released her bra and his mouth found her breasts. Rapture spiraled within her. Her blood sang in her ears. The fires of love burst inside her as Wes joined himself with her. She'd been loved before, but with them it was always a first. A new perception, new emotions, new sensitivities. Their world was reformed each time they came together. Each time his body thrust into hers a new joy was created, a new level of breathless wonder enveloped them.

Brenda's breath became ragged. She forced air into her lungs as every part of her became one with Wes. She clung to him, her legs clinging to his, her body open and accepting. She writhed under Wes as if she'd been away for a long time and had to compensate for it.

He seemed to feel the same way. His body worked at fever pitch. Brenda felt the pleasure, gave and took of it until she could feel her own scream. She held it, clamped her teeth together to hold it back. She didn't want to stop. She wanted to reach that higher place. That place where light and earth and fire and water all came together, where there was the testament of their love, without beginning or end. Light flashed, colors coalesced. She heard the thunder, the deep tearing of the sky as forces greater than she could comprehend raged for release. Her scream, his shouting her name, and the burst of pleasure that filled her were unequaled by anything in the universe.

Brenda felt death was surely coming. No one could sustain such pleasure. It poured from every fissure of her being. No one could withstand the fierce velocity with which the blood raced through her system, heating her, burning her, forcing her body to work with Wes's. She matched the rhythm he created, annexed herself to the primal dance that lovers had learned since time began. Each dance was unique to the lovers, each step never before done, never seen or known by anyone else. Brenda and Wes were original in their cotillion. She was never sure of anything more in her life than this moment.

And she knew it would never end.

Half an hour after the cocktail party began, Wes and Brenda arrived. Too late to be fashionable, they made an entrance as they came into the ballroom. For a short moment they stood together in front of the entire Johnson clan. Then her parents headed for them.

Pamela Reid had a wide smile on her face and her father was beaming.

Brenda had everything she wanted. And she had won the bet.

Dear Readers:

It's nearly the anniversary of the September eleventh tragedy that changed all our lives. Family became so much more important. Not only our own families, but the community as a family too. Living in the shadow of New York City, I was witness to firsthand impressions of the tragedy. Writing was difficult after that, but I believe A FAMILY AFFAIR is the perfect book to renew our sense of love and personal relationships.

Brenda Reid and Wesley Cooper both have a deep sense of family. They both want one. Wes's method is unorthodox and his little white lie goes a long way toward destroying the best thing that's ever happened to him—Brenda!

Writing this book reminded me of my own family reunions. They take place annually in South Carolina. Every other year my six sisters and brother try to get together with our children, their children, and their children's children. The food is great—I get hungry just thinking about it! The games are fun, with talent shows and plenty of conversation. We review what's happened to us, who's married, who's divorced, and who's got a new job or a new man. Brenda and Wes are a lot like us.

Family is a major part of the African-American community. Keeping in touch with each other, visiting, and knowing that the family survives is important. The next time you get together for a holiday meal, a family reunion, or just dinner with your sister or brother, remember that special bond that unites families.

I receive many letters from the women and men who read my books. Thank you for your generous comments and words of encouragement. And thanks to those of you who think the books would make great movies. Some of you even cast them. I love reading your letters as much as I enjoy writing the books.

If you'd like to hear more about A FAMILY AFFAIR, other books I've written, or upcoming releases, please send a business size, self-addressed, stamped envelope to me at the following address: Shirley Hailstock, P.O. Box 513, Plainsboro, NJ 08536. You can also visit my Web page at the following address: http://www.geocities.com/shailstock.

Sincerely,
Shirley Hailstock

For a sneak peek at the first book in the Family Reunion Series

HEARTS OF STEEL
by Geri Guillaume

Just turn the page. . . .

Football sucks. It has to be the most idiotic game ever invented. No, I take that back. I think that game where you have to say, "Big bucks, no whammy" when it's your turn takes the prize for idiocy. But football runs a close second.

I'm not talking about fùtbol, otherwise known as soccer. Noted players like Pele can even make bouncing a ball on top of your head look sophisticated.

I'm not talking about Australian-rules football, either. Given a hundred years and a book of the rules, I won't ever be able to figure that one out. I just like watching the referees in their cute white coats and fedoras perform what looks suspiciously like a Wild West fast draw to authenticate a score.

I'm talking about good old-fashioned Monday-night, Hank Williams, Jr., caterwauling, "Are you ready for some football?" turkey-day marathon, American-style football.

Am I ready for some football? No. Never. Not even if you paid me.

Before you jump to any conclusions, let me be the first to say that I *know* what the game is all about. Nobody can accuse me, Shiri Rowlan, of letting ignorance prejudice my thinking. That is, I know how the game is played.

I know how many players are supposed to be on the field. I know the player positions (mostly prone, since those behemoths can eat their weight in food). I understand the mechanics of the game. How many downs do you get to score? Four. How many points do you get when you score? That depends on how you get the ball across the goal line. Field goal. Touchback. Touchdown. Who cares?

I can even tell you what the Icky Shuffle is all about. Trust me, you don't want to know. What I don't get is what makes otherwise sane individuals run full tilt toward each other, deliberately trying to bash each other's brains out for temporary possession of the stuffed hide of some poor animal. It's ridiculous.

And the people who dress up, parading around in feathers or face paints, all in the name of supporting their team, ought to be locked up as well. For real! If you saw a grown man on the street, in a giant chicken costume, flapping his arms and clucking in your face, wouldn't that make you want to call the local law enforcement?

I wasn't always this way. I wasn't always a player hater. Before I saw the light, I enjoyed a rousing game of football just as much as the next girl. There was something about sitting on the huge, sectional couch with my father and older brothers, scarfing down snacks, yelling at the television, cursing or blessing the team, was as close to heaven as I could get on a Sunday afternoon.

I *had* to like football. If a girl following behind two big brothers wanted any attention at all from her father, she had better learn to like what he liked. So I did. When my dad cheered for a play, I cheered for a play. When my dad cursed the coach, I cursed the coach. That is, I substituted some of my dad's more colorful epithets for my own. "Son of a rock-sucking witch" was one of my more careful, color substitutions. Still, if I shouted it loud enough, it sounded very close to the real thing.

But I remember, almost to the day, the very hour, when I came to my senses. It was the summer of eighty-nine. If my math is correct, that means I've been carrying a grudge against that stupid game for thirteen years now. I'd almost forgotten about my conversion, or rather . . . the birth of my aversion.

What suddenly reminded me just how much I disliked that game? When the little boy sitting directly across from me launched a grapefruit-sized football at my head to get my attention.

Yeah, that's the way to make me a fan. Go, team.

For a sneak peek at the third book
in the Family Reunion Series

THE TIES THAT BIND
by Eboni Snoe

Coming in September 2002
from BET/Arabesque Books

Just turn the page. . . .

Essence Stuart held the doorknob with one hand and wiped away tears with the other. It was her house, but now every time she stepped into the bedroom upstairs Essence dreaded what might lie inside.

Her chest quivered as she opened the door. Essence hoped her mother did not see the movements. Hoped with the sight only a mother has for her child that Sadie could not see beyond the strong face her daughter presented. Essence's shoulders sagged when she realized there was no chance of that. Sadie's frail body lay motionless on the modest full-size bed. The rich brown eyes Essence loved so much were hidden beneath thin, dark eyelids.

Quietly, Essence sat in the cushioned chair. Over the last few days this chair had become her bed, her dining table, and the place where Essence was watching her mother die. Daring such a thought created a tightness close to her heart. It seemed like an impossible notion. Not that Essence expected her mother to live forever. No one did. What was impossible was accepting the tireless woman that she had known all of her life would simply stop. Be no more. All of Sadie's energy, her life force, that cooked, cleaned, danced, sang, worked exhausting hours, cried, laughed, and most of all loved Essence would be gone.

Essence closed her eyes. Perhaps not gone if any of the religious or spiritual teachers, even philosophers had a clue. It meant Sadie would simply not be here for Essence to hug and touch, not here for her to look into her mother's eyes without words because words were not necessary. But even with that belief tears formed behind Essence's eyelids.

"Essie."

Sadie's thin voice opened Essence's eyes. She leaned in quickly. "Yes, Mama?"

In slow motion, Sadie lifted her hand and wiped away Essence's tears. "Don't cry, Boo. Don't cry."

Essence turned her face into her mother's hand and held it there. Finally, she shook her head. This was all too much. Everything was caught within the lump in her throat. Essence feared if she spoke, a tidal wave of tears would be released. Yet her heart overflowed and her love for her mother was greater than her fear. "What am I going to do without you, Mama? It's always been the two of us. We've been through so much together."

"And we will go through this . . . together. You'll just keep going, Essie. I've got another path to take." Sadie gathered her strength. "I have no doubt the Essence I know, the one who's always found the strength and courage to move forward, will have the ability to weather my passing."

"I don't want the strength, Mama. I want you to stay here, with me." Essence couldn't stand to hear her mother speak of dying. She struggled under a wave of grief.

Sadie pressed on. "You've always been a good daughter. I want you to know I know that. Minding me and taking to heart anything I felt was important. And Essie?"

"Yes." Essence sniffed.

"We haven't come across anything more important than this."

Essence closed her eyes again. "I know." She opened them only to see Sadie's face distorted with pain. "Are you hurting?" she inquired, tossing her own suffering aside.

"A little." Sadie searched Essence's eyes. "But I fear not as much as I've hurt you, Essie."

"Hurt me?" Essence was dumbfounded. "You've never hurt me. You gave me all you could give, Mama. I'm twenty-nine now, and when I look back over my childhood I don't know how you did it. Raised me while you worked two jobs without any outside help or support. You gave me with a loving, stable home. I couldn't ask for more."

Sadie's smirk was almost a grimace. "That's not what you said at twelve when you got your first job."

"Nope, it wasn't." Essence's smile created more tears. "I didn't understand then. But now I know I'm better for it because I learned the value of work and money early in life. And I also learned money isn't everything."

"No, money isn't everything. But I could have made it easier on us." Sadie paused again. "But my pride wouldn't let me. Just like it wouldn't let me tell you about your father."

"My father." Essence was shocked, but she collected herself and determined to focus on the present situation. "Oh, Mama. I—" she started to reassure Sadie.

"This is not the time to sweep the truth aside or to cover up our feelings. There's been enough of that, and I think you learned how to do it so well from me."

Essence could see Sadie's chest rising and falling. She placed a comforting hand on her mother's arm.

"I know through the years you've wondered about your father," Sadie continued. "You had to. It's only human. But I couldn't bring myself to tell you about him." Her dim eyes probed Essence's bright ones. "And through the years, because you never asked, I told myself it didn't matter. The truth is my mind accepted that excuse, but my heart knew better."

Essence looked down at the green and blue comforter that covered her mother's bed. Yes, she had wondered about her father. Wondered who he was. Why he wasn't a part of their lives. Was it because he didn't care to be? Or was he even alive to care?

"Essie."

Wistfully, Essence looked up. "Yes."

"I want you to do something."

"Anything you want, Mama."

Sadie closed her eyes and sighed. "There's a key taped in the bottom of the jewelry box your grandmother gave me." She spoke slowly. "Bring it over here. And bring the round leather box that's tucked in the left hand corner of my top drawer."

A box and a key? Essence didn't know what to make of Sadie's request. For a moment she studied her mother's face. Somehow it appeared more relaxed. Relieved even.

"Go get them, Essie," Sadie said without looking at her.

Essence followed her mother's instructions. Her movements were almost involuntary. Didn't deathbed revelations occur only in the movies? Still, somehow this strange turn of events felt fitting to Essence. From the moment she discovered her mother had terminal cancer, life seemed to be coated with a fictional veneer. Essence procured the tarnished gold key and the deep green box, and returned to the cushioned chair.

"I remember the day I bought that box." Sadie's voice was full of the past. "I pictured myself giving it to you on your fifth birthday. I told myself that would be the perfect time. You would be just old enough to understand, but young enough not to be bitter. But your fifth birthday came and went, and I kept my secret. Then you got older in real life and in the daydream where I saw myself giving you the box and the key. Funny." Sadie turned a smile that was no smile at all. "I never saw you opening it under these circumstances."

Sadie's voice became a low, monotone backdrop as Essence slid the tiny key inside the lock. It turned as if the box had been bought yesterday. When she lifted the lid two star sapphire cuff links sparkled.

"Those were your father's."

Essence looked at her mother, then back at the cuff links.

"He didn't mean to, but he left them behind on the night I got pregnant with you."

"So you never saw him again after that?" The words came but Essence felt disconnected from them.

"That was the last time we were together in a personal way. I've seen him many times. I couldn't help it. He's everywhere."

"What do you mean?" Essence looked confused.

"He had just started his political career when we got together. I fell in love the first time he smiled at me." A ghost of a real smile touched Sadie's mouth. "I was lost to him after that. Fascinated that a man like your father would be interested in me."

"Did you stop seeing each other because you got pregnant with me?" It was a difficult question, but Essence had to know.

"You were part of the reason. But he was also married." Sadie paused. "It's one thing to have a woman on the side. It's another to have one who claims to be having your baby."

Essence looked straight into her mother's eyes. "So who is he, Mama?"

"Cedric Johnson."

"Cedric Johnson!" Essence's stomach dropped. "Brenda and Shiri's uncle?"

Sadie nodded. "It's very complicated, isn't it? Cedric being your best friends' uncle was another reason it was hard to tell you. Oh-h-h." Sadie sighed heavily. "Brenda and Shiri's families had practically made you a member. Many, many a day you were at their house when I had to work. They fed you and guided you when I couldn't, and I just couldn't bring myself to tell Pamela and Doris, tell their mothers, that their beloved brother was your father." Her eyes sought understanding. "Not after all the things they'd said to me in private berating the man who abandoned a wonderful daughter like you. So there I was knowing they were talking badly about their own brother; the pride of Birmingham, Alabama's black community. One of our city councilmen."

Cedric Johnson is my father! The words played repetitiously in Essence's head. "Oh my God. I sat near him during a wedding." Essence's eyes widened. "And as a kid I thought he told some of the best jokes at the Johnson family Christmas parties." An audible intake of breath followed. "The Johnsons think the world of him. And so does everybody else."

"I know. I know. And there was a time I did too." Sadie licked her dry lips. "Then when I found out I was pregnant, and Cedric denied that you were his baby, I was so hurt. Shocked." Her speech slowed. "But I pulled myself together, and I told myself I didn't want anything else to do with him. I wanted him to see I could make it on my own. That I didn't need him or anybody else." A dim light appeared in Sadie's eyes. "I moved on and time passed, but then fate stepped in. You, Brenda, and Shiri became good friends. And for a while I had many a sleepless night over that, picturing all kinds of things. Because of my secret, I visualized Pamela and Doris turning their backs on you if they ever found out about your father. And that the whole Johnson family would hate us for dragging their beloved Cedric into a big mess."

"Oh my God." Essence grabbed her mother's hand.

"But do you know what gives me a strange kind of comfort?"

Essence shook her head.

Sadie closed her eyes again. "I never, ever, loved anyone like I loved your father." Her voice filled with life, more life than her body had exhibited for months. "He gave me you."

She still loves him after all these years. My mother still loves Cedric Johnson.

"But, Essie."

"Yes, Mama?"

Sadie locked eyes with her daughter. "I don't want what was a peaceful life to be the center of a scandal at death."

"Ma'am?"

"I mean, I told you who your father is because you've always had the right to know, but I want to be buried, Essie, without a cloud hanging over my head. Please." Sadie touched her daughter's hand. "You can do whatever you want about your relationship with your father after I'm gone."

"You don't have to worry about that, Mama." It took some effort, but once again the thought of Essence's mother dying took precedence.

DO YOU KNOW AN ARABESQUE MAN?

1st Arabesque Man HAROLD JACKSON
Featured on the cover of "Endless Love"
by Carmen Green / Published Sept 2000

2nd Arabesque Man EDMAN REID
Featured on the cover of "Love Lessons"
by Leslie Esdaile / Published Sept 2001

3rd Arabesque Man PAUL HANEY
Featured on the cover of "Holding Out For A Hero"
by Deirdre Savoy / Published Sept 2002

WILL YOUR "ARABESQUE" MAN BE NEXT?

One Grand Prize Winner Will Win:
- 2 Day Trip to New York City
- Professional NYC Photo Shoot
- Picture on the Cover of an Arabesque Romance Novel
- Prize Pack & Profile on Arabesque Website and Newsletter
- $250.00

You Win Too!
- The Nominator of the Grand Prize Winner receives a Prize Pack & profile on Arabesque Website
- $250.00

To Enter: Simply complete the following items to enter your "Arabesque Man": (1) Compose an Original essay that describes in 75 words or less why you think your nominee should win. (2) Include two recent photographs of him (head shot and one full length shot). Write the following information for both you and your nominee on the back of each photo: name, address, telephone number and the nominee's age, height, weight, and clothing sizes. (3) Include signature and date of nominee granting permission to nominator to enter photographs in contest. (4) Include a proof of purchase from an Arabesque romance novel—write the book title, author, ISBN number, and purchase location and price on a 3-1/2" x 5" card. (5) Entrants should keep a copy of all submissions. Submissions will not be returned and will be destroyed after the judging.

ARABESQUE regrets that no return or acknowledgement of receipt can be made because of the anticipated volume of responses. Arabesque is not responsible for late, lost, incomplete, inaccurate or misdirected entries. The Grand Prize Trip includes round trip air transportation from a major airport nearest the winner's home, 2-day (1 night) hotel accommodations and ground transportation between the airport, hotel and Arabesque offices in New York. The Grand Prize Winner will be required to sign and return an affidavit of eligibility and publicity and liability release in order to receive the prize. The Grand Prize Winner will receive no additional compensation for the use of his image on an Arabesque novel, website, or for any other promotional purpose. The entries will be judged by a panel of BET Arabesque personnel whose decisions regarding the winner and all other matters pertaining to the Contest are final and binding. By entering this Contest, entrants agree to comply with all rules and regulations.

SEND ENTRIES TO: The Arabesque Man Cover Model Contest, BET Books, One BET Plaza, 1235 W Street, NE, Washington, DC 20018. Open to legal residents of the U.S., 21 years of age or older. Illegible entries will be disqualified. Limit one entry per envelope. Odds of winning depend, in part, on the number of entries received. Void in Puerto Rico and where prohibited by law.

ARABESQUE
A PRODUCT OF
BET BOOKS

BOOK YOUR PLACE ON OUR WEBSITE AND MAKE THE ARABESQUE ROMANCE CONNECTION!

We've created a customized website just for our very special Arabesque readers, where you can get the inside scoop on everything that's going on with Arabesque romance novels.

When you come online, you'll have the exciting opportunity to:

- View covers of upcoming books

- Learn about our future publishing schedule (listed by publication month and author)

- Find out when your favorite authors will be visiting a city near you

- Search for and order backlist books

- Check out author bios and background information

- Send e-mail to your favorite authors

- Join us in weekly chats with authors, readers and other guests

- Get writing guidelines

- AND MUCH MORE!

Visit our website at
http://www.arabesquebooks.com

COMING IN SEPTEMBER 2002 FROM ARABESQUE ROMANCES

__ONE HEARTBEAT AT A TIME
by Marilyn Tyner 1-58314-365-3 $6.99US/$9.99CAN
Elizabeth Roberts has worked hard for a successful career and a sizzling romance with Adam Gregory. Nothing is going to stand in the way of their happiness . . . until someone sets a scheme in motion that threatens to destroy both her career and Adam's trust in her.

__HOLDING OUT FOR A HERO
by Deirdre Savoy 1-58314-245-2 $6.99US/$9.99CAN
N.Y.P.D. detective Adam Wexler finds himself playing bodyguard to Hollywood sex symbol Samantha Hathaway, the sole survivor of the crash that killed his brother—and the star of Adams fantasies. But from the moment he enters her room, he senses the woman beneath the image.

__A CHARMED LOVE
by Courtni Wright 1-58314-267-3 $5.99US/$7.99CAN
The murder of a famous jeweler plunges detective Denise Dory into an investigation that brings her back into the arms of her partner and secret lover, Tom Phyfer. Now, torn between duty and desire, Denise joins forces with Tom on a cross country race to stop a killer . . .

__JUST THE THOUGHT OF YOU
by Loure Bussey 1-58314-367-X $5.99US/$7.99CAN
Novelist Diamond Tate has given up her dream of a happy ending in real life. Instead, she puts all of her passion into her writing, trying to forget the past. But it soon catches up with her on a Caribbean cruise that leaves her alone and adrift once more . . . until she encounters attorney Jake Dupree.

__THE TIES THAT BIND
by Eboni Snoe 1-58314-338-6 $6.99US/$9.99CAN
Essence Stuart gets her opportunity to confront her biological father, Cedric Johnson, at the Johnson family reunion. Unknown to Essence, Cedric has hired handsome detective Titan Valentine to investigate her, and a powerful attraction between Essence and Titan is an unforeseen complication. Are resentment and suspicion a match for a love that goes beyond the physical?

Call toll free **1-888-345-BOOK** to order by phone or use this coupon to order by mail. ALL BOOKS AVAILABLE SEPTEMBER 1, 2002.

Name_____
Address _____
City_____ State _____ Zip _____
Please send me the books that I have checked above.
I am enclosing $_____
Plus postage and handling* $_____
Sales tax (in NY, TN, and DC) $_____
Total amount enclosed $_____
*Add $2.50 for the first book and $.50 for each additional book.
Send check or money order (no cash or CODs) to: **Arabesque Romances, Dept. C.O., 850 Third Avenue, 16th Floor, New York, NY 10022**
Prices and numbers subject to change without notice. Valid only in the U.S. All orders subject to availability. **NO ADVANCE ORDERS.**
Visit our website at **www.arabesquebooks.com**.

Do You Have the Entire
SHIRLEY HAILSTOCK
Collection?

__Legacy

                0-7860-0415-0 $4.99US/$6.50CAN

__Mirror Image

                1-58314-178-2 $5.99US/$7.99CAN

__More Than Gold

                1-58314-120-0 $5.99US/$7.99CAN

__Whispers of Love

                0-7860-0055-4 $4.99US/$5.99CAN

Call toll free **1-888-345-BOOK** to order by phone or use this coupon to order by mail.
Name_____
Address_____
City_____ State_____ Zip_____
Please send me the books that I checked above.
I am enclosing $_____
Plus postage and handling* $_____
Sales tax (in NY, TN, and DC) $_____
Total amount enclosed $_____
*Add $2.50 for the first book and $.50 for each additional book.
Send check or money order (no cash or CODs) to: **Arabesque Romances, Dept. C.O., 850 Third Avenue 16th Floor, New York, NY 10022**
Prices and numbers subject to change without notice.
All orders subject to availability. **NO ADVANCE ORDERS.**
Visit our website at www.arabesquebooks.com.